Praise for The Lady Adelaide Mysteries

"A lively debut filled with local color, red herrings, both sprightly and spritely characters, a smidgen of social commentary, and a climactic surprise."

—*Kirkus Reviews* on *Nobody's Sweetheart Now*

"Set in England in 1924, this promising series launch...is...frothy fun."

—*Publishers Weekly* on *Nobody's Sweetheart Now*

WHO'S SORRY NOW?

WHO'S SORRY NOW?

A LADY ADELAIDE
~ MYSTERY ~

MAGGIE ROBINSON

Poisoned Pen
PRESS

Published by Poisoned Pen Press, an imprint of Sourcebooks
P.O. Box 4410, Naperville, Illinois 60567-4410
(630) 961-3900
sourcebooks.com

Library of Congress Cataloging-in-Publication data is on file with the publisher.

Printed and bound in United States of America.
SB 10 9 8 7 6 5 4 3 2 1

WHO'S SORRY NOW?

Who's sorry now?
Whose heart is aching for breaking each vow?
Who's sad and blue, who's crying too,
Just like I cried over you.
Right to the end,
Just like a friend
I tried to warn you somehow.
You had your way,
Now you must pay.
I'm glad that you're sorry now.
Right to the end,
Just like a friend,
I tried to warn you somehow.
You had your way,
Now you must pay.
I'm glad that you're sorry now.

Songwriters: Bert Kalmar / Harry Ruby / Ted Snyder, 1923

CAST OF CHARACTERS

MOUNT STREET
Lady Adelaide Compton (Addie), widow of
  Major Rupert Compton, older daughter
  of the late Marquess of Broughton
Major Rupert Compton, ghost
Beckett, Addie's maid
Lady Cecilia Merrill (Cee), Addie's sister
Lord Lucas Waring, viscount, Addie's suitor

THIEVES' DEN
Fredo (Freddy) Rinaldi, manager
Patricia (Trix) Harmon, hostess
Ted Boyce, waiter
Ollie Johnson, band leader
Mary Frances Harmon, Trix's cousin and member
  of the girl gang the Forty Dollies

THE BRIGHT YOUNG PEOPLE
Thomas Bickley
Penelope Hardinge
Roy Dean

Philippa (Pip) Dean, Roy's sister
Lady Lucy Archibald
Bernard (Bunny) Dunford
Millicent (Millie) Avery
Gregory Trenton-Douglass
Christopher (Kit) Wheeler
Nadia Sanborn
Prince Alexei Andropov, Nadia's cousin
Dr. Paul Kempton
Sir Digby Sanborn, Nadia's father
James Archibald, Earl of Marbury, Lucy's father

SCOTLAND YARD
Inspector Devenand (Dev) Hunter
Sergeant Bob Wells

Chandani Hunter, Dev's mother
Harry Hunter, Dev's father

Prologue

Gay, gay, gay.

Or so some people might say. The music was blaring, the illegal champagne and other forbidden liquids and substances were flowing, and Lady Adelaide Compton was bored stiff, sitting alone at the table. Her sister Cee and their new friends were dancing as if tomorrow and its resultant hangover would never come, but Addie knew better.

There were always consequences to bad behavior.

Take her late husband, Major Rupert Charles Cressleigh Compton, Great War flying ace and even greater philanderer. Last summer he was forced to come back from the dead (and probable eternal damnation) to redeem himself by performing a good deed or two by assisting in a murder investigation.

And then he had disappeared.

He was, as far as Addie knew, still dead, and mercifully absent from New York City. And she had looked. Around every corner of the bustling streets. Behind the voile curtains of the glamorous Fifth Avenue apartment in which she and her family were staying. Under the bed of the same. The entire voyage across the

Atlantic had been fraught with potential Rupert-sightings. Every handsome mustachioed man in a dinner jacket was a potential wraith, which made Addie understandably nervous since there were so many of them. One expected one's late and unlamented husband to remain cozy and confined in his expensive satin-lined coffin and not pop up at inconvenient interludes.

However, he *had* saved her life, and she supposed she should be grateful.

But she'd be even more grateful if she never saw him again.

The lamps in the night club flickered, and then went out altogether. There were a few shrieks, but light spilled from the hundreds of votive candles in the ballroom, and the jazz band never missed a note. Addie felt a hand on her exposed back—her beaded black dress was modest in the front but quite naughty in the rear, dipping nearly to her waist.

It was a cold hand.

She'd felt that hand before.

Rupert! She'd just been thinking of him. Had her random thoughts somehow summoned him? If so, she'd prefer to turn off her brain completely, but how? Her mind did have an alarming tendency to wander.

"It's only I. Again. Don't be frightened," Rupert whispered.

"Easy for you to say!" she hissed back. The noise in the club was infernal, but someone might hear them anyway. Or hear her, and think she was losing her mind once more. She'd been caught too many times last August "talking to herself."

Oh, lord, was he here because someone was going to die? That was certainly no way to start the new year.

"Not as far as I know," he said, his voice low and smooth.

The blasted man was reading her mind. If only he'd possessed that skill before he died, things might have turned out differently in their marriage. A truly understanding man was a rare commodity indeed. In fact, Addie wasn't sure she knew of any, with perhaps one exception.

Rupert cleared his throat to reengage her attention. "This seems to be a minor intervention on my part. The notice to rescue you was very sudden—I'm not really prepared, and I had my own party to go to, you know." He sounded a trifle peeved.

Like the nightclub, Addie was in the dark regarding Rupert's post-life schedule. The Fellow Upstairs, as Rupert referred to him, had an unusual sense of humor. Keeping Rupert from entering the gates of Heaven by assigning him to be Addie's guardian angel for what seemed now to be an apparently inde-terminate period of time was extremely annoying. Rupert must be anxious to move on, and Addie had hoped last August's antics had assured him of his proper place in the afterlife, wherever that might be.

She had her own opinion where he deserved to go, but per-haps she should be more charitable.

It was difficult to see him in the flickering light, but he appeared to be wearing the same bespoke Saville Row suit she'd buried him in, his maroon tie and matching pocket square still crisp. His mous-tache had grown back, and there was no denying he was amazingly attractive even if he was amazingly dead.

"Why are you here?"

"The joint's about to be raided. Think of the headlines: *British Beauties Behind Bars. Society Dames Detained.* Your sainted mother would have a fit if you and Cee wound up in the pokey with the hoi polloi."

Addie had no idea what a pokey was, but she could infer with the best of them. "*Now?*"

"The buttons are upstairs even as we speak. Do you know they carry bean-shooters in this country?"

"Speak English, Rupert!"

"I am, my dear. The American version. This is quite a place, what? Rather marvelous in its own grubby way."

Addie wondered how long he'd been in New York, but appar-ently time was of the essence if she didn't wish to find herself on the front page of every rag in the city, so she didn't ask. "How can we get out of here?"

"They've got all the exits blocked. When they turn on the lights, it'll be curtains. Go get Cee and meet me in the men's loo."

The men's loo! Rupert dissolved before she had a chance to question him further. Well, if caught in the men's toilet, she could always pretend to be a building inspector, although beaded chiffon was an odd choice of uniform.

Addie waved wildly at Cee, but of course went unnoticed in the shadowy room. She gathered up their purses, gingerly ducked around gyrating couples on the dance floor, and grabbed Cee's flailing arm.

"Quick! It's—it's an emergency!"

Her sister stopped mid-step. "What's wrong?" Her partner didn't seem to notice Cee's ceasing and continued to Black Bottom his bottom off.

"You've got to come with me. No time for questions."

Cee at one time had been Addie's little minion at their childhood home, Broughton Park. She'd marched off to battle in whichever direction she was sent, put crickets in their governess' bed, watered down the butler-before-Forbes' secret stash of wine (and drinking a little, if truth be told), and performed other nefarious tasks too numerous to mention. But Cee at twenty-five was entirely different and far less malleable. She opened her mouth to protest, so Addie simply dragged her away with every ounce of strength she possessed and shoved her down a black hallway into the Gents'.

Fortunately an electric sconce stuttered inside so they weren't completely at the mercy of the night. It must be on a separate circuit from the ballroom, Addie thought, pleased with her scientific deduction even in the face of catastrophe.

Cee's own face was a vision. Half-intrigued by the sudden location and half-indignant, she gave Addie a shove. "What the hell, Adelaide! I was enjoying myself with Roddy!" Roderick

Huntington Smythe, III was just one of the American swains who'd circled Cee once the Marchioness of Broughton's daughters had arrived on their shores. Addie had had a few swains herself, even though technically she was still in mourning.

"We have to get out of this place. It's about to be raided."

"What? How do you know?"

"A little birdie told me." Addie looked about the room. There were four urinals and two sinks, but no sign of the birdie.

"I'm behind the cubicle door," came the sepulchral voice. "There's a window over the crapper. I'll boost you up."

"This way," Addie said, sounding far more confident than she felt. She entered the stall, and there was her old nemesis, appearing far too cheerful considering the situation.

"I've already unlocked the window. All you have to do is shimmy out, hail a taxi, and Bob's your uncle."

Addie felt a pang for the fur coats they were leaving behind, but needs must. "You go first, Cee. I'll help you."

Cee looked up to a window that seemed impossibly high. "You expect me to climb up on a filthy toilet bowl and somehow crawl out that tiny window?"

"Yes, I do. Don't be squeamish. At least you have shoes on." And lovely they were, too, brand-new, with brilliants scattered on the satin.

Just then the loo door banged open, and a red-faced man entered, looking much the worse for wear. "I say, ladies, have I the wrong room?" he slurred.

"No, we do," Addie said brightly. "Go on about your business. We won't look."

"Better than seeing pink elephants, I s'pose." The man began to deal clumsily with his trousers. Addie turned and resolutely kept her eyes on the spangles of Cee's evening gown, wondering how she was expected to push her sister up the several feet required for freedom.

Rupert took care of that, tossing Cee through the window as she cried out in surprise. "You next, my dear."

Addie found herself hurtling through the air and squeezing through the narrow casing, breaking two fingernails and no doubt bruising a hip. Perhaps she should go on a slimming regimen in the new year, though one did hope not to find oneself in a similar window-shimmying predicament in the future.

The shrill whistles and screams inside were audible from the street, and Addie breathed a sigh of relief at the very close call.

Rupert rolled out of the building as well and dusted himself off. "Happy New Year!" He gave Addie a quick kiss, which was not precisely unpleasant but very, very strange. She couldn't even squeak in protest since Cee was so near, grumbling about the hole in her stocking.

He waggled a white finger at her. "Be careful. I'm perfectly prepared to keep you out of danger in England—under my current contract. A sacred duty. All part of my rehabilitation plan. But this trip across the Atlantic has taken quite a lot out of me. Absolutely no visit to Chicago and that Capone person while you are over here. No train to California to chat up film stars, either. I forbid it."

As if Rupert could forbid her anything anymore. Addie was about to remind him in no uncertain terms, but that felt somewhat ungrateful after his latest effort to protect her. Plus, Cee would hear her and think she was crazy.

Blast. Addie resolved that she and Cee would lead lives of utmost boring decorum during the rest of their stay in America. After all, they'd be home by the second week of March. How hard could it be to avoid mobsters and mayhem and movie actors?

And Rupert's reappearance.

"But I do have an inkling I'll be seeing you when you get back home." He blew her another kiss and vanished.

Oh no. Was Rupert going to play knight errant wherever and whenever as part of avoiding hell? For the rest of what she hoped would be her long and unremarkable life? She'd go mad! Why couldn't he stay dead?

And did he mean Addie was going to be mixed up in yet another murder? Unhappy new year ahead!

Chapter One

London, an early Thursday morning in mid-March, 1925

Two dead Bright Young People decades before they got to be Dim Old People. Both by poison. Both in a very public place a week apart.

And Detective Inspector Devenand Hunter was anticipating a third death.

He felt it in his bones, which could be a useful sensation, but impossible to explain to his superiors. So he stuck to the evidence at hand, what little there was of it.

His instincts had failed him rather spectacularly at the end of last summer, when he'd been called to a country house in the Cotswolds to investigate two murders, that of a society beauty with flexible morals, and an elderly Scottish gardener. Two more disparate victims could not have been found, but they were linked in death as they had never been in life.

The culprit had been captured and hanged. It was the capturing part that had almost gone so wrong that Dev had contemplated turning in his warrant card. He had put his hostess Lady Adelaide Compton at risk, and were it not for an inexplicably tipped tea trolley, she might have died.

And that would have been...a damned shame. Lady Adelaide was...

Dev was thinking in ellipses, searching for suitable words. He liked Lady Adelaide far more than he should. She was the daughter of a marquess, widow of a war hero, and he was the son of a retired police inspector and his Indian-born wife. The fact that Dev's elegant mother could out-queen the queen meant nothing in the scheme of the British social hierarchy—he would always be an outsider because of the color of his skin.

Thus he'd made no effort whatsoever to contact Lady Adelaide in the ensuing months, fixing it so she'd have no part in the trial. She had been abroad anyhow, and his reach did not extend across the Atlantic Ocean.

He often wondered about her, a pointless exercise. He expected to read a notice of her engagement to Lord Lucas Waring now that her year of mourning was officially up. Looking at the black-boxed announcements day after day in *The Times* was a little like picking at a scab, but Dev couldn't help himself. It was best to be armed with the truth, no matter how unpleasant it was.

He brushed his thick black hair from his forehead, as if he could brush his thoughts away, and considered his surroundings. The private nightclub called the Thieves' Den was murky even in daytime, the harsh scent of spilled liquor an offense to his nostrils so early in the morning. It was a place he and his sergeant Bob Wells would never be welcome during regular hours, and that suited them both.

Apart from the astronomical membership fee far beyond a policeman's salary, he and Bob had better things to do lately. Bob was wearing a groove in the carpet with his teething daughter so his wife Francie might snatch a few consecutive hours' sleep, and Dev continued his self-improvement plan, reading philosophy and religion into the wee hours and remembering most of it. Neither of them owned evening clothes or diamond cufflinks or patent leather shoes like the second victim, Thomas Bickley, who was still lying under a glass and bottle-strewn table waiting for the medical team to arrive. His face was almost black, a sure sign of cyanide poisoning.

The club's owner Fredo "Freddy" Rinaldi had called Dev as soon as the body had been discovered by the young Polish woman who came in to clean at dawn. Dev had already sent her home, in hopes she'd drink a pot of tea or a bottle of vodka and calm down.

The last time Dev had been here, the victim had had the grace to die on the Soho sidewalk outside. Either way, though, Rinaldi was facing ruin. Members were not apt to enjoy themselves much if they expected to be knocked off when out on the town. The newest "in" venue had a grim future if word got out.

"What can you tell me about Mr. Bickley, Freddy?"

The club owner shrugged. "Practically nothing. He's just a kid. Or was. Twenty, twenty-one, tops. His dad owns Bickley's Brewery. The money was good enough for me, even if the gene-alogy left something to be desired. We're not the Embassy Club or the Gargoyle Club, you know. His father bought a knighthood a couple of years ago. Sir Barry Bickley he is now."

All it took was ten thousand pounds. Thank Lloyd George for that, Dev grumbled inwardly. For a stretch, those wanting to elevate themselves into the peerage or honours list made hefty contributions to the parties in the coalition government, all legal but pernicious just the same. It was somewhat amusing that Freddy, whose dubious origins were far less distinguished than the beer-brewing Bickleys, held their success against them.

"Did he come here often?"

"Three or four nights a week, sometimes more. I'd say he was a regular. Never had no trouble with him, though, not like that Penelope Hardinge, sniffing around the band all the time." Rinaldi, when stressed, lapsed into the rough language of his misspent youth, and two deaths were enough to stress the most hardened soul, of which Rinaldi was one.

Penelope Hardinge had been the first to die after drinking

from a silver flask on the wet pavement outside the club a week ago. At first her friends thought she'd slipped and hit her head, but the autopsy had proved otherwise. The vibrant Penny was known for her indiscriminate drug use and interest in very unsuitable men, but it was unlikely she'd drunk a cyanide cocktail by choice.

Her father had made his fortune supplying wool for His Majesty's troops at exorbitant rates, and the words "war profiteer" were still mumbled when his name came up. Still, it was no reason for his daughter to die so ignominiously.

So, the Thieves' Den membership was not precisely the cream of the creamiest crop. Dev had a list of Rinaldi's other clientele and had every intention of interviewing as many of them as he could, tedious as that was bound to be. He also had a record of who'd been present each night the deaths occurred, too—members and their guests, and where they'd sat. Dev was interested in the overlap.

Freddy Rinaldi was a surprisingly organized sort of chap, each table and its inhabitants labeled night after night. Dev was sure the man had an ulterior motive besides billing—blackmail? Drug sales? Tips to the press for publicity? There were scores of licensed nightclubs in London, some blameless, some mixing prostitutes and criminals with the ordinary cocktail and jazz aficionado. As a private club, the Thieves' Den had been generally safe from the Metropolitan's recent raids on after-hours liquor sales, but maybe that was about to change.

"Have you called his family?"

Rinaldi shrugged. "Thought I'd save that for you lot. Look, you'd better get to the bottom of this quick. The club is just getting started. Bad for business it is, people dropping like flies all over the place."

An understatement. The Thieves' Den was the latest venue for mindless decadence. Opening on St. Valentine's Day, it had made a quick splash amongst those Bright Young People who were at such loose ends. Dev could hear his mother quite clearly:

"Those who are easily bored are boring." To claim to be bored was practically a badge of honor nowadays, not a confession that one's life was aimless.

"Tell me about last night. Who did the boy come in with?" Dev slid the list back to Rinaldi over the sticky bar. The Polish girl would have her work cut out for her if she recovered.

Rinaldi dug a pair of half-moon spectacles out of his dinner jacket pocket. He was still wearing his work uniform, white tie, and had not yet gone to bed. Dev guessed he was around forty, good-looking in a louche movie actor sort of way, all slicked back hair and clipped mustache. He wondered where Rinaldi had got the funds to start the establishment, and would probably soon have to find out.

"Let's see. Trix was hostess last night, and her handwriting ain't the best. Pretty girl, though. Looks like class at the door, all curves and blonde hair. Can talk posh too if she has to—quite a mimic. Here they are, at Table 31. Tom Bickley. Bunny Dunford." He looked up with a roll of his eyes. "Bunny's Bernard when he's at home, by the way. These toffs and their nicknames, I swear. Might as well be Mopsy, Flopsy, and Cottontail. Lady Lucy Archibald. Pip Dean. That's Philippa. Roy Dean, her brother, all of them at the same table as young Thomas in the back room."

Dev and Bob both copied the names down in their respective notebooks. "And none of them saw young Thomas sliding to the floor at some point?" Bob asked.

"Oh, they may have thought he was squiffy and needed a rest. They don't give a toss for anyone but themselves, you know. They was as likely gassed themselves."

"Did you notice them leaving?"

"To be honest, no. For a Wednesday night, we were busy. A bunch of 'em went off on a scavenger hunt around two. Cleared out half the club. Off to steal a bobby's baton or some such. Madness."

Dev agreed so much effort and energy should be put to better use by England's quasi-elite offspring. "I'll want to talk to this Trix, and the rest of your staff. Please gather them together by six. I'll come back then."

Rinaldi took off his glasses. "You ain't going to pin this on me or my workers!"

"I'm sorry, Freddy. I need to interview everyone. And it goes without saying your club is a crime scene. You'll have to close, at least for tonight."

"Jesus! You're trying to kill me without poison! Come on, Inspector, give a guy a break."

"Couldn't even if I wanted to. You're about to be invaded—my people will be going over the place with a fine-toothed comb. It will take hours. Don't touch anything." Dev was thankful that the cleaner had tripped over Bickley's patent leather-clad foot before she had a chance to clear the table. One of those dirty glasses probably contained the dregs of poison.

Freddy Rinaldi knew enough not to argue. He'd just barely skirted propriety for over half his life and had no wish to find himself on the wrong side of the law in middle age. The man sighed, and put his glasses away. "I have a cot in the office. My temporary home. Tell your boys to knock if you need anything. But no free booze. I mean it."

"Of course not," Dev said, though he wouldn't be surprised if some of the fellows thought they could get away with a nip or two while on the premises. According to the press, the Metropolitan Police Force was plagued with corruption from top to bottom.

But maybe if they thought the liquor was poisoned, they'd abstain.

"Bob, you're the welcome committee. I'm off to see Sir Barry and his wife."

"Don't envy you that task, guv."

It was Dev's least favorite part of the job, but it had to be done. If one believed in karma and reincarnation—which Dev was nearly sure he did—perhaps Thomas Bickley was being reborn somewhere in the world where he wouldn't find himself murdered in the flower of his youth twenty years from now.

But what had he done in this life to deserve it last night? Dev would have to find out.

Chapter Two

Saturday afternoon

"Bored, bored, bored!" Cee kicked a white ottoman, and Addie winced. While she had made advances redecorating her "too-white," sterile flat, that scuff mark would show. Perhaps she should bring the piece of furniture to the upholsterer. White was definitely de trop if one's shoes were involved. A flame stitch pattern in shades of red? Charcoal gray velvet piped in bright pink? Addie rather enjoyed decorating now that she had free rein and plenty of money to pay for it. Rupert had only cared about investing in his car collection.

And mistresses.

"Come now, Cee. Mother says only boring people get bored."

"Mummy can say whatever she pleases, and I don't have to pay attention to her, do I? You've stopped. So shall I."

All that was missing was a stamped foot. Cee was going through a difficult period. At twenty-five, she should be settled by now. The lengthy visit to New York this past winter had resulted in a refused proposal from a perfectly nice young stock broker whose ancestors had come over on the *Mayflower*. He was damned proud to associate his family with religious fanatics and mercenary chancers, and never let one forget his alleged pedigree. But Cee claimed she'd given her heart away last year and there was no point in trying to divert her with straight white American teeth, a Harvard degree, or a healthy trust fund.

The recipient of that heart, a widower almost twice Cee's age, had remarried and was expecting another child, a veritable miracle baby considering how old his new wife was. Everyone was so pleased for them. But Cee resolutely refused to cheer up, and was becoming, frankly, a bore to rival all bores herself.

Did that mean that Addie too was boring? No doubt. And what a relief it was. After the excitement and derangement of last August's double murders on her estate, Addie was embracing her bland and blameless life. She'd enjoyed her five-month foray into the New World, even if somewhat hampered by the constraints of Prohibition and that infamous raid where she and Cee had made a lucky escape.

Addie had never been much of a drinker anyway, and after her husband died speeding under the influence of too many French 75 cocktails, a lesson had been more or less learned by one of them.

She still blushed to think of the evening that she and Inspector Devenand Hunter had had dinner here in her Mount Street flat. Due to the inconvenient reappearance of her late husband Rupert in his ghostly form, Addie had consumed far too much wine. The policeman had put her to bed—unmolested—and she'd more or less sworn off alcohol when she awoke, her head pounding and her heart sore.

Once, Addie had been convinced she was losing her marbles— being haunted was not for the faint-hearted. But Rupert was no longer jumping out of closets and bushes to aggravate her—at least not yet, even after his implied threat on New Year's Eve— and she hardly missed their arguments.

At first, she'd thought the entire event last summer was a temporary mental aberration, a delayed reaction to her grief. For while Rupert didn't deserve it, she *did* grieve. Addie would have chalked the episode up as a summer storm, if not for his unexpected New Year's Eve visitation.

Their five-year marriage had not been a success, punctured as it was by Rupert's infidelity and Addie's naïveté. She'd been around Cee's age when she married, dazzled by Rupert's heroism and good looks. So many of her crowd had died in the Great War that she'd considered herself lucky to have attracted Rupert's attention, or anyone's.

Addie sometimes wondered if they could have handled things differently, but it was water under the bridge. Spilt milk. And any other appropriate cliché. Let bygones be bygones.

Let Rupert *be gone*. There were no such things as ghosts, she chanted to herself, even if Rupert had given her that quick New Year's kiss on the street. Never mind what the Bible said, or that dodgy medium Gerald Dumont who used to be engaged to her friend Babs.

"Let's go out tonight," Cee implored. She was spending the week with Addie in London while their mother was supervising the spring cleaning of the dower house at Broughton Park. After their long absence, Lady Broughton had a few decorating ideas inspired by New York as well, and Addie assumed Cee would be with her longer while their mother brought the dower house into the twentieth century.

If Cee wasn't too *bored*. But how could one be bored in London? What was that famous quote? Something about tiring of life altogether if one tired of London. Addie had had a decent enough education at Cheltenham Ladies' College, but like most females of her class, had never attended university. She'd been expected to be decorative and to marry, which she was and had.

But neither was quite enough.

"I thought we might order something in from the Connaught." The hotel was just around the corner and delivered perfectly delicious dinners if one knew the right people to ask, and of course as a marquess' daughter, Addie did.

"Bah. That's no fun. I did so enjoy those New York speakeasies.

Gin in the tea cups. Dancing until dawn. Even the raid was kind of amusing."

Dawn? Addie could have fallen asleep on her feet without very much trouble right this minute. They had only been home for three days, and she longed for her bed at Compton Chase, her Cotswold country house. But Cee needed to be kept out of trouble, yet somehow entertained. It was a challenge Addie was prepared to meet, once she had a little more beauty sleep.

"I just don't think I'm up to it. And where would we go?" At least she wouldn't have to wear black anymore if they went out. Her year of mourning was officially over.

"Anywhere. There probably are all sorts of divine new places that have sprung up since we were gone. Let me call around."

Oh, joy. Addie left Cee cradling the telephone and went into the kitchen.

Her maid Beckett was sitting at the enamel table glumly reading a new movie magazine. Addie knew the reason for her maid's lack of enthusiasm. She'd expected to go to Compton Chase and pick up her flirtation with Addie's gardener Jack Robertson by now. But given the choice of where to go after the transatlantic trip, Cee had opted for Town, and now they were all stuck a hundred miles away from home. Spring was sprouting up in the country, and Addie was missing it. Missing her terrier Fitz, too, who had probably forgotten her. Five months was a long time to be away, although Addie had enjoyed every minute of it, except when she was thrown out a window.

New York society had been vastly different from London's, and it had been a novelty not to be eternally marked as Rupert's widow or her father's daughter. Most of her new acquaintances had no idea who she was, not that she really was anyone special. An accident of birth was nothing to brag about. But she had been able to be herself without the British baggage. It had been... exhilarating.

"You'll have the night off, Beckett. Cee wants to go dancing. Don't wait up."

"And what will I do, Lady A? File my nails?" The cheeky Beckett was back. It was almost a relief. For a while last September, Addie's maid had been too good to be true, on her best behavior in order to impress Jack. It had been very odd indeed, for Addie had become used to Beckett's cheerful insubordination.

"Why don't you go to the cinema?" Beckett usually went twice a week, no matter the weather or what was playing.

"I seen everything there was to see in New York."

"Stop being mulish and ungrammatical. Surely there's something new here. We were on the ship over a week."

Beckett slapped the magazine shut. "When can we go home? I don't trust that Jane. Jack writes that she's after him day and night."

Jane was a perfectly nice, somewhat mousy parlor maid, who was far from being a *femme fatale* in Addie's opinion. The girl was missing a front tooth, if she remembered correctly. Addie really should see about sending her to the local dentist at estate expense. "He wants to make you jealous."

"Well, he's succeeded. Why can't we have Lady Cecilia to stay at Compton Chase?"

For one thing, it was too close to Cee's crush Sir David Grant's house, he of the new wife and prospective baby. Addie wasn't sure her sister could behave in a ladylike fashion if she encountered them. Instead of becoming more mature, Addie was convinced Cee was going backward through a second, peevish childhood. She wasn't even reading the high-brow books her mother disapproved of anymore, though she clung to her vegetarian diet. According to Constance, Lady Broughton, Cee would never land a man by trying to be "different."

But surely landing a man was not the be-all of a young woman's life, was it? It hadn't really worked for Addie.

"Give us a week in London. I need new clothes."

This was blatantly untrue. Addie had stepped off the *Aquitania* with a trunkful of the latest New York fashions. She had wardrobes and boxes full from before Rupert's death filled with things she hadn't even worn yet. Most of them hadn't gone out of style in the year she hadn't tried them on, and if they needed hemming or letting out, that was a simple enough task.

Beckett gave her the withering look she deserved.

"Do you want to come with us?"

Now she had Beckett's full attention. "Me?"

"Why not? You used to come out with us sometimes in New York." Beckett and Cee were approximately the same size, although Beckett was a touch shorter. It only meant the borrowed dresses didn't show so much leg. Cee was quite firmly in flapper territory, curly bobbed hair and all.

"But that was in America. Everybody does strange things in America."

Addie smiled. "I see no reason why I have to explain your presence to anyone. I doubt they'd care anyhow." At thirty-one and a half, Addie was a little too old for the Bright Young People set, and didn't care much for their opinion in the first place. She was beyond costume soirees, bathing parties, and midnight treasure hunts. The almost manic quest for fun was a mystery to her. She'd much rather be curled up in bed with a good book and a cup of cocoa, Fitz snoozing at her feet.

If he would forgive her long absence.

Gosh, she was still a stick-in-the-mud. The trip abroad had widened her horizons but hadn't changed her character. Addie was a responsible adult, if one didn't count conversations with her dead husband.

But one could be practical and yet have fun. It was time for a slight adjustment.

"Come on. Just do it. If anyone asks, you are our cousin Maeve from Ireland."

"Faith and begorra. Golly, I sound like my old granny," Beckett said with a grin.

Chapter Three

Even with her spectacles, Addie could hardly see a damn thing because of the thick fug of smoke hanging over the Thieves' Den's small back room. She couldn't hear anything either—the American Negro jazz band was in full and fulsome swing in the main room, where it was even smokier, and she was hoarse from shouting at Cee and Beckett over the music.

There was no one to shout at right now, though. Cee had been hauled off by a young man to do the Charleston, and everyone else at the table followed, including her maid. She could see the dance floor through the arches; it was jam-packed, as, like the Black Bottom, the dance could be performed without a partner. Plenty of single dancers were giving it their all, and Addie felt like an ancient dowager sipping on her ginger ale, vicariously feeling her back go out from the kicks and swiveling hips.

In Regency times, as a widow, she would have been assigned to monitor the wallflowers, but no one tonight was interested in her advice or proper decorum. One didn't come to places like the Thieves' Den to hide one's light under a bushel.

Before this evening, Addie had met only one of Cee's friends, Lady Lucy Archibald, an earl's daughter. The family, who had been neighbors in the country, had fallen on rock-hard times.

Both of Lucy's brothers had been killed in the war. The mold-ering Queen Anne house had been razed after a devastating fire destroyed more than three-quarters of it. After severe financial reverses, their town house was sold, too, and Lucy's parents were making do with a modest rental in Bloomsbury. It was said the Earl of Marbury was parting with his rare book collection volume by volume to pay the grocer's bills, and that his wife had taken to her bed in anticipation of the Rapture. Addie supposed it was up to Lucy to marry well and restore the family fortunes, if that was even possible.

From what Addie knew of Lucy, it would require a strong soul to take her in hand without a generous dowry and some ear plugs. She was pretty enough, tall and lissome, but prickly and proud. Her wit was cutting, and she never hesitated to make her opinions known.

Oddly, because of that she was much sought-after by the young *nouveaux-riches,* who confused her sneering pronounce-ments with *savoir faire.* If Lady Lucy was attached to a project, it was bound to be a smashing success.

Addie believed Lucy used her position to cadge free drinks and entertainment. Not having the funds for her own member-ship, she was a guest tonight of a club member, Bernard Dunford, who had an obvious pash for her. Lucy treated him like slime on the bottom of her worn velvet shoe, which only seemed to make the young man keener.

There was no accounting for the vagaries of young love.

The rest of the party consisted of the Dean siblings, whose parents owned an exclusive seafront hotel in Brighton, and Millicent Avery, who had organized the evening. Cee and Millie had been at school together, although they'd never been espe-cially close. In fact, Addie was not sure why Cee had called Millie in the first place, but here they were in London's newest private club. Beckett's eyes had been big as saucers, so at least *she* was having a marvelous time.

The room was wood-paneled, which made the space even darker. Olive green suede banquettes hugged white linen-draped tables, a stubby votive candle flickering in the center of each tablecloth. Attempts had been made to resemble a gentlemen's club—the poorly-executed copies of Old Masters on the walls, for example—not that Addie would really know. She'd never tried to storm any of the bastions of masculinity in St. James's, although that was one of the recent popular pranks. Girls dressing up in boys' clothing always caused a stir.

She hoped Cee wouldn't get any ideas. Their mother would certainly not approve.

Wending her way around the dancers, the pretty blond hostess was making the rounds, heading straight for her. Addie tried to make herself invisible by closing her eyes, but it didn't work.

"All alone, love? Can I get you anything?" This was asked kindly, but made Addie feel older and more out of place than ever.

"I'm fine, thanks." The girl didn't go away. Addie sighed inwardly at having to make the requisite small talk. "Is it always so loud?"

The girl smiled, revealing a deep dimple, and nodded. "I expect I'll be deaf before I'm twenty. It's what the membership expects, though. The band is great, isn't it?"

Addie supposed it was. The young musicians were certainly enthusiastic, and were making the most of taking turns with their solos.

"How long have they played here?"

"Ever since Valentine's Day, the day we opened. I heard other clubs want to grab 'em, but Oliver—the leader Ollie Johnson—likes it here." The hostess dropped her eyes to her scarlet-manicured fingernails and blushed. Addie could see one obvious attraction of the Thieves' Den. There were no flies on Ollie, a handsome ebony-skinned trumpet player of considerable skill.

"Well, good luck to you all."

The hostess pointed to the empty champagne bottles. "I'll

send a waiter over to clear all this up. Are you interested in a membership form, madam?"

"I? Good heavens, no. I'm usually in the country." And far too decrepit, she wanted to add. "But I'll take one. For my sister." Addie wondered what their mother would have to say about *that*.

The girl reached into the folder she was carrying and pulled out two pieces of paper. "One for her and one for us. The first is the rules and what-not."

Rules! Maybe Cee wouldn't be interested after all. Addie thanked her and tucked the papers into her evening bag.

"What did Trix want?"

Addie looked up to see Roy Dean loosening his white tie. His conventionally handsome face was flushed from his recent exertions, and he picked up a drink from the table and downed it in one swallow.

"She was soliciting membership. Are you a member?"

"Me and m'sister both. Gave us a family discount. Hottest place around."

Like London's very own version of hell, Addie thought. "So it would seem. The club has been open for a month, I take it?"

"Caught on like wildfire. Much more fun than some other places I could mention. Do you not dance, Lady Adelaide? I'd be happy to go back on the dance floor."

"No, thank you, Mr. Dean. I've enjoyed watching."

"Lady Cecilia says you just got back from New York. I bet they've got nothing like this!" He slid around the banquette until he was next to her, so close that Addie could smell his cologne and perspiration, layering into the funk of the space.

None of it was tempting.

Addie had been in darker, odder, more fashionable spots in New York, but she decided innocent young Mr. Dean did not need to know. She caught Beckett's eye across the room and waved.

"Your little Irish cousin's a cutie, isn't she? Doesn't look a bit like either of you Merrill sisters. Not that you both aren't cute," he said hastily. "You must have broken a few hearts in your time."

Deliver me, Addie said silently. She would have to ask for a push chair to get her feeble body out of here before this stupid boy buried her in kind condescension. Beckett would be pleased at the compliment, however.

"I never kept track. What about you, Mr. Dean? How do you keep yourself busy?"

"I have to spend the summers in Brighton—learning the hotel business from the ground up, y'know. My pa is a stickler. No shortcuts. Worked as a bellboy when I was still in short pants. The rest of the year I try to amuse myself." From the softness under his chin and bleary eyes, he appeared to be doing a thorough job of it.

"And your sister?"

The young man shrugged. "She's on the hunt for a rich husband. Pa is old-fashioned. The hotel will come to me, and poor Pip is on her own. You know how it is."

She did indeed. Her cousin Ian was enjoying the amenities of the Merrill family seat, Broughton Park. If Addie had been born Adelbert, she'd be the marquess and not wasting a moment of her time in the Thieves' Den.

A thick-set waiter came over with a tray of reinforcements— which Addie had not ordered—and tidied up the table.

"Hey, Ted! How's it going?"

"Can't complain, Mr. Dean."

"Rough time the other night, what?"

The waiter kept his face neutral. "Pardon?"

"Tommy. Tommy Bickley. Do y'know what happened?"

"I'm sorry, sir. The police haven't told us anything."

"The police?" Addie asked, suddenly alert.

"Nothing to worry about, ma'am. One of our members had an attack. Heart, they think. A real surprise, him being so young and all. Can I bring you anything else? A buffet supper will be served in the dining room soon."

Addie checked her wristwatch. It was almost midnight. How much longer would Cee want to stay? She eyed a bottle of champagne. She'd switched to ginger ale, but one more glass wouldn't hurt, would it?

The waiter intuited her thoughts, popping the cork and pouring them each a glass of bubbly. One sip told Addie the club was cutting corners on its liquor quality by this late hour. Things may have started off top shelf, but that was a while ago.

"This Tommy—is he all right?" she asked Roy Dean once the waiter left. The Thieves' Den seemed a terrible place in which to be ill.

Dean shook his head. "I heard he died in hospital. It's all rather mysterious. Never noticed he was sick. Wondered where he went—couldn't find him when we all left."

"Gracious! How dreadful. Had he been in good health?"

"Far as I knew. We weren't really pals. Father's a beer baron— you know Bickley's Brewery?"

Addie did not, and didn't want to. As much as she dreaded it, she had to have a talk with Cee and the company she was presently keeping.

Chapter Four

Sunday

Addie had been looking forward to a quiet evening in, but it was not to be. At least tonight's venue, the Savoy, was far more than several notches up from the Thieves' Den, the food and drink superior, the music by the Orpheans somewhat more restrained than Ollie Johnson's All American Band.

The makeup of Millie's party was somewhat elevated too, although everyone and their uncle seemed to be a deposed Russian royal of late. Prince Andrei Alexei Andropov was Millie's special guest, along with his half-English cousin Nadia Sanborn. Nadia's father, a diplomat like Millie's, had married a Russian aristocrat at the turn of the century. Her relative Andrei had made a harrowing escape in the aftermath of the Revolution with empty pockets, a shaky grasp of English, and his very good looks, seeking refuge with the family,.

Addie believed every girl at the table was a little in love with him, and it was not hard to see why. From his white-blond hair to his piercing green eyes to the breadth of his shoulders, he was very easy on the eyes. His melancholy air was designed to foster sympathy, and his fractured English was utterly charming.

Addie was immune—she'd fallen once for a handsome face, and look where that had gotten her. Besides, the prince was too young for her by more than half a decade. She was feeling more ancient by the evening again, and wondered how many silver hairs she'd have to pluck out of her gold tomorrow morning.

Cee was hanging on Andrei's every accented word. Oh dear. Their mother, the Dowager Marchioness of Broughton, was not apt to welcome an impoverished Russian émigré into the family, no matter how elegantly he wore his tails and top hat and how uselessly blue his blood might be.

Two other young men had joined their party: Gregory Trenton-Douglass and Christopher Wheeler, known as Kit. Addie had seen them last night at the Thieves' Den at another table as well, and wondered if any of this crowd ever stayed home in their slippers and listened to the gramophone. If Addie didn't have misgivings about Cee's state of mind, that's where she'd be. Her sister shouldn't need a chaperone, and frankly, Addie didn't feel like much of one, even though the children around her treated her with deference—as if she might totter into an open grave at any moment at the advanced age of thirty-one.

Well, she wasn't dead yet, and planned to make the most of her time on earth while she could. Rupert's early demise had shown her that much—*tempus fugit. Carpe diem.*

Which reminded her of Lucas. She hadn't called him yet to tell him she was back, although he probably knew by now. News in their exclusive little circle traveled fast, and his estate marched with Broughton Park in case he couldn't hear the tribal drums. Her mother's return would have been noted in the neighborhood, especially as she was now employing half the village to refresh the dower house. He'd probably turn up in Town at any moment expecting an answer to his proposal.

Addie wasn't ready to give it.

For years she'd had a girlish crush on Lucas Waring. Their childhood friendship might have turned to something stronger had the Kaiser not intervened. And by the time Lucas was ready to make his intentions known, it was too late. Major Rupert Charles Cressleigh Compton had landed in his Avro 504 on leave and flown off with Addie's heart.

That heart, bruised and battered, was still beating, and rather averse to falling prey to another man. Or at least that's what Addie's brain told her, when she could think clearly over the noise of twentieth century life. She had time, didn't she? Lucas had said he'd wait, would not place pressure on her. He knew how deeply hurt she'd been.

Life as Lady Waring would be predictable. Safe. Lucas was nearly as good looking as the Russian prince, and far more intelligible.

No surprises.

Addie frowned. Where had that thought come from? Oh! From Lucas's first rather lame proposal. Rupert had said—

No. No. No. Rupert had not said anything, and if he did, she didn't have to pay attention anymore. Addie prided herself as being a sensible widow, and sensible widows did not listen to their dead husbands' advice.

"Do you care to dance, Lady Adelaide?"

It was the prince, who had managed to move next to her as she stared at her wedding ring. For some reason, she'd been unable to take it off and lock it away in her jewel case.

"No, thank you, Prince Andrei," she said with a smile. "I'm too old for such nonsense."

"Too old! Now that *is* nonsense. You are beautiful woman. I would be fool not to appetize you."

"I think you mean appreciate, and I'm very flattered. But I'm out of practice. Perhaps one of the other young ladies—"

"Pfft. I did not ask them, did I? If you dance with me, it would give me opportunity to make improvements at my English. You could explain the idiots. Those sayings that make no sense."

Idiots? There were plenty of them, too, to be sure. "I believe you mean idioms. English is a difficult language."

He nodded. "It is so. Through. Though. Thought. Bough. Enough! I fear I shall never get used to it. My French is naturally much better. But, ah!" He clapped a hand over his heart. "I must. I can never go home. My country is gone. Ruined."

Addie couldn't fathom never seeing Compton Chase again, even if she'd only been its mistress for six years, and felt a tug of empathy. "Perhaps one day the world will be different."

"Not for me. I have lost everything but good name. Come, cheer up me. One dance only."

Addie found herself unable to resist. Fortunately the tempo slowed to a waltz and she was swept up in the Russian's arms. She hadn't danced since a few sociable nights in New York, and before that, the odd evening of Kathleen Grant's funeral, when Rupert's jazz records were dusted off and put to good use.

Rupert had been an excellent dancer. He'd been excellent at most everything, except being a faithful husband.

With Rupert's death, now she'd never have the last word. Make the last point in an argument. Receive the last kiss.

Well, perhaps she had on New Year's Eve.

Addie shut her eyes against the glittering room and allowed herself to relax in Prince Andrei's embrace. She didn't wish him to be anyone he was not—the past was best shut up behind a thick locked door. She'd been luckier than most, and knew it. And if she sometimes allowed herself to think of a tall Anglo-Indian police detective, there was no real harm in that.

She turned as a commotion at the table caught her attention. Now that the music had slowed, her sister and her friends had returned to cool off. There seemed to be some sort of friendly argument between Gregory and Kit, with Cee smack in the middle, laughing as they pretended to slap at each other. The drink she was holding tipped and spilled onto the tablecloth, and Kit replaced it with his own.

Cee took a long sip and made a face, then clutched her throat. To Addie's horror, her sister pitched forward on the table.

"Cee!" Addie slipped out of Andropov's hold and ran toward the table. The young men seemed frozen in shock. She heard an almost-forgotten familiar voice in the crowd and stumbled over a chair leg.

"It might be poison, love. Get a doctor quick."

Rupert! Addie couldn't see him on the dance floor, but that didn't mean he wasn't here bedeviling her with his well-meaning interference.

"I need a doctor! My sister's been poisoned!" Her scream was loud enough to penetrate the music, and the Orpheans wound down their notes. The entire room fell silent as Addie reached the table and stuck her finger down Cee's throat, hoping it wouldn't be nipped off.

Poison. At the Savoy. It didn't make any sense, but then nothing did if Rupert was in the vicinity. She prayed Cee would be all right, and was relieved as the first trickle of vomit poured forth. Cee opened her eyes and sputtered, then retched in earnest. Kit and Gregory jumped away, and the rest of the party looked on in mingled alarm and disgust.

"I'm a doctor. What happened?"

Addie looked up. The man appeared too young to be employed at anything, but then everyone looked too young to her lately. He was accompanied by the maître d' and two waiters, who hovered solicitously behind him. "I think—I know it sounds ridiculous— that there was poison in the drink."

"Poison? Are you sure she's not had too much of a good time?" The doctor discarded his dinner jacket and took Cee's pulse. "Erratic. Could be from dancing." He checked her pupils. "Hm. Somebody call an ambulance," he said to a hovering waiter. "You've done well to make her purge, but she'll need her stomach pumped. Tests. I'll go with her. I expect you'll want to come too."

"Th-thank you." A flash went off and Addie blinked. The Bright Young People often found themselves in the newspapers, but she doubted Cee would appreciate being immortalized covered in sick.

The doctor gave orders to the Savoy staff to leave the table as it was, but remove it from the scene. In his opinion, additional glasses might have been tampered with and Scotland Yard should be called. Addie was reminded of last night's conversation about the Bickley boy, but he'd had some sort of attack. There had been no mention of poison.

Cee groaned. "Ugh. I feel awful. What was in that horrible drink?"

"It was a Hanky Panky," Kit said, "a new Savoy specialty. Fernet Branca, gin, sweet vermouth. Thought I'd give it a try."

"It's revolting." That explained the intense herbal smell. Perhaps Cee was allergic to one of the herbs in the concoction. Addie wished she could wash the inside of her nose out, but she was not in such dire straits as Cee, whose Patou dress was probably a lost cause no matter how adept Beckett was with stains.

Their companions were shuttled to a private room to wait for the police, and the entire table they had been sitting at was carried out of the ballroom to await police inspection. Much subdued, the orchestra started up again, and the Savoy's guests reclaimed their evening in a quietly tasteful way. Fun must be had at all costs. It was 1925, after all.

The ambulance crew arrived and poor Cee was carted out on a stretcher, with Addie and the doctor, Paul Kempton, in attendance. It was a little crowded in the vehicle, but Addie was grateful to be able to keep Cee under her watchful eye.

Perhaps she'd overreacted—she was hearing things again, if not actually seeing Rupert. It was extremely unlikely that one of Cee's friends would be the victim of poisoning at the Savoy, or anywhere else, for that matter. They were a harmless bunch, idly rich but with no real malice. Even tart-tongued Lady Lucy could be forgiven for her grumpiness, considering her family's string of bad luck.

Addie wouldn't borrow trouble. Until she knew the cause of Cee's sudden illness, she would hope for the best.

But Rupert *had* said he'd see her again.

Damn it all.

Chapter Five

The Savoy this time. A steep step up from the Thieves' Den. And a stunning surprise—the victim was someone Dev knew.

She wasn't here, though, but having her stomach pumped as a precautionary measure. Most unpleasant. The nine shaken young people who had been present during the incident had been sequestered in a private room by the Savoy management, with free drinks and food. However, no one had been eager to partake of the artfully arranged spread.

Five of the group were familiar faces from just the other day, and none seemed happy to encounter representatives of the Metropolitan Police Force again. All had claimed ignorance under Dev's and Bob's previous questioning about Thomas Bickley; they remained ignorant of this event as well.

Four were fresh interviewees. A new potential victim, Christopher Wheeler, whose cocktail Lady Cecilia Merrill had sampled, swore he knew no one who'd wish him harm. His drink, as well as some others, had arrived while he was dancing, and no one noticed anything unusual. The whole of the table had been on and off the dance floor for several sets, save for Philippa Dean, who'd gone to the ladies' lounge to repair her make-up, and Millicent Avery who'd accompanied her. Dev had always found it odd that women needed a friend for moral support to "powder their nose."

For the last song, Roy Dean had been paired with Nadia Sanborn, Bernard Dunford with Lady Lucy Archibald, Lady Cecilia with Gregory Trenton-Douglass, and—Dev could not quite believe it—Lady Adelaide Compton was part of the group as well and had danced with an actual Russian prince.

Her period of mourning was definitely over if she was whirling about on a dance floor, and soon he'd have the opportunity to see her. Dev would have to take special care that he keep up a professional barrier.

Poison was supposedly a woman's method of murder, but he wouldn't jump to conclusions. So far, the victims did not have much in common besides their age; Dev wasn't even sure if they had known each other. It was obvious to him that Lady Cecilia's involvement in this had been unintended—he'd have to look into Christopher Wheeler's background more thoroughly to see why someone might try to poison him.

Penelope Hardinge was a good-time girl, vying with famous deb Elizabeth Ponsonby for wicked notoriety. Her numerous exploits made all the papers with gushing glee. She'd never refused a party invitation or a drink or drug in her short life. Thomas Bickley, by comparison, was so young and innocent he'd barely begun to shave. Where did Christopher Wheeler fit in?

Dev required the group to turn up tomorrow to be fingerprinted, not that he expected any proof of guilt would be found on the cocktail glasses. The young women were all wearing gloves anyhow. This request was greeted with mulish compliance, and he heard a few mutterings along the lines of "my father's solicitor will have something to say about that."

He ignored the objections, gave them all a warning not to leave London without notifying him, and sent Bob home to his wife and baby daughter. The forensics team arrived in short order, and Dev left them to bag up glassware and cigarette butts.

The hotel was anxious to duck any negative publicity and had promised Dev full cooperation. After he interviewed the barman and the waiter, one of the Savoy limousines delivered him in unaccustomed style to Charing Cross Hospital in Agar Street.

He admitted to himself he was nervous. Had he known he would encounter the Merrill sisters tonight, he might have chosen another suit. Shaved again. Polished his boots. Too late to spruce himself up—it was more important he find the person who was responsible for almost killing Lady Cecilia.

After a quick word and the flash of his warrant card at reception, he was directed to a private suite off the regular ward. The hospital bed was empty, but Lady Adelaide Compton was sitting upright on a gray metal chair, her tortoise shell spectacles on her lap. Her eyes were closed, and there was a glistening sheen across her lids that matched the seafoam green of her evening gown. She'd bitten off her lip rouge and was perilously pale.

Dev thought she looked…well, there were those ellipses again.

He didn't want to alarm her, although he didn't think she was asleep—her body was too rigid. Feeling somewhat like a voyeur, he stayed in the doorway, waiting for her to open her extraordinary hazel eyes.

She must have sensed his presence. With a start and a flutter, she caught her glasses before they fell to the floor and put them on.

"Inspector Hunter!"

Her voice was as alluring as he remembered, a soft alto. With the influence of some wine, he knew she could sing, too, although there was not much to sing about at present.

"Forgive the intrusion, Lady Adelaide. How is your sister?"

"The doctor came in a little while ago. She should make a full recovery—thank God she only swallowed a small amount of that drink. Is that why you're here?"

Dev stepped into the room. "Yes. What happened tonight is not the first time poison has been used to make a point. If it's any consolation, I don't believe Lady Cecilia was the intended victim."

"No. It was Kit. Kit Wheeler. His drink was tampered with. He seems a harmless enough young man. Why would anyone want to kill him?"

"That's what I need to find out. Do you know him?"

Lady Adelaide shook her head. "I only met him to talk to tonight. I did see him at the Thieves' Den yesterday, but we were not introduced. Cee knows him, but not well. We've been abroad, you know."

The Thieves' Den again. It was almost impossible to picture Lady Adelaide Compton there; it didn't seem like her kind of place at all. The dark. The smell. The noise. But what did Dev truly know of her character? He'd only spent about two weeks in her company during a murder investigation, which was bound to alter one's conceptions.

"Yes. I trust your stay in New York was pleasant?"

"More pleasant than this homecoming, that's for sure. Does what happened tonight have anything to do with the Bickley boy?"

Dev looked at her sharply. There had been nothing in the newspapers—between the Deputy Commissioner and Sir Barry Bickley, they'd hushed it up. "How do you know about Thomas Bickley?"

"I don't, really. Just that something was said about him having a heart attack."

"It was no heart attack."

She waited, but Dev was not inclined to elaborate. The fewer people aware of the trajectory of the investigation, the better. Once the press got hold of the fact that someone was targeting Bright Young People for certain death, all hell would break loose. If society's junior set was already pushing boundaries, imagine how they'd delight in testing the Grim Reaper himself.

"They're going to keep Cee in here overnight to be on the safe side. Do you know Paul Kempton? Thank heavens he was at the Savoy. He knew at once something was terribly wrong."

"He's a doctor?"

"Yes. Just qualified, actually. He seems very young to me, but then everyone does."

Dev sympathized. When he met with fresh-faced young patrolmen, it was impossible for him to believe he'd ever been that naïve or innocent.

"Tell me what happened. I'll spare Lady Cecilia an interview until tomorrow." He pulled out his notebook. It was crammed with extra papers that he meant to organize—the whole leather book was becoming too thick and unwieldly, and there were precious few blank pages left. Dev had an attachment to it; his early cases were neatly annotated. Almost his entire history as a detective inspector was within.

"I really didn't see anything. I was on the dance floor when she took a sip of Kit Wheeler's drink. Hers had spilled."

"How did it spill?"

"She and Wheeler and Gregory Trenton-Douglass were having some kind of good-natured argument, or at least it appeared that way to me. Everyone was laughing. Cee went to bat one of them away and tipped her glass. Wheeler promptly handed his to her—they were all hot from dancing, you see. She—" Lady Adelaide closed her eyes. "She clutched her throat and fell over as if her strings had been cut. I rushed over and made her vomit."

"Quick thinking."

"I didn't even think."

"All the better. I'd like to have you around in case of emergency."

Lady Adelaide blushed scarlet. Dev remembered how easy it was to gauge her emotions from her fair skin.

"It was some sort of new drink. With an herbal liqueur."

Dev had the recipe in his notebook. The Savoy Hanky Panky. Its amusing name belied its potency and potential for harm. With its bitter flavor and secret combination of herbs, it would be easy to camouflage the taste of poison.

"The witnesses heard you say the word poison immediately. What made you think that?"

She stared off into a corner at an ugly metal cupboard. "I—I don't really know. A hunch, I suppose. Everything happened so fast. Cee can be dramatic, but I knew at once she wasn't faking."

"Well, I'm glad you were there, and I imagine your sister is grateful as well." He closed his notebook and slid it inside his suit jacket. "I want to talk to this Doctor Kempton, so I'll leave you now. Are you staying in Town?"

"Yes. Although after this Cee might come to her senses and enjoy some quiet in the country."

"You were away some months."

"And I'm longing to get back. As is Beckett—you remember my maid? She has designs upon Jack Robertson and is irritated we're here instead of there."

"Ah. Young romance." Dev did not know what that felt like, if he were to be honest. Despite his mother's every effort recently, he'd avoided her choices for a daughter-in-law.

"Indeed. But if someone is poisoning young society people, I'd like to help."

Dev's heart tripped. "I beg your pardon?"

"Like I did before. Like *we* did. I might be in a better position than the police to see things. Discover clues."

Out of the question. He'd send her back to America if he had to. "Have you forgotten what nearly happened—"

"Of course not!" she interrupted. "I'd be much more careful this time. Face it, I can go into places like the Thieves' Den and The Embassy Club that the police cannot, except when they're raiding them. Even 43. I presume Mrs. Meyrick is out of jail?"

Kate Meyrick's club kept evading the law, and Kate had seen the inside of a prison several times. Dev gave her his most serious look. "Lady Adelaide, I appreciate your desire to help. But believe me," he said, fibbing, "we have this situation completely under control."

"Rubbish. There has been at least one murder so far, yes? And a second attempt tonight."

"How on earth do you know this?"

"I have my sources. And we, that is, I, want to stop this madman. Or madwoman, I suppose."

There was a madwoman right here, and Dev was not sure what to do about her.

Chapter Six

"Well done, my dear. It's just like old times. Fighting crime. Seeking justice." Rupert bounced up and down on the iron bed and gave her a grin. He was still wearing the very same clothes she had buried him in.

She'd been lucky since January 1. Apparently her time was up.

"Inspector Hunter didn't say yes. Stop jumping about like a grasshopper!" Addie hissed. "You'll undo the hospital corners or something. Cee should be arriving any moment."

Rupert sprang off the bed and sat on the other metal chair in the room. The hospital could not have provided more uncomfortable seats unless they'd studded them with nails, but Rupert probably didn't feel discomfort anymore. He'd talked about rules and molecules—really, what on earth was she thinking? Rupert didn't talk about anything since Rupert was *dead*.

Yet here he was again, in the proverbial flesh that only she could see.

"Poor thing. I once had my stomach pumped, you know, when I was barely out of leading strings. Too much cheap liquor stolen from our butler. Father was furious. So, of course, was the butler, who had stolen it from Father. One doesn't cross one's butler if one can help it. Between the two of them, I couldn't sit down for days. Nobody cared that I almost died."

Addie had not heard this story before, and she didn't want to hear it now, though it did remind her of Cee's misadventure with the wine. "Why are you here?"

Thank God he had slipped into a cupboard—or she had shoved him there in her mind—when Devenand Hunter turned up so unexpectedly. Until then, she'd been at her wit's end arguing with Rupert to go away, removing her spectacles and shutting her eyes so she couldn't see him lurking. Trying to make sense to the inspector with Rupert capering in the corner would have been impossible.

If the hospital had a mental ward, she might as well check herself in now—she was right here.

"I know. It's most unsettling for you, me showing up again out of the blue. But think of me! Just when I was acclimating so nicely. After our last successful adventure, I was in kind of a halfway establishment, which was rather better than I expected. But then I was rudely torn away again, without even a chance to discover my mission or shave—I know how you dislike my moustache. Never mind. Sacrifices must be made. Cee was in danger, and I know how fond you are of her. It was my duty."

What a speech. Addie's head spun. Did facial hair grow after one was dead? She'd heard ghastly things about fingernails. "How did you know it was poison?"

Rupert shrugged. "How do I know anything? It's a mystery. Or a miracle. You can thank me now."

Addie would have thrown a bedpan—empty or full—at him if one had been handy. But Rupert's words at the Savoy *had* made her act quickly. She supposed Cee owed her life to him, which was rather an extraordinary thought. Something she could never tell her, or anybody.

"There you go! You're coming around to the idea. There's no point in fighting it."

"Stop reading my mind. I don't like it, and you know that," Addie said crossly.

"I explained about that. It's not actually mind-reading. But I do catch a sentence or two on occasion."

"Well, drop them. It's very disconcerting." Addie rubbed her temples to chase away the headache Rupert always brought with him.

"I'll try. I don't want to upset you more than necessary. You really are mentally sound. Except for the misplaced affection for that idiot dog of yours. He's managing without you, fat and sassy, useless as a watchdog. He'd go off with anyone who had a biscuit in his pocket. Disloyal cur."

Addie knew Rupert's description of Fitz was accurate, but she was annoyed nonetheless. "You're just jealous."

"Of a mangy dog? Don't be absurd! Why—"

"Shh ! Someone's coming! Go back in your cupboard, please."

"It's not *my* cupboard," Rupert grumbled, but he did as she asked.

Cee was wheeled into the private room by the same stern-looking nurse who had given Addie progress reports all night. Her sister's face had long lost any color derived from artificial and natural causes, and she was as white as the sheets that Rupert had mussed. Addie leaped up to hug her.

"Stay where you are," Cee croaked. "I smell like a sewer. I've purged from every conceivable orifice. Even my ears hurt."

"A sponge bath will take care of that. I'll give you two minutes with your sister, and then it's off you go, Lady Adelaide. I'll be in the hall if you need anything."

Once they were alone, Addie swallowed back tears of relief. "Oh, Cee, you poor thing."

"I could be dead, and then I'd be a lot poorer. Thank you for coming to my rescue. I suppose now I have to do everything you say since you've saved my life." She gave Addie a wobbly smile.

That would be refreshing, but Addie wouldn't count on it lasting. "Don't be silly, love. How do you feel?"

"Lucky. Have the police come round?"

Addie felt the beginnings of a blush. "Yes. And you'll never guess who."

"That dishy Indian fellow, the fabulous Inspector Hunter, am I right?"

Half-Indian, but who was doing fractions at this hour? "Yes. He's been investigating some unusual occurrences in the young smart set. I've asked to help him."

"What? And perhaps get in trouble yourself? No, Addie! Let's go to Compton Chase. I've had enough of London. I promise I won't bother David and Eloise."

"Maybe *you* should go. Mrs. Drum will take perfect care of you."

"I'll think about it." Cee yawned. "Get the nurse in here, please. I'm ready for more torture. If I don't get cleaned up soon, I'll need a nose plug."

"A bath sounds delightful." Addie planned on taking one herself when she went back to Mount Street to wash away the odd hospital odors.

Would Rupert come with her? How did he get from place to place? *She* would be taking a taxi.

Addie walked down the dim hallway, hoping Beckett was not up and worrying. It was dreadfully late. Even after the few wild nights in New York, she didn't think she'd ever get used to staying up until all hours, but if she was going to assist the police—

Duty, as Rupert said. She could always nap in the afternoon.

It had been a shock to find Inspector Hunter standing in the doorway. A pleasant one. The man was as good-looking as she remembered, steady and solid, too. He'd firmly dismissed her offer of help, but if he thought she could be dissuaded so easily, he was mistaken. She couldn't sit on her derriere while her sister and her friends were targets of some fiend.

Addie needed to know more about the victims. Society was in flux—the war had accomplished what decades of union members and suffragettes marching had been unable to. There was still plenty of economic disparity, but one could advance if one used one's wits and grit. "Knowing one's place" was nearly a thing of the past. Actresses married aristocrats and no one batted an eye. And if one had peculiar sexual proclivities that lasted beyond boarding school, well, that was becoming more acceptable, too.

Addie had learned a lot last summer. She'd never been a prude, just uninformed.

The twentieth century waited for no one.

Stepping out to the street, she wrapped herself against the cold foggy air. Her embroidered satin evening coat was more for looks than substance, though it did have a silver fox collar. She turned it up to her ears, muffling the sound of her own footsteps. There were no handy taxis anxiously awaiting her, which was a bother. She'd just have to walk to a cross street and try her luck. London nightlife was no doubt still in full swing somewhere, even though Addie was as knackered as she'd ever been.

A shadow fell across the pavement and she squeaked in what was, she acknowledged, fear. She hadn't much money with her, but her wedding and engagement rings would keep some thief in tea and toast for decades, possibly till the Afterlife. She really, really should lock them away at her bank.

But she'd miss their familiar sparkle, maybe more than she missed Rupert, which made her totally shallow.

"*Bon soir*, Lady Adelaide! I didn't mean to do the scaring." The man's head was bare, his hair gleaming platinum under the fog-shrouded streetlight. He dropped a cigarette and ground it out with a patent leather-shod foot.

Oh, good. Not a thief. Or worse. "Prince Andrei? What are you doing here?"

"I ask police where your poor sister is took and I wait."

Maybe there was more to Cee's crush than Addie thought. "Out in the street all this time?"

"Alas, no. I go to the what-you-say cantonment—"

"Canteen," Addie supplied helpfully.

"Yes, that. The coffee, it disgusts, so I sit in lobby. They did not permit me to go upstairs as I am relation to nobody, but I persisted. I only came outside for the smoking. Is luck I caught you in time. Allow me to escort you home."

"That's very sweet of you, but unnecessary." Addie was so exhausted she didn't think she could make small talk in proper *or* fractured English. French was out of the question.

"I insist." The prince gripped her elbow and steered her down the sidewalk. "I have car. Well, is my cousin's. Her father's to be exact. He is important man in diplomatic circles. I, as you know, am nobody now. I have nothing to call my own."

He thumped his chest as he spoke. So dramatic, so definitely un-English.

"A car?" To be frank, her dancing shoes were pinching her toes. It would be heaven to slide onto a soft leather seat. And she'd be home in just a few minutes.

"I sent driver to sleep. I am perfectly qualified."

"Thank you. That's very kind of you."

"Is nothing. How is Lady Cecilia?"

"Much better. She'll be released tomorrow. Well, I guess tomorrow is today already."

"I shall visit if you allow. With the flowers. What does she like?"

Oh, dear. Addie felt she needed to nip this situation in the flower bud. Her mother would thank her even if Cee didn't. "I'm not sure she'll be up to company."

"Then I come next day. Here we are." The shiny sedan was obviously a diplomatic vehicle, flying its little Union Jacks. Addie was quite sure if the king knew its current purpose, he would disapprove most heartily.

A perfect gentleman, Prince Andrei held the door open for her and she sank into comfort. "If you will direct me, Lady Adelaide?"

Addie struggled to keep her eyes open, yawning and pointing out the turns. Traffic was light at this late hour, and Prince Andrei was as qualified as he promised, handling the vehicle capably.

She was nearly asleep when he parked right in front of her Mount Street flat. Addie noted lights were still on, and have would speak to Beckett tomorrow about turning them off at a reasonable time and turning in. Addie could flip all the switches necessary to see herself to bed.

"Thank you so much," she said, truly meaning it. If she could climb the front steps, it would be a miracle, and she said so.

"I come in with you."

"No, honestly—another time. I'd love to offer you a nightcap, but it's been a very long and frightening night."

"I insist."

"But—" He slammed his door and raced nimbly to her side. In one smooth swoop, he gathered her up in his arms.

"Put me down at once!" she cried.

"No, Lady Adelaide. You are tired and I am Russian gentleman."

"An *English* gentleman just doesn't go around picking up ladies against their will."

"You are sleepy. I am man, no matter where I come from. Strong."

"Don't be such a—*such* a man!" Addie whacked Prince Andrei's shoulder, which was pretty much as hard as marble. His trim frame was most deceiving.

"I can hardly be anything else. This my nature as God made me. And I carry you up these bloody steps." With that, he grimly soldiered on, shifting Addie very much like a bag of unruly potatoes.

"You shouldn't say bloody in good company."

Prince Andrei only grunted in reply. She knew she was no lightweight.

"This isn't Russia, where as a nobleman you could do just as you please," Addie reminded him. She'd heard about the horrific treatment of peasants. No wonder there had been a revolution.

"No, sadly is not. Do you have house key?"

Addie fumbled in her evening bag, but before she could fish out the key amidst her lip rouge and hankie, Beckett threw the front door open.

"What is the meaning of this?" she asked, sounding very much like Addie's mother. Addie had never been so glad to see her.

"Put me down now," Addie ordered.

"Not until good-night kiss." And with that, the prince leaned down with a wolfish smile, and Addie could do nothing to stop him.

Chapter Seven

"Huh. I leave you alone for one night and you take up with wicked foreigners."

As Beckett and her old granny were proudly Irish, and republican at that, she really was in no position to lecture about wicked foreigners. But Addie knew better than to argue. Beckett had her opinions, and was not shy about expressing them.

"I'm sorry I was so late. There was...an incident."

Beckett raised a neatly-plucked eyebrow. She followed Hollywood fashion assiduously, from her shingled dark hair to her crimson-stained lips. Lady Broughton was forever after Addie to get a "proper" maid, but Beckett had wormed her way into Addie's heart. "What sort of incident? Too much champagne? A duel over who you'd dance with next?"

"Don't be so saucy. Cee was poisoned at the Savoy." Addie was gratified to see her maid's pert scarlet mouth snap shut. "I—I more or less saved her life, and then we went to hospital."

"Blimey! Poisoned! But you were at the Savoy! You don't get poisoned at the Savoy!"

"It wasn't their fault. Someone put something into a drink, and Cee had the misfortune of swallowing it. She'll be all right, but they're keeping her overnight just to be safe. I'm totally exhausted."

Beckett gave her a knowing look. "I bet. It's a real hardship being kissed by a Russian prince."

"How did you know he's a prince?"

"His picture is in the society papers all the time. Him and his cousin Nadine."

"Nadia, I believe." Addie shrugged out of her coat. She wouldn't describe the kiss as a hardship, just very unexpected.

And expert. Andrei Andropov might be penniless, but his kiss was worth something. She hadn't been kissed like that—well, ever.

"I resent that."

Addie dropped her evening bag to the floor. Damn Rupert for startling her again. Had he been in the back seat of the car the whole way home, or did he fly here on not-quite-angel's wings?

"Look, Beckett, I was going to take a bath, but we both need our beauty sleep." The last thing she needed was Rupert jumping out of the bathroom hamper to ogle at her, or offering to wash her back. "Thank you for waiting up, but you shouldn't have. I'm a big girl and can take care of myself."

"Who's going to undo all those hooks and eyes on that dress?"

"I don't mind," Rupert said with a bright smile. The hound.

"I do! I mean, I will. I think I can take it off over my head." It was loose enough, meant for dancing, all the metallic threads catching the light as one spun and dipped. "Sleep in tomorrow, won't you? And don't disturb me unless someone from Charing Cross Hospital calls. Or the police."

"The police!"

"Yes, I ran into Detective Inspector Hunter again. He's in charge of Cee's case." Addie tried to sound disinterested, but felt a typical blush rising.

Beckett looked contemplative. "Is he now? What a small world."

"Yes, it is," Addie said hurriedly before Beckett quizzed her any further. "Good night now."

Addie went to her room and closed the door firmly behind her, only to find Rupert loosening his maroon foulard tie on her bed. He was always one step ahead of her.

"*How* do you do this?" she muttered, pulling her dress up. There was no point to modesty; Rupert had seen it all, though not in quite a while.

"I believe it's called teleportation. Though sometimes disorienting, it's very useful, wouldn't you say?"

"No, I wouldn't. You can't sleep in here, you know."

"I wouldn't dream of it," he replied. "Dream of it. Get it?"

"Ha ha," Addie said, rolling down her stockings. She kicked her shoes off into a corner, only just stopping herself from flinging one at her dead husband. She was now in her slip and knickers, and there she would stay until Rupert faded into the silver-striped wallpaper.

He stretched across the coverlet, on his usual side of the bed. "I thought we might discuss our strategy."

"Rupert, I am practically unconscious. I've only just got my land legs after the crossing. Do you know I've been out late two nights in a row? Even in my debutante days, I needed a nap." Addie recalled house parties, broad lawns, tennis. Flirtation over the tea table. Young men in cricket whites out to show their prowess, virginal young misses in broad-brimmed hats applauding with gloved hands even if the game was incomprehensible.

Before the war, everything was white and green and innocent in her mind. But now some of those great houses she'd visited as a girl had been torn down, their heirs buried beneath fields of poppies. Nothing would ever be the same again.

"I think you're onto something," Rupert said, jumping up from the bed as if he were on springs. Well, he hadn't been dancing all night, or at least she hadn't noticed him in the Savoy crowd.

"What are you talking about?"

"These kids being killed off. Someone yearns for the good old days. Is jealous of their youth."

Addie sat at her dressing table and removed the bobby pins from her hair. "I'm sorry. You aren't making any sense." She was nearly too tired to run the brush through her hair but managed to free the worst of the tangles. The cold cream came next, wiping away the last of the green sparkle.

"Think about it. First came Penelope Hardinge."

"Who?"

"That's right, I forgot. You don't know. Penelope dropped dead in front of the Thieves' Den a few weeks ago. She was, by all accounts, a very naughty young lady. Drugs, drink, debauchery— all those popular "d" words the Bright Young People embrace so cavalierly. She had her eye on young Ollie Johnson, the band leader, and made quite an enemy of Miss Harmon. That's Trix, the hostess there—you remember her."

Addie did—the pretty blonde who'd given her membership papers. "But you weren't there!"

"No, that's true. I was happily elsewhere." He examined his fingernails, and Addie was pleased to see they weren't growing like that horrible children's tale *Struwwelpeter*.

"How do you know this stuff?"

Rupert shook his head. "I don't know everything, just bits here and there. It's rather like a jigsaw puzzle with half the pieces eaten by the family dog, and let me tell you, I'm *not* pawing through the poo even if I'm supposed to be solving crime to get to heaven eventually. One has one's dignity."

One certainly did, even if one was deranged. Addie really shouldn't even attempt any conversation with him, but Rupert was as compelling in death as he had been in life. "Go on."

"Penelope's pa made a fortune fleecing the government during the war. They couldn't prove corruption, but some ministers' heads should have rolled."

"This poisoning business doesn't feel political to me—the victims are much too young. Why does one murder? For money. Love. Revenge. Maybe Trix killed whatshername in a jealous rage." Addie paused. "And Tom Bickley, too, just because. He might have seen something he shouldn't."

"Now, now, I won't rule it out, but that would be too easy, hardly requiring my help at all. And she wasn't at the Savoy tonight, was she?"

"I have no idea. She could have been—the place was jammed." Addie might not have even recognized her. The girl could have worn a wig or something. Trix had seemed rather sweet, though. It would be a shame if she really were a murderess, but Addie had reason to know people were often not what they seemed.

"Who do you know who is unhappy with his current status in life?" Rupert waggled a dark eyebrow at her. "And I don't mean me."

"You can't accuse Prince Andrei!"

"Oh, can't I? He's got some nerve, Barney Google with the goo-goo-googley eyes. Kissing you like that in front of God and Beckett! Thinks he's the world's greatest lover, just like the song."

Addie laughed, then covered her mouth in case Beckett was hovering. "His eyes are not googley. They're green." An unusual pale green, like gooseberries. Sinfully long eyelashes too. Addie couldn't help but notice. Didn't some men have all the luck in the eyelash department? Rupert, Mr. Hunter…

"I saw the way he looked at you all night, like he wanted to eat you right up but was missing his silver spoon."

"Don't be ridiculous! I'm too old for him!" She'd seen the unwelcome wrinkles as she wiped off the cold cream not two minutes ago.

"*He* doesn't think so. Probably knows you're a rich widow, too. I bet he keeps a list of possible conquests in his sock drawer and plans accordingly."

"That's enough, Rupert. The poor man has lost his home. His family. His fortune. Of course he's not happy! But why would he want to kill random young British people?"

"Who knows? Russians are madmen. Everyone knows that.

They won't be satisfied until rivers of blood flow through Piccadilly. Damned Bolsheviks."

Addie shivered. "That's quite enough. I have no real interest in international affairs."

"Nor I. My expectations couldn't be lower with that bunch at Whitehall."

This was an unfamiliar side to her late husband. If Rupert had lived, would he have sought a career in government? As a war hero, he would have probably garnered many votes, especially now that some women had suffrage. He could be irresistible.

Would he have curtailed his playboy ways for the greater good? She supposed anything was possible.

"I really am tired. Could you go wherever it is you go and leave me in peace?"

"If you insist. But tomorrow, we must have a little chat. I'm looking forward to getting out and about again."

Addie tossed her tissues in the trash. "What do you mean?"

"Why, we'll go out together in the evenings and sleuth. I'm dreadfully sorry I can't lead you around on the dance floor as we used to—I do miss dancing."

"That does *not* sound like a good idea to me. I can't have you muttering at my side all night—I'll go insane."

Some might say she was there already.

"I shall be discreet, I promise. A second pair of eyes should be welcome, what? And I have the advantage of being able to eavesdrop. Nobody can see me but you, though I'm working on that."

"Lucky me," Addie mumbled. She rose from her dressing table. "Good night, Rupert."

"Good night, my dear. Sweet dreams." She blinked, and he was gone.

Squelching the instinct to shake her curtains or check in the closet, she put on the silk pajamas that Beckett had laid out for her, brushed her teeth, splashed water on her face, and climbed into her bed. Tomorrow she would go to Scotland Yard and see if she could persuade Detective Inspector Devenand Hunter to accept her help.

If he wouldn't, why, she would just act alone. Or as alone as one could be with a ghost in tow.

Chapter Eight

Monday mid-morning

Bob knocked on the office door, his cheeks pink. "Guv, you have a visitor. A lady. I mean, a *real* lady. It's Lady Adelaide Compton herself."

"Tell her to go home," Dev snapped. She was the very last person he needed to see today. The reports on his desk threatened to avalanche, and he had interviews to conduct later. Lady Adelaide was a delicious distraction he could not afford.

"I told her you was too busy and that she'd need to make an appointment, but she wouldn't budge. She's as stubborn as my Francie."

As Francie was renowned for her stubbornness, this said a lot. Dev knew Lady Adelaide's sister was on the mend; he'd spoken to her first thing this morning over her breakfast tray of decidedly unappetizing mush in hospital. Lady Cecilia had been unable to recollect anything useful which might add to the case, and was anxious to go to the country.

That was good news. The Merrill sisters could decamp to the Cotswolds and leave him alone to do his job. He'd been nearly speechless last night when Lady Adelaide offered to help in the investigation.

Over *his* dead body. He wasn't taking any more chances. If they hadn't been interrupted by that nurse, he would have given her a piece of his mind, what was left of it. He'd nearly bitten his tongue clean through.

Damn it.

"All right, show her in. But in five minutes, come in to tell me the Commissioner is on the line."

"Right-o."

Dev didn't ask Bob to lie for him often, but in this instance, it was self-preservation. He didn't trust himself. All Lady Adelaide had to do was bat her eyelashes behind her tortoise shell spectacles, and Dev was very much afraid she'd lure them both into peril.

She was looking more rested this morning, in a powder blue lightweight wool suit trimmed in blonde mink. A matching hat was perched upon her golden head. The calendar might say it was spring, but it felt more like winter. Today was damp and cold, a miserable day to match his mood.

Dev swore softly to himself. This could not possibly go well unless he threw a rug over her to stop him from being blinded by her beauty.

"Good morning, Inspector. I've just come from seeing Cee. She's to be discharged this afternoon. She told me you'd already been in to talk to her."

"Yes. I'm very busy. What can I do for you, Lady Adelaide?" He hoped he sounded as grouchy as he felt, and he did not invite her to sit down. The sooner she left, the better.

She didn't seem to notice his rudeness. "I'm sending her to Compton Chase with Beckett on the evening train, so I'll be free to assist you in the investigation," she said brightly.

Christ and Krishna. "As I told you last night—this morning— while I appreciate your offer, you are to stay away. The police have everything in hand."

Lady Adelaide smiled. "You can't keep me home of an evening,

Inspector. What if I want to go dancing at the Thieves' Den? I'm applying for membership, you know."

Dev raked a hand through his hair, struggling with his temper. "I think that's very unwise. That sort of place shouldn't appeal to you."

"Well, it appealed to poor Thomas Bickley and Penelope Hardinge, and that was their undoing. Someone needs to observe what's going on."

He bit back an oath. How did she find out about the Hardinge girl? "You can't look in on all the nightclubs in London," Dev reasoned.

"Of course not. But two deaths have already occurred at the Thieves' Den. I think that's the obvious place to start."

"What can you do that the police can't?" Dev asked, knowing very well the answer she would give.

"I'm part of that social world, at least tangentially. I may be a bit older, but it makes sense for me to go to a place like the Thieves' Den and kick up my heels now that I'm back in Town. You might call me a wicked widow. No one need know I'm cooperating with the police."

"You are *not* cooperating with the police!" Dev growled. And she was the least wicked of anyone he'd ever met, including his own mother.

She smiled. "Not yet, anyway. But you can't stop me."

"No, damn it, I can't! You're a grown, independent woman. But use your head, Lady Adelaide. Your sister could have died if not for your prompt intervention. Is that the fate you want for yourself? Who will look out for *you*?" He'd stick out like a sore thumb in such places, and anyhow, the handful of suspects already knew who he was.

No one would question Lady Adelaide Compton's presence, however—as a wealthy widow and marquess' daughter, she could do as she pleased. She could go slumming every night and twice on Sunday and no one would have the nerve to criticize her.

"I promise I'll be careful."

As careful as they both had been when that murderer pointed a gun to her head last August? Dev still had nightmares. He couldn't count the number of nights he'd woken up in a cold sweat.

She took a step closer to his desk. "I presume you're working on a list of who was present at both the Savoy and the Thieves' Den when the poisonings happened."

Dev slapped a hand down on a folder. "Yes, I'm working on it. And no, you're not going to see it." There were a surprising number of young people who were at both places on the three nights in question. Dev was finding it tedious to interview all of them—most did not take the questioning seriously. In fact, they seemed incapable of taking anything seriously beyond their next drink or drug or themed party. Too young for the war, they were old enough to suffer its dismal consequences. Any bit of fun was seized upon, from dressing like babies with booze in their bottles to midnight scavenger hunts.

"It would be useful so I could focus my attention and narrow it on the likely villains."

She was like a terrier with a cornered rat. As the rat, Dev sighed.

"Fine. I have a few more people to see this afternoon. When I finish, I'll let you know."

The smile she gifted him with was radiance itself. It was all he could do not to smile back at her.

"Excellent! I won't keep you."

There was a knock on the door. Dev was now sorry he'd made arrangements to be interrupted.

"Sorry, guv. The commissioner is on the line for you," Bob said, blushing furiously. Honest as the day is long was old Bob. Francie would know the second he fibbed.

"Is he now? Please tell him I'll return his call in a few minutes."

"But—"

"That will be all, thank you."

Scratching his head, Bob left. Dev would make it up to him later.

"You really needn't delay your phone call," Lady Adelaide said. "I was just leaving."

"Stay for a bit. We didn't have much time last night to, um, catch up." Dev wondered if he sounded desperate to keep her in his office. She was safe for the time being and lovely to look at.

Lady Adelaide dropped into the hardwood chair in front of his desk and crossed her legs. Dev tried hard not to notice her skirt head north.

"Well, you know I went to New York with Mama and Cee. It was amusing for a time."

"Bright lights? Broadway?"

"That and more. There are quite a few British people living there that Mama knows, but we met a load of Americans too. We were quite spoiled with invitations. But after a while, I guess you could say I got homesick."

"Which is why I don't understand your aversion to going to Compton Chase now."

"I want to! If only to see my dog, who probably won't recognize me. But this poisoning business is more important, don't you think?" She looked at him, her expression serious.

"It is, but it's not your responsibility."

"How can you say that? It's up to everyone to watch out for their neighbors. If you didn't believe that, you wouldn't be a policeman."

He hadn't given his motivation much thought lately—he'd been too busy to think. Dev, like the rest of his colleagues, had been preoccupied with the all-female Forty Dollies gang, whose specialties were shoplifting, theft, and blackmail. They were causing a stir all across England, looting stores and homes and very much enjoying the profits. They rivaled the Bright Young People for their evening antics, too. Dev wondered how many of those glamorous girls were on the Thieves' Den's membership roster. He'd have to speak to Freddy Rinaldi again.

That was another reason to worry about Lady Adelaide's safety. Were the Forty Dollies branching out into murder? Dev supposed it was possible. They'd been at the heart of London crime for decades, but had only infiltrated the popular imagination recently through the tabloids.

But what would *their* motivation be? What did they have to gain? The victims had not been stripped of their jewels or wallets, something those brazen young women were experts at. They stuffed everything that wasn't nailed down underneath their clothes in special pockets, thus growing in girth by the time they were done. Most of them came from the Elephant and Castle neighborhood, where they were in league with the local male criminals.

"I appreciate your confidence in my character," Dev replied. "I hope it's not misplaced."

"To be honest, I wasn't always a good judge of character. I like to think I'm improving."

Did she mean her late husband? For all that he'd been a famous war hero, there were glaring lapses of character afterward. If Dev were married to Lady Adelaide, he couldn't imagine ever breaking his wedding vows. He would honor and cherish her—

Ha. As if that were ever possible. Their worlds were much too far apart, no matter how much he was smitten.

And he wasn't the only one. "How is your friend Lord Waring?" *The pompous arse.*

"I'm afraid we haven't been in touch. I only got home Thursday. Gracious, a lot has happened since." She rose, and Dev reluctantly followed. "If I'm to turn into a night owl, I'd better get Cee sorted and take a nap. You will get that list to me?"

"I'll deliver it myself. Shall we say tomorrow morning? Ten o'clock, or is that too early?" Lady Adelaide didn't strike him as the type of woman who lounged in bed until noon, but he reminded himself again that he really didn't know her.

And wasn't apt to.

Chapter Nine

Tuesday morning

The flat was quiet without Beckett's cheerful presence. She usually hummed along to the gramophone or wireless as she went about her duties, but Addie was in no singing mood.

She'd had a difficult telephone conversation with her mother yesterday afternoon trying to explain Cee's "accident" without alarming her too much. Pressure as only Lady Broughton could apply had been placed on her to return home with Cee on the evening train, but Addie had not succumbed. Her mother was dropping her redecorating venture for the time being and headed to Compton Chase to nurse her youngest. Addie had warned her staff to be on the lookout, and had a feeling bonuses would be required.

She'd helped Beckett pack up Cee's things as her sister supervised from a chair, wan and listless. Clearly Cee understood just how close a call she'd had. Addie promised to return to Compton Chase as soon as her "pressing business" in Town was finished, not meeting Cee's eyes at the lie.

It hadn't helped that Prince Andrei had turned up at the cocktail hour, his arms full of red roses. Ostensibly they were for Cee, but Addie couldn't help reliving that shocking stolen kiss. She'd been so flustered at his arrival Cee was bound to be suspicious that she was about to carry on an affair with the Russian prince.

Which she most definitely was *not*.

Addie had deputized him to escort Cee and Beckett to the train station, which left her with a flat full of flowers and a guilty conscience. The scent throughout the rooms was even more intoxicating this morning, and Addie wondered where the man got the money to be so extravagant. Sponging off his relatives was no way to conduct his current life.

Addie had managed to dress herself without Beckett's help in a sober gray shift trimmed with white ribbon and swallow most of a cup of tea. Then she laid out a variety of treats in case Inspector Hunter had time for a biscuit or some pound cake. She expected him to be prompt, but the doorbell rang at nine thirty-three. Willing her blushing cheeks to cool, she opened the door.

"Lucas!' His name came out as a croak, but her old childhood friend Viscount Waring didn't seem to notice. She was enveloped in a rough hug, her nose rubbing against the fine wool of his tattersall suit. He'd have a lipstick mark on his chest, but it wasn't really her fault. If she'd had her wits about her, she'd have managed to escape his unwelcome embrace, just as her mother had taught her. Fainting, feinting, it was all the same. A girl had to be prepared.

"Your mother rang me up last night, and I decided to take the first train. You can't stay away from trouble, can you? Oh, my darling, I've missed you so!"

Addie knew she was expected to return the sentiment, but the words got caught in her throat. Gently, she untangled herself and took a step backward. "Wh-what a surprise," she stuttered.

"I made a pact with myself to wait for you to summon me, but your mama seems to think you are hiding something and sent me to winkle it out."

"Does she? How absurd!" Addie had not revealed her plan

to help the police to anyone. Was Lady Broughton consulting a psychic like Gerald Durant, or becoming one herself? Her mother's perspicacity could be a fearsome thing. Poor Cee was going to have to live with it for the next few days.

"She couldn't understand why you changed your mind about staying in London. She said originally you were awfully keen to go home to Compton Chase after the trip."

"Yes, yes, I was." Addie realized they were still standing in the doorway, where they might be discovered by any of her upstairs neighbors.

Or Inspector Hunter.

Damn. Lucas was a complication she did not need.

"Do come through. May I get you coffee or tea?"

"No thanks. I had some awful swill on the train and I may never recover. Why *did* you decide to stay? Cee might need you."

Addie wondered if he was quoting from her mother's script. She could practically hear her giving Lucas his marching orders over the telephone. "Cee will be fine. Beckett is with her, though I do expect her to return to me once she's helped get Cee settled. Mama has abandoned supervising her decorating scheme for the Dower House for the moment and is there too. My sister will be very well looked after."

"I'm just surprised you chose to remain here alone. You weren't avoiding me, were you?"

Goodness, how sincerely blue his eyes were—could a color be sincere? All of him was sincere, from his concerned expression to the pitch of his voice. Addie hadn't seen him in five months, but apart from the surprise of finding him on her doorstep, she was not feeling...well, anything but slight annoyance. Her heartbeat remained stubbornly regular, her skin was cool, and her breathing completely normal.

Lord Lucas Waring was every young woman's dream—handsome, rich, eligible. Addie had had a crush on him most of her life, and last summer he had asked her to marry him.

So why couldn't she say yes? Her mourning for Rupert was over, and she considered herself to be a practical woman. Her mother would be pleased if she accepted him.

"Let your mother marry him then."

Rupert! She supposed it was too much to hope for that he'd stowed away in the First Class carriage with Cee and Beckett.

Another man she could do without this morning.

Addie ignored him, her nose resolutely in the air as she walked by the bench in the hall. He was sitting cross-legged on it like some snake charmer, minus the snake and requisite turban and *pungi*. The position did not look comfortable, but perhaps the dead were double-jointed.

"Come through the sitting room and tell me all about what's happened in the country."

Lucas grinned. His teeth were straight and white. No heart flip. Oh, well.

"I won't bore you with how many sets of twin lambs were born, or what we're planting in which field. Things are much as usual. I've been down your way quite a bit visiting Eloise and David. They are very happy."

Bully for them—she really meant it. "When is the baby due?"

"The end of July. David got right to work. I envy him, with three sons already."

He sounded wistful. But Lucas was only in his early thirties; there was still plenty of time to pass on the Waring name.

"How are they? The boys, I mean. Do they miss their mother at all?" David's ex-wife Kathleen had been murdered, and Addie was partly responsible for capturing the criminal. Her one claim to fame, which would never be revealed. Marquess' daughters didn't go about getting mixed up in murder inquiries, at least in her mother's opinion.

"They seem fine. Hellions, the lot of them. Eloise has her hands full, but that's just as she likes it. She always was a managing sort of woman." Lucas sat down on the white sofa, pushing some colorful pillows aside. "I say, are these biscuits and cake I see? Are you expecting someone?"

"Um, Detective Inspector Hunter said he might drop by. He's in charge of Cee's case."

"That Indian chap? What a coincidence, eh? I bet you never thought to see him again." Lucas helped himself to a slice of pound cake and two ginger biscuits. "I've changed my mind about the coffee, if it's not too much trouble."

"Of course not. I won't be a moment."

Damn again.

Addie went into her bijou kitchen, lit the gas rings, put the kettle on the boil for tea and measured coffee and water into the pot. She prided herself being reasonably proficient when it came to coffee, tea, canapés, or cocktails. It was far too early to drink, but she was tempted.

Inspector Hunter was a very intelligent man. He would not turn over that list in front of Lucas, who would be scandalized to discover that she was helping the police again. She would have to warn Mr. Hunter at the door that she had a visitor who would run right to her mama with the news.

Addie did not wish to engage in a battle of wills with the Dowager Marchioness of Broughton. For all that she was an adult woman, a widow herself, independently wealthy, and relatively smart, Addie was unsure she could stand up to the barrage. Her mother had had years of practice getting her way.

Addie heard the doorbell as the kettle whistled. "I'll get it!" Lucas called.

Too late to stop him. Grudgingly, she poured the tea into a pretty china pot and did the same to the coffee, and set both on the tray she'd prepared earlier. Shoving open the kitchen door with a shoulder, she came to a full stop. Across the room, the two men were eyeing each other in the manner of dogs establishing their territories.

"Prince Andrei! What a...surprise." She really should come up with better lines.

"Let me take burden." He rushed across the sitting room and snatched the heavy tray from Addie's hands. "To put on table with the sweets?"

"Uh, yes, thank you." She'd have to get another cup from the china closet.

Lucas lifted a golden eyebrow. "*Prince* Andrei? I don't believe we've met." He held out his hand, as any gentleman must.

"Lucas, this is Prince Andrei Andropov. Prince Andrei, Viscount Waring." She'd been drilled for years on who was to be introduced first to whom, and suspected she'd got it wrong. A prince, even a foreign one, would have precedence over a mere viscount, or so she thought. Her mother surely would know.

But Prince Andrei didn't seem to stand on ceremony. He pumped Lucas's hand with enthusiasm and turned to her. "Excuse intrusion. I have come to ask about Lady Cecilia. And see how my roses is doing."

Lucas looked around the flower-bedecked sitting room. "You brought these? Very impressive. Too bad Lady Adelaide prefers the color pink."

"I do?" She'd really never given it much thought. Roses were roses. Now if one really wanted to impress her, they'd bring peonies, but it was too early in the season, and the ants would be a problem.

"I remember next time. How is sister?"

"Please sit. I spoke to my mother very early this morning, and Cee was still asleep. Dr. Bergman will look in on her later." Even if their family doctor was retired, he made exceptions for the Merrill family. "Do you want coffee or tea?"

"You do not have samovar, but I shall take my chance. Tea, please. Lots of sugar."

Addie did as she was bid, then fixed Lucas a cup of coffee. She didn't have to ask how he liked it. That was the thing with Lucas—she knew him so well. She'd never have to ask anything. They had twenty-five years of friendship behind them.

No surprises.

"Friends, remember? Not lovers. Your marriage to him would be yawn-inducing. You'd have to stick pins in yourself to stay awake, and that would be at breakfast. The rest of the day would require something stronger and pointier. Arrows, stakes, swords. Maybe one of those jousting lances."

Rupert was perched on the arm of the sofa now, not far from where Lucas sat. *I don't need your opinion.* Addie thought as hard as she could. Let Rupert pick up on that, puzzle pieces or radio waves.

"So, how long have you two known each other?" Lucas could not keep the suspicion out of his voice.

"Just the two days. I had honor of dancing with Lady Adelaide at Savoy when sister got sick."

"I did see you in the Thieves' Den, though. The night before." The prince had been at a nearby table with his cousin Nadia, Kit Wheeler, Gregory Trenton-Douglass and a few other people she didn't know.

Lucas set his cup down with a little crash. "The Thieves' Den! Don't tell me you've been spending time there. Why, it's a den, all right. A den of iniquity. I've heard all about it, even buried in the Cotswolds. It's a wonder you weren't assaulted and robbed in the dark."

"Really? It's all the rage with young people like Cee. Her friend brought us there. The music is excellent," Addie said, stealing a look at her jeweled wristwatch. Detective Inspector Hunter should be arriving at any moment.

Would he think she'd invited the prince and Lucas as a sort of protective barrier? Nothing could be further from the truth.

"I don't want you going to such places," Lucas huffed. "It's not safe."

"But Lord Waring, I am there to protect Lady Adelaide. Is honor." Prince Andrei straightened his broad shoulders and looked like every girl's version of a champion. Without a jousting lance.

Hm. It would be helpful to have a male champion to escort

her. If she turned up with Prince Andrei night after night, no one would wonder why an "old lady" such as herself was out and about. His charms were hard to resist.

But after Rupert, she knew better. Much better. Charm could only go so far.

Across the room, Rupert raised his hands in submission and mumbled, "Mea culpa."

Damn it! He was eavesdropping in her head again. It was most aggravating.

Addie smiled and let her mind wander. It was a true shame that Inspector Hunter couldn't escort her—she'd seen him dance very creditably, and he was as handsome as any man of her acquaintance.

"Even me?" Rupert covered up his mustache with two fingers. *Even handsomer than you. And much nicer.*

"Ouch," said Rupert, reading her loud and clear.

"As to that, I plan on staying at my club for a few days. *I* can escort Lady Adelaide wherever she wishes to go," Lucas offered with a scowl.

"Dogfight," Rupert murmured. "The prince weighs less, but is probably more agile due to his youth. However, Waring has been pushing that plough for a few weeks to impress his tenant farmers. It might be a draw."

"Gentlemen, there's no need to argue!" Addie said quickly. "I'll be delighted to spend time with both of you."

And then the doorbell rang.

Chapter Ten

Addie would have to give Mr. Hunter credit. He didn't bat a dark brown eye when he entered the drawing room. If he was surprised to see Lucas and Prince Andrei there, one would never know it. And he got rid of both of them with panache that Addie would not have believed possible.

Taking out his thick notebook, he said "I'm here on confidential police business relating to Lady Cecilia Merrill, I'm sure you gentlemen both understand." Firm. A little fierce. The men swallowed their pride and their cake as fast as they could and left Addie's flat in minutes. Only Rupert lingered, twirling the cufflink on his custom-made shirt, pretending not to listen.

"I hope you don't think—" Addie began.

"I hope you don't mind—" Mr. Hunter said at the same time. He gave her a dazzling smile. "You first."

"I didn't invite them. Prince Andrei just turned up. And my mother sicced Lucas on me. She wants me to go home."

"And quite right she is. I had hoped you might have had a change of heart."

"Oh, no! I'm eager to get started. And both Lucas and the prince have volunteered to keep me company."

"I'll come too," Rupert grumbled. "I'd be much better company than those lugs. Lucas has that stick up his arse, and Andrei is just a gigolo. Plus, I can be stealthy and useful. Not that you seem to care."

Addie squelched the urge to put her fingers in her ears.

"You didn't tell them of your hare-brained scheme! Andropov's a suspect!"

"Told you," Rupert said smugly.

"It's not hare-brained. And no, of course I didn't tell anyone. Lucas is so old-fashioned—he thinks women belong at home playing bridge or arranging flowers or doing needlepoint, not working with the police. He'd have a fit."

"So he should. Lady Adelaide, while I appreciate everything you're trying to do, you must be aware the person—or persons—we're dealing with are dangerous. Evil. If anything happened to you, I couldn't live with myself."

"Neither could I—but then I'm not exactly living anyhow, am I?" Rupert interjected. "Look, Addie, maybe Hunter is right. We should pick another challenge to get me into heaven. I—I could ask to get reassigned. If I knew who to talk to." Rupert looked serious, for Rupert. He'd slipped from the sofa arm to the window and was staring out pensively.

"It's a good challenge! I mean, no one should die before their time, me especially. If I can stop the next attack just by being observant, how can that be a bad thing?" Addie asked.

"And how observant can you be with so much going on in the dark? I know what these places are like when they're in full swing. Have you thought this through at all?"

Addie nodded. "If I know who to focus on, it shouldn't be too difficult. You have the list?"

Mr. Hunter pulled it from his jacket pocket but didn't pass it over. "We've pretty much ruled out the Thieves' Den and Savoy staffs, although I suppose we should keep an open mind. Death isn't good for business though, and people need their jobs."

So much for Trix Harmon, Addie thought. How convenient

if she could pin this on the pretty blonde despite her cheerful innocence and that appealing dimple.

"We've cross-checked everyone who was present on the three nights in question, and narrowed it down to eight people, including the alleged victim Christopher Wheeler. He didn't imbibe, so it's perfectly possible he knew the drink was tampered with. I think the Savoy was an anomaly, though—we tested Mr. Wheeler's cocktail. Even if your sister had drunk the whole glass, she wouldn't have died. This time, it wasn't cyanide that was added, thank God, but ipecac syrup. Ironically, it's often given to people who *have* been poisoned to purge the system. Wheeler's cocktail was intended to make one violently ill."

"Could it be some kind of copycat scheme?" Addie asked. The murders had been hushed up, but it was possible someone had cottoned on to them and was deliberately trying to confuse the police.

"We've considered that. But we're hoping that the murderer has run out of the truly deadly stuff. It's damned difficult to get hold of cyanide."

"Could the poisoner be having a crisis of conscience? Maybe the first deaths weren't meant to be deaths at all."

"It doesn't matter what the original intention was. The person who did this is a murderer and will hang." Mr. Hunter sounded as if he'd like to tighten the noose himself.

He pressed the folded paper into her hand and Addie felt a pleasant little zing. "It goes without saying that you not share it with anyone."

"Of course not! I'll…I'll memorize it and then burn it. Or should I eat it?"

Mr. Hunter grinned. "Just like in a spy thriller. I don't think you need to go that far. But don't leave it around where anyone might see it. I take it Beckett has gone to the country with your sister?"

Addie nodded. "She's coming back in a few days, so I'm camping out alone."

"More dinners from the Connaught?"

Golly. So he remembered the embarrassing night when he'd put her to bed. It was the last time—almost the *only* time—she'd overindulged in wine or in any sort of spirits. She blamed Rupert, getting underfoot and under her skin.

"Don't blame me! I was only washing up the dishes, trying to be helpful." Rupert was now plumping a cushion on a chair, as if he were some bloody parlor maid. Addie wished he'd stay put. This fading in and out of corners was disorienting.

"I like being alone," Addie said pointedly. If only Rupert would take the hint.

"Oh. Then I won't ask you to dinner one night."

"Oh! Gosh, I didn't mean you! I'd love to have dinner with *you*." Rupert blew her a raspberry, which she ignored. "It probably should be here again, though. If someone sees us in public, they'll know I'm in cahoots with the police." She had an awful thought. "What about the prince? He's seen you here with me."

Mr. Hunter tapped his worn leather notebook. "I'm here to follow up, aren't I? Your sister was a victim, and I'm asking you pertinent questions."

"I wish I had pertinent answers."

"Maybe you will. We'll give this idea of yours two weeks. The perpetrator has struck once a week for the past three weeks. If he or she takes time off for some much-needed good behavior, nothing much may happen this week. Let's discuss the list. I've dubbed them the Great Eight. A little lame police humor."

Addie unfolded the paper.

> *Prince Alexei Andropov*
> *Lady Lucy Archibald*
> *Philippa Dean*
> *Roy Dean*
> *Bernard Dunford*
> *Nadia Sanborn*
> *Gregory Trenton-Douglass*
> *Christopher Wheeler*

Millie Avery wasn't on it, which was a relief, at least in terms of validating Cee's judgment. "Alphabetical, I see. And typed."

"Bob is an efficient lad. He knows my handwriting leaves something to be desired. It's conceivable we've missed someone, but to the best of our knowledge, all eight were present at each event, though not necessarily sitting with each other or the victims."

"I assume you've interviewed them all."

"Oh, yes. Some after the Bickley boy's death, and the rest Sunday night and into Monday. Miss Hardinge's demise didn't immediately arouse suspicion."

"Did they know her?"

"Only in passing. Not one of them claimed to be very friendly with her—she ran in a wilder circle. They don't even seem to realize she is dead, and I did nothing to alert them."

Addie frowned. "What do they have in common? I mean Penelope Hardinge, Tom Bickley, and Kit Wheeler."

"That's presuming Wheeler wasn't trying to divert us from his guilt by poisoning his own drink. An excellent question. On the face of it, all they have in common is their youth. And membership at the Thieves' Den. Miss Hardinge was twenty-two, Bickley twenty, and Wheeler is twenty-three."

"How does one get hold of cyanide anyway?"

"One can sign for it at a chemist's, although that would be far too convenient for me, wouldn't it? It's found in common fruits' seeds and pits. Plant roots. The French used the gas version without much success in the war, and some manufacturing processes rely upon it—electroplating, printing, mining, photography, even textile production. If one is determined and has the right connections, it's not impossible to find. But," he paused, raking back his hair, "it's not easy to make someone ingest enough of it to die. I understand the taste is terrible. One must conceal it in something else with strong flavor. "

"Like the cocktail Cee had."

"Yes. Except that cyanide wasn't used this time."

"Thank God." Addie picked up her cup and took a sip. The coffee was cold. If one was terribly thirsty from dancing, one might bolt a drink down without noticing anything odd at first.

Mr. Hunter cleared his throat. "One more thing. I must warn you—some real thieves have made themselves at home in the Thieves' Den. Have you heard of the Forty Dollies?"

She laughed. "That sounds like a children's story."

"If only they were so innocent. We've been arresting members of this female gang for quite a while. I grilled Freddy Rinaldi last night—he's the manager of the Thieves' Den—and he admitted several of his members might not be on the up-and-up. I think he knows more than he's admitting, and I intend to put some pressure on him. But you'll have to be very, very careful. Keep your wits about you the whole time." He sighed. "I don't like any of this, Lady Adelaide."

"Thank you for caring about me," Addie said.

"Gag. I'm going to be sick." Rupert pretended to throw up into a sterling silver cachepot on the mantel. Addie noted it was tarnished, and would have to get after Beckett when she returned.

"Of course I care! After last August—" He swallowed. "We were lucky. Very lucky. As much as I want to solve these crimes, the thought of you in danger makes me ill."

"Join the crowd. Maybe he's right, Addie. Go on back to Compton Chase. You can't get into too much trouble there. What's the worst that could happen? Snagging your stocking on a hedgerow? Stumbling into a rabbit hole? Snoring and drooling during that idiot Rivers' sermon?"

"Nonsense. I'll be fine." She hoped so, anyway. It was too bad Inspector Hunter couldn't disguise himself as a maharajah and escort her, but there were too many people who had seen him at work. The thought of him in robes and paste jewels was rather intriguing, however.

But she didn't have time to be silly. Which of the eight was guilty? Could any of them be acting with a partner? She might enlist Lucas's help for a few of the nights ahead, not telling him anything meaningful, however. The same for the prince. It was hard to believe him to be a poisoner, but then she didn't know him, did she? Maybe he'd been turned down by rich and rackety Penelope Hardinge and he'd sought revenge. Maybe he'd been turned down by Tommy Bickley! Although after that kiss, Addie was fairly sure Prince Andrei was interested in women, not young men. But one could never quite tell.

Of the lot, Addie knew Lady Lucy the best. Beneath her haughty sarcasm, she had been wounded by the war as much as her poor dead brothers. It must be galling to lose one's position in society. It was too bad she and the prince couldn't make a match—they had similar problems and would understand each other. But with no money between them, it was impossible.

Was Lucy capable of murder? So far, her sharpest weapon had been her tongue.

The Deans were ordinary upper-middle-class, pleasant, polite, polished. Sent to the right schools. Wearing the right clothes. Pip's future was more clouded than her brother's; she needed to marry well. But Addie couldn't see either one of them slipping cyanide crystals into drinks unless they possessed a streak of madness that was hidden beneath their healthy, hardy fronts.

Nadia Sanborn was a cypher. Quiet compared to her flamboyant cousin, she was pretty, although not as pretty as Andrei. Fluent in Russian, Andrei mentioned she had a job as a translator working for the British government. How she was able to party her nights away and get up in the morning was a mystery. Was she a Communist spy tasked to murder the children of capitalists? Unlikely.

Addie would have to make an effort to get to know Kit Wheeler and Gregory Trenton-Douglass. They had been friends since their school days, and seemed to do everything in tandem. Divide and conquer, if she could.

And that left Bernard "Bunny" Dunford, who appeared as harmless as the animal he was nicknamed after.

"How well do you know our suspects?" Mr. Hunter asked.

"Not well at all, except for Lady Lucy Archibald. But I promise you, that will change."

Across the room, Rupert groaned.

Chapter Eleven

Wednesday

"What fun to catch up! My treat, of course, as I said when I called." Addie smiled above the luncheon menu. She and Lady Lucy Archibald were seated in the magnificent arched Reading Room in Claridge's, a solicitous waiter hovering nearby. "Shall we order some champagne?"

"What is there to celebrate?" Lucy asked, a sour twist to her pretty mouth. She wasn't wearing lipstick, didn't need to. Her lips were naturally coral and Addie almost felt jealous of the younger woman.

"Why, I should think Cee's recovery," Addie said after a startled moment.

"Of course. How stupid of me. You said on the phone she was doing well."

"Yes. I spoke to her this morning, right before I rang you up. My mother is at Compton Chase with her, which gives me more time in London."

"Lucky you."

"I *am* lucky," Addie agreed. "Almost too lucky. With the exception of my husband's death, of course." Although that might be a matter of opinion.

Lucy flushed. "I'm sorry. You must think me the rudest person in the world, and usually I don't mind the title. I've sought it out and earned it. But I didn't mean to offend *you*. I—I forgot."

"You've had your own troubles, I know. And I'm not wearing black as a reminder anymore. What a relief." Addie waved the waiter over and ordered the champagne. Not the most expensive. She didn't think Lucy was quite worth it, and as she didn't plan to drink much of it herself, it wouldn't matter. "How are your parents? My mother sends her best."

"My mother *is* wearing black, on the few occasions she goes out. I don't think she'll ever get over my brothers' deaths. It's been ten years."

Addie recollected the Countess of Marbury's sons died early on in the hostilities, only a few months apart. The elder had been married, leaving behind a pregnant wife. Fortunately for the earldom, she'd borne a son. Unfortunately, she'd remarried after the war and moved to Canada, taking the child with her. It was one more blow to the countess and her husband.

"Grieving is such an individual process. Bad enough to lose a spouse, no matter how difficult they might have been. But to lose a child—to lose two, it's just unthinkable."

"She still has *me*," Lucy said with some force.

"I bet your mother is like my late father. Sons are always more important to some people than daughters. My father would never admit to it, and loved us to pieces, but Cee and I know he would have given anything for a boy to carry on the family name."

"The title will go to my nephew, not that he'll care in Toronto. There's nothing much else left. The house is gone except for the foundation, and my father sold off all the acreage that wasn't entailed ages ago. One has the gatehouse, of course, if one wants to camp out with the mice and the pigeons." Lucy gave a bitter chuckle.

"Not that our circumstances are similar, but you know my cousin Ian inherited and is at Broughton Park. He means well, and is kind to Mother, so I have no complaints." This really was a fib—Addie saw no reason why as the eldest daughter she could not have inherited. Though Cee would be even more difficult if Addie had more to lord over her.

Ah, well, she'd have to take it up with Parliament. She understood the principle of keeping estates intact for succeeding generations, but she didn't have to like it.

The champagne was delivered, opened, tasted. They placed their lunch orders—filet of sole meuniere for her and lobster mayonnaise for Lucy. Addie kept the conversation light, asking to be updated on all the goings-on while she and Cee were away. Lucy was a remarkably astute and cutting observer of Bright Young People, and Addie found herself reluctantly laughing over many of Lucy's somewhat malicious descriptions.

They finally got around to the Thieves' Den over coffee and éclairs.

"I'm thinking about joining," Addie said, touching up her lip rouge. In public. Lady Broughton would be horrified at her oldest daughter's boldness.

"*You*? Really?"

"Why are you so surprised? I'm not dead yet, even if Rupert is." Addie took a quick look around the dining room and was grateful he wasn't counting the napkins or pinging the glassware at the wait station. "I hope you don't think I'm too old."

"Oh!" Lucy blushed prettily. Light brown curls gilded by strands of gold, sky blue eyes, and peachy skin, she really was an English Rose, but with a few thorns still attached. "Of course not. I'm just not sure you'd like the usual crowd there. You're a marquess' daughter."

"And you're an earl's daughter! Why do you go?"

She shrugged. "I'm not a member, you know, just a guest. Bunny insists on dragging me there nearly every night, and one goes along to get along."

"There. You must find it amusing."

Lucy glanced at the cleared table next to them for a moment. "Sometimes. But mostly not."

"If you don't mind me asking, are you and, um, Bunny serious?"

Lucy rolled those sky blue eyes. "*He* thinks so."

"He seems very nice." The kiss of death for some girls. Bad boys were far more appealing. Everyone thought they could reform a bad boy. If asked, Addie was here to tell them it was difficult, if not impossible.

"Yes, he is nice. And rich. And reasonably good-looking. The answer to my family's prayers, in fact."

"I hear the 'but.'"

"He's too good for me," Lucy said, her smile twisted. "And he's thick as a brick not to know it after the way I treat him."

"So, I won't be hearing wedding bells?"

"Who knows? I hear anything can happen in 1925, even Lady Adelaide Compton joining the Thieves' Den."

Addie laughed. "Well, you can expect to see much more of me! I'm bringing the paperwork over this afternoon. Cee will be jealous when I tell her."

"How long do you think you'll stay in Town?"

"I'm not sure. Originally, I couldn't wait to get to Compton Chase, but now that my mother is there taking care of Cee, I'd be superfluous. London is lovely in the spring, all the parks waking up. Window boxes in bloom."

"Rain. Fog."

"Well, we have rain and fog in the Cotswolds, too. I say! How would you like to go down to the house for a few days? It would do Cee a world of good to see some friends. She's apt to be very bored with only Mama for company."

Lucy shook her head. "I cannot leave *my* mama. She depends on me, even if I am second-best."

"Oh, well. It was just a thought. Maybe I could talk to your mother and plead my case."

"No!" Lucy pushed back almost violently from her chair.

"No, thank you. In fact, I've been gone too long as it is. She'll be worried. It was a lovely lunch, but I'd best be going."

"If you give me a minute to settle the bill, my taxi can take you to Bloomsbury."

"No, that's all right. Thank you again." Lucy moved as if the devil himself was after her.

"Huh." Rupert materialized in Lucy's vacated seat. "That was quite the exit."

"I *knew* you were here somewhere."

"Could you feel it in your bones? I confess, I can't feel much of anything anywhere, which is just as well. So, what did you learn?"

Addie covered her mouth with one hand. "I can't talk to you out loud here! I'll look like a madwoman."

"Fine. I'll meet you at the flat." In the bat of an eyelash, he was gone.

"So dreadfully unnerving."

"Pardon me, Lady Adelaide, is everything all right? Lady Lucy left in rather a hurry." It was the maître d', with an appropriately concerned expression on his face. He'd obviously overheard her talking to herself, too. Madwoman indeed.

"Uh, yes. She remembered an appointment. Took me by complete surprise. I was…unnerved."

"Everything else was to your satisfaction?"

"Oh, absolutely! Lovely, as usual. Could you put the bill on my account, please?"

"Of course, my lady. May we send you home with a box of treats for your tea later?"

That sounded too tempting to resist. Addie knew her way around the kitchen in a manner of speaking, depending upon who was doing the talking. Her cook and housekeeper at Compton Chase frowned upon too much interference or democracy, so Addie's forays into the kitchen were limited. She depended upon Beckett to keep starvation away when they were in Town. Since her plans tonight involved getting dolled up for the Thieves'

Den without the maid's assistance, it would be nice to have some sustenance until the club's indifferent midnight supper.

A few minutes later, she was armed with a box stamped with the Claridge's logo. The doorman procured a taxi for her from the queue. She asked the driver to wait while she stashed her goodies in the kitchen and got the membership form and its accompanying exorbitant check from her desk at Mount Street, then journeyed on into Soho.

Addie half-expected the club to be shuttered in the middle of the afternoon, but she was pleasantly surprised to find the door unlocked.

What she didn't expect was to find Freddy Rinaldi, sprawled facedown on the floor in his dressing gown.

Chapter Twelve

"I can't stay here." Freddy Rinaldi made an attempt to throw off the hospital sheet and drew a sharp breath in pain.

"You have three broken ribs and a possible concussion, Mr. Rinaldi," Dr. Paul Kempton replied mildly. "Not to mention those black eyes that will frighten anyone with eyes of their own. I can't stop you, but I dare say you won't get very far by yourself."

"Who's going to open up my club?"

"I imagine your staff is there by now. I'll have Bob drop by and let them know of your…accident," Dev said.

"Tell Trix she's in charge. Temporarily. I'll be right as rain tomorrow," Rinaldi growled. "But not a word of what happened. Tell them I tripped."

Dev had seen enough domestic abuse cases to know all the excuses. But what had happened to Freddy Rinaldi was not domestic abuse.

Bob had his orders, and would wait for Dev to turn up to interview the employees. He didn't expect to glean much information from them, but he would try. Kempton left them alone, a nurse at the other end of the ward in case of emergency.

Rinaldi cradled his ribs. "I got nothing to say."

Dev raised an eyebrow, but put his notebook away as a gesture of good faith. "Nothing at all?"

"Not to a copper."

"Freddy, we know about the mill theft."

The man looked genuinely blank. "What mill?"

"Brown and Sons Textiles. Not only were bolts of cloth stolen, but chemicals, including a small amount of cyanide, as well." The company had ceased day-to-day operation, and was in receivership. It had come as quite a shock when the bankers inspected the building this morning and found it ransacked. There was no telling the exact date of the crime, which was highly inconvenient—no one had been on the site for months. But Dev was convinced it had bearing on the murders.

"I don't know nothing about that."

"You *do* know that cyanide was used to poison two of your club members."

"It ain't got nothing to do with me, I swear! Like I'd kill off my own business."

Rinaldi was getting progressively more agitated. Dev pulled a chair up to his bedside and settled in.

"So, no idea who's behind this robbery?"

"How would I know? I admit, when I was a kid, I ran with the wrong crowd. I've kept my nose clean for decades. Worked hard. Saved."

An operation like the Thieves' Den must have required quite a lot of saving. The building had been redecorated from top to bottom in an approximation of good taste. "You have no silent partners?"

Rinaldi flushed beneath his bruises. "It's none of your business."

"Isn't it? You know, originally I was very impressed with your record-keeping. Trix makes a list every evening of your members present and their guests. Don't you find it odd that sometimes a member comes home to find their house has been robbed while they've been out? Not too much taken, just the odd diamond pin or silver candlestick. In fact, the member might not even notice. Or think they simply misplaced the item. Accuse one of the servants unjustly." Dev had been reviewing some recent thefts—one of his hunches was bearing some fruit.

The victims all belonged to the Thieves' Den.

"I don't know what you're talking about."

"Don't you? It's come to my attention there have been more than several break-ins since your club opened. The word on the street is that the Forty Dollies are responsible."

Rinaldi shrugged, then winced. "Could be. Those girls are everywhere, ain't they? Stuffing fur coats into their knickers right under the salesman's eyes. Walking out of jewelry shops with a whole tray of sparklers. You have to admire 'em for it."

"You might, but I'm afraid I don't." The women were clever and attractive, used numerous aliases, and usually got off with just a warning, or a very short stay in one of His Majesty's prisons. The mill job sounded more like their male friends' work, though. The women were compatriots of a male gang that was known for its brutal style. Anything was fair game, though the men usually stopped just short of murder.

As Rinaldi could attest, if he would confess to what happened to him.

"Look, Freddy, I'm prepared to make a deal with you. Something's going on, and the Thieves' Den is smack in the middle of it."

"Believe what you want. I told you, I got nothing to say."

Dev rose. "Suit yourself. I hope the next time you and your... friends get together, you come out on top."

Damned stubborn idiot. The police couldn't protect him if he wouldn't protect himself.

Instead of waiting for the lift, Dev took the stairs two at a time. He'd been stuck indoors too much lately poring over paperwork and needed the exercise.

What he wouldn't give for an evening filled with foxtrots, Lady

Adelaide Compton in his arms. She'd told him on the telephone she planned to go to the club tonight, and he hoped she wouldn't fall afoul of any criminal element present. He'd recognized a few of the false names the Dollies used to escape incarceration when he was going over the membership list.

Dev shuddered. Lady Adelaide could have been a victim just like Rinaldi if she'd arrived at the Thieves' Den a half hour earlier. Fortunately, she'd had the presence of mind, once she'd checked the man's pulse, to run across the street to the tobacconist's to call an ambulance, then the Yard, instead of using the club's phone. The perpetrator could still have been at the scene, and Dev told her to go straight home. She was gone when he and Bob arrived.

He would have liked to catch a glimpse of her, even under such unprepossessing circumstances.

Damn, but he was a fool.

He checked his watch. The Thieves' Den opened at eight, though most of the action happened closer to midnight. Even if another crime had been committed, Dev had decided to let the club open as usual. Two of his youngest men would circulate in the club tonight, trying to blend in. He doubted they'd succeed. The best he could hope for is that they'd be ignored. They were to keep Lady Adelaide in sight as much as possible without arousing suspicion.

He hailed a taxi outside the hospital, expense account be damned. He couldn't very well return to the Thieves' Den in the ambulance he'd arrived in, and Bob had left in their police-issued car.

There was a pall when he entered the club. A few of the wait-staff appeared shell-shocked, their expressions familiar to Dev after the Somme. According to Bob's quick briefing, no one knew anything about why Rinaldi would be attacked. The band was not due in for another hour, so their questioning would have to wait.

Under her make-up, the club's hostess Trix was pale as a ghost, her crimson lips the only spot of color on her face. She was dressed for the evening, even though it was still daylight. Her mostly-sheer red dress left little to the imagination.

"Miss Harmon, can we speak in the office for a few minutes?" Dev asked.

"Why? I'm really busy, what with Freddy laid up." Her usual girlish dimpled charm was absent.

"I won't take up much of your time."

"Oh, all right."

She led the way to Rinaldi's office, which was, frankly, a mess. It doubled as his bedroom too, and a cot with a mound of blankets was shoved in a corner. Papers covered every surface, and empty coffee cups were stacked on the desk itself. "Is it always like this, or did the intruder toss it?"

Trix looked around and shrugged. "I can't tell. Freddy is not the neatest."

"Yet you keep meticulous records of attendance every night."

"Sure. We send out invoices every week. The members don't like to be bothered to pay cash when they're out celebrating. We cross tabulate with the bar bill and remind them what they owe."

"And they pay promptly?"

"Most do."

"What are the consequences if they don't?" Dev knew that rich people were notorious for not meeting their financial obligations. Many a dressmaker or tailor had gone out of business waiting for payments that never arrived.

"We've only been open for five weeks. It's a little early to tell. But Freddy won't carry them forever, if that's what you're asking. They'll be kicked out of the club if they get too far in arrears, no matter who they are."

"Has anyone been thrown out yet?" It seemed unlikely that a disgruntled Bright Young Person would resort to beating up the club's owner, but one never knew.

"I don't think so."

"Who else has access to the nightly attendance list?"

Trix looked at him sharply. "What do you mean?"

"It would be convenient for certain people to know when houses and flats are vacant while the residents are enjoying themselves here."

"Anybody can see it, I guess. It's not a secret. I keep it at the podium in the vestibule until we close."

"So no one has come to you to ask to look it over?"

"No."

"Not even your sister?"

Suddenly, Trix Harmon wasn't so very pale. "I don't have a sister!"

"My mistake. I must have gotten some names mixed up."

"Look, Inspector, I've got to get the house organized. The band is due any minute to practice, too."

"I won't keep you. If you remember anything that might be helpful to your boss, let me know. Have a good evening."

Dev left her muttering and scooping up coffee cups. He would bet his next paycheck that Mary Hart, AKA Mary Smith AKA Mary Frances Harmon, member in good standing to both the Forty Dollies and the Thieves' Den, was Trix Harmon's sister.

Chapter Thirteen

Almost Thursday

Addie had drunk a pot of coffee in her attempt to stay awake long enough to make her grand entrance at the Thieves' Den. And grand it was. She wore a jeweled net cap over her hair, her favorite fox stole, and a slinky silver floor-length satin dress.

Satin was not very forgiving, so every pound that Addie gained on her cross-Atlantic journey—the food had been incredible—was visible. She hoped it added to her allure as a wicked widow. Unfortunately, she still had to wear her specs if she was to catch a criminal in the act, but she was determined to bat her mascaraed eyelashes as often as possible behind the lenses to live up to her new naughty persona.

She gave her membership application and a check for the outrageous fee to the pretty hostess Trix, who was stationed at the mahogany podium. The girl wore a flashy red dress that contrasted with her pearlescent skin. Jazz was blaring from the main room.

"Changed your mind, eh?" Trix shouted.

"Why not?" Addie said with a brilliant smile, shouting back. "I believe it's a woman's prerogative."

"Well, welcome to the Thieves' Den. I'll see that you get a membership packet in the post."

"No hurry. I'm not much for rules," Addie fibbed. Any daughter of the Marchioness of Broughton was primed for propriety under most circumstances. Even rebellious Cee didn't press ahead too far into the modern abyss.

"Are you meeting anyone tonight?" Trix asked.

"Is the prince here?"

"Which one? We have a few, you know, from all over," the hostess said with pride. "The Prince of Wales doesn't belong yet, but he comes in with his friends sometimes."

Addie was positive the King would soon be having sharp words with his rebellious son. "I'm looking for Prince Andrei."

Trix's scarlet fingernail traced the list in front of her. "I don't see him. I haven't been at the podium all night, or I'd remember him coming in. Isn't he the cat's meow?"

"Um, yes, isn't he? He doesn't have a bean, though." It had been drilled into Addie that one never spoke of money. Oops. But she felt protective of the prince and Trix's possible interest. "How does he manage to pay the fees?"

"His cousin, I think." Trix shrugged. "I shouldn't be talking out of turn."

"It's all right—it's just between us girls, isn't it?" Penelope Hardinge and Thomas Bickley were heirs to great fortunes. Addie didn't see what that might have to do with their deaths, but one never knew.

Had they been blackmailed over some indiscretion and neglected to pay? Penelope had a substantial portfolio of peccadilloes, but as far as Addie knew, the Bickley boy was as blameless as a wooly white lamb. "I want to sit with amusing people. Let me just come around and see who's here."

"No! That is, I can't show you the list—I'll get in trouble. It's meant to be kind of confidential."

"How silly when I have eyes in my head. As soon as I step

over the threshold, I'll see who's in the room. I just don't want to get flagged down by tiresome people and be forced to sit with them. You understand, don't you, dear?" As Addie gave her little speech, she fished into her bag and brought out a fiver.

Trix's eyes widened, but she palmed the bribe with alacrity. Addie wished she'd had more small denominations, but she was saving them for the taxi fare home—five pounds was an obscene amount of money to give away for so little. She stepped around the podium and skimmed the names. Trix's handwriting was not exactly illegible, but it took Addie a minute to figure it out.

"Oh, good! Kit and Greg are here! Such lovely boys. Will you bring me to them?" They were the only names she recognized from the suspect list.

"Of course, Lady Adelaide." Trix would probably escort Addie to the gates of hell for five pounds.

She followed the girl through the smoky main room, stifling a cough. Dozens of couples were dancing with abandon, and Addie avoided meeting anyone's eyes. Trix led her through the arches to the smaller, separate room to the rear she'd sat in before. The band was still more than audible, but the atmosphere was not quite so manic, the smoke not so thick. The tables back here were half-empty tonight, votive candles flickering against the gloom.

Christopher Wheeler and Gregory Trenton-Douglass were seated at a table for two, appearing to be in the middle of an argument. Trix hung back, but Addie forged ahead, adopting a brazenness that would seriously dismay her mother.

"Good evening, gentlemen! Do you mind if I join you? I need a port in the storm. Two ports are even better."

They both rose quickly, pasting polite smiles on their handsome faces. The men were a study in contrasts. Wheeler was fair, reminding Addie a little of a younger Lord Lucas Waring, square-jawed and blue-eyed. Trenton-Douglass, despite his double-barreled name, looked darkly foreign, even down to his tailoring. French, she thought. A gentleman, wherever his ancestors came from—he immediately grabbed a chair from a vacant table for her.

Wheeler took her hand. "Lady Adelaide! What a pleasure. How is your sister faring? I've been crushed with guilt that she came to harm because of me."

"It's not your fault, Kit. How were you to know that your drink was tampered with? And anyway, one doesn't expect such shenanigans at the Savoy. Please, let's sit and save our strength." Addie's new dancing shoes needed breaking in. How she longed for her comfortable pair of brogues and a country lane to walk in.

"We almost didn't come out tonight," Gregory Trenton-Douglass confided. "We stayed in Monday and yesterday, you know, just so you don't think we're heartless. It's all been such a shock."

"Life is short, as I have reason to know. There's no point to hibernating under the covers. Where is that waiter? I'm simply parched." Any more liquid after the coffee was apt to send Addie into the ladies' loo, but who knows what she'd discover in there?

Kit rose again and signaled the waiter across the room. Addie remembered the man's name was Ted, and greeted him warmly. "What can you recommend, Ted?"

He checked his watch. "The champagne is still apt to be good, milady."

Just as she'd suspected. The longer the nights wore on, the weaker or more inferior the drinks. It made good business sense, she supposed. Why waste the premium stuff on a clientele too tipsy to notice?

"What are you boys drinking? Will you join me in a bottle? I can't drink it all alone."

"Certainly. Put it on my tab," Greg said gallantly. Ted scurried away as fast as a man his size could go.

"Thank you." Addie adjusted the fox stole, which was tickling her nape. "Where is everybody this evening? I don't recognize any of Cee's friends."

"Funny you should mention that. We were just fighting—well, not fighting, exactly, but I thought we should go," Kit said a bit sheepishly. "The usual crowd isn't here. That wog policeman put the fear of God in them, I reckon."

Addie felt her blood chill. And here she'd thought Kit and Greg were nice boys instead of snotty prejudiced public school clichés. "Pardon?"

"We were all interviewed after your sister's accident by some Indian chap. M'father's called the commissioner to complain. Man shouldn't be allowed to speak to his betters the way he did."

"I believe I met him in hospital," Addie said, her voice chilly. "I found him to be perfectly polite and professional. His ancestry should not be an issue to anyone with a modicum of intelligence and perspicacity."

His betters, indeed. These two callow boys couldn't hold a candle to Dev—Detective Inspector Hunter, that is.

"Well, he would kowtow to you, wouldn't he? You're a marquess' daughter, after all, and sister to the victim. He treated Greg and me like scum with all his stupid questions."

"How else is he to catch a k—um, whoever put poison in your drink?"

"It was probably just a prank," Greg offered. He gave Kit a look, but the other young man gave a slight shake of his head.

"I hardly think it's very funny," Addie said, incensed. "Do you actually have friends who would do such a thing? At the Savoy, of all places."

"I wouldn't have thought so, but anything goes nowadays, doesn't it? As long as we're not bored." Kit brightened. "Oh, good. Here comes Ted with the champagne."

Addie would have much preferred beaning the boys on the head with the bottle, but forced herself to stick to her mission. She took sips as the young men bolted the liquid down as if it were water.

Time to get them back on track. "So, what did Mr. Hunter say that was so offensive?"

Greg gazed around the dim room and leaned in. "He was pretty cagey, mentioning some names, but we figured it out between us."

"Don't, Greg. You'll only alarm Lady Adelaide."

"I'm not made of spun sugar, and if it has anything to do with what happened to Cee, I want to hear it."

"What happened to Lady Cecilia was probably not the first time some maniac has struck. We've done some sleuthing. Did you know that two people died *here*?"

Addie pretended ignorance, clutching her pearls with a gloved hand. "No! Really?"

"Some tart we really didn't know, as we told that Hunter person, and then a poor kid we did, Tommy Bickley. He was behind us at school. He never quite fit in, though. There was money, but no class, if you catch my meaning."

Addie certainly did. She would have to consult her Debrett's and see if either Kit or Greg turned up in some muckety-muck's family tree. Somehow she divined they would be on somewhat lower branches. The biggest snobs were always those that had no right to be.

"He practically accused *us* of killing them!" Kit said, his face darkening in anger. "'Where were you on the night of so-and-so?' As if a fellow can remember all of his social engagements."

"I'm sure you misinterpreted that." Inspector Hunter was far too astute for to make accusations that wouldn't stick. "Did he actually tell you those two young people were dead? I haven't read anything in the papers."

"Naw. We knew about Bickley being found under the table, of course. Heard he had heart problems. But the girl—what was her name, Kit?"

"Peggy. No, Penny something."

"We asked around. She died on the pavement outside. Her pa had it all hushed up."

"How very peculiar," Addie said, wrinkling her nose. "Do you think the Thieves' Den is dangerous?"

"No more so than the Savoy. If anything can happen there—" Kit shrugged.

"Maybe these incidents have nothing to do with each other. Why would someone try to poison you, Kit, if you say you aren't close to the two dead people?"

"Damned, I mean, dashed if I know."

"Aren't you worried it will happen again?"

"Greg will watch out for me, and I'll watch out for him. We do everything together."

Addie raised an eyebrow. "Everything?"

Kit looked straight at her. "You're a woman of the world, Lady Adelaide. Greg is my partner. In all things. We're not ashamed." He reached for Greg's hand and gave it a squeeze.

Ah. But someone might have quite a different idea of propriety. Homosexuality was a crime. Which was better—poison or prison?

Chapter Fourteen

Thursday

Addie opened one eye and promptly shut it. Rupert was seated on a chair next to her night table, tossing her alarm clock back and forth between his well-manicured fingers.

"Go away."

"Didn't you hear it go off? It was loud enough to wake the dead. Hahahaha."

"Very funny. What time is it?"

"Just after nine. How did it go last night? I regret I was unable to join you. Something came up."

Addie had heard the "something came up" excuse for most of her marriage, and didn't bother to quiz him. Although he was supposed to be on some sort of improvement plan, she expected he weaseled his way around in Limbo just as he always had on earth.

Addie sat up and stretched. "I met with Kit and Greg. It's too soon to rule them out, although I can't see them as murderers. They didn't even remember Penelope Hardinge's name."

"They're good actors. They have to be, considering their personal proclivities."

"Damn it, Rupert, do you know everything?"

"Not everything, pet. We've discussed that. Come along— I've brewed you a pot of coffee and stand prepared to butter you a scone from your Claridge's' bounty."

"You didn't eat the last cream puff, did you?" Addie asked accusingly.

Rupert didn't meet her glare. Apparently Rupert ate and drank when he wished, which led her to wonder about all sorts of physiological things. She excused herself to perform her own, slipped into her least seductive robe, and joined Rupert in her little kitchen. He'd set the enamel table with linen napkins, the jam pot, a glass jug of cream, her good china. There was even one of the prince's red roses floating in a brandy snifter.

"Thank you for fixing the coffee—it smells heavenly." Rupert had never shown any domestic inclination whatsoever before he died, but she was grateful he did now. Truth be told, Addie had a hangover. She was feeling the after-effects of a very late night and too many glasses of champagne. In her current state, she probably would have scorched her fingers on the toaster.

They sat in cozy quiet, Rupert reading *The Times*, crunching crumpets the only sound. It was bittersweet, Addie thought, this sudden reunion with comfort and companionship. She had just about come to terms with the fact that she wasn't losing her mind, that her late husband was an apparition that only she could see. There really was no other explanation. She wondered how many other widows across the British Isles were being haunted right this minute—perhaps they could form a club. Produce a pamphlet of do's and don't's. Support each other before they checked themselves into a grim mental hospital.

"Huh."

"Anything interesting in the paper?" Addie asked.

"That fellow Mussolini is out and about again in public making mischief. There was speculation he was ill, but I guess he's recovered. And tuxedos for women are all the rage in Paris. Don't buy one, I beg you. Some things are sacrosanct and should be kept in the male sphere. Cigars. Cars. Combat."

Addie spread a dollop of strawberry jam on half a scone. "I drive perfectly well and you know it. I never would have thought you were so old-fashioned."

"I know. It's an unexpected turn. I grow more like my poor old pa every day. How is he?"

Addie faithfully corresponded with Rupert's elderly parents in Cornwall. So far, she had withheld his recent reappearance—and numerous past sins—from them. "Both your parents are well, I believe. I wrote to let them know I was back from the States, but I haven't received a letter yet."

He folded the paper and laid it next to his plate. "What's on the agenda today?"

"Prince Alexei. He's dropping by later for lunch."

Rupert sat up. "Here?"

It was gratifying to hear the objection in Rupert's voice. "Yes. And then later I'm having dinner with Lucas."

"Faugh. I don't envy you."

"Why not? They're both very attractive, intelligent men." Red flag. Bull. It was almost enjoyable—if ironic—to see Rupert so proprietary in death after his own amorous lapses in life.

He seemed to think the better of charging. "Don't get me started. I suppose you'll want me to scram."

"That would be most helpful," Addie agreed. She was having lunch delivered from the Connaught for the Russian prince. After having dinner with Lucas tonight, she'd have to go on a diet, especially if she had to get through any more bathroom windows or other tight spots in the future. Womanly curves were to be rued lately, although Addie was damned if she'd bind her breasts to be fashionable.

She'd simply been born in the wrong decade.

After Rupert slipped away, Addie got out Beckett's feather duster and swiped various surfaces with lackluster vigor, then

attended to her own bath and beautification. She ensconced herself in the drawing room window seat, where she could observe
the comings and goings on Mount Street between turning the
pages of an old issue of *Flynn's*. Agatha Christie had a short story
in it, *Traitor's Hands*. After last summer, Addie had sworn off
fictional mysteries, but she couldn't seem to resist the siren's lure
of Mrs. Christie.

The service bell rang promptly at noon, and Addie ushered
the young waiter into the kitchen with his boxes. He arranged
everything with precision on the dining room sideboard, cheer-
fully received his tip, and returned to the hotel. Lunch would
not be fancy—sandwiches, salads, and a very tempting coconut
cake. Addie wanted to put the prince at ease with picnic food,
although it was still too cold to eat outside on her handkerchief-
sized backyard terrace. She poured wine for him, but none for her.

Prince Andrei was also prompt, turning up at half past noon, a
pink rosebud in his lapel and pink rosebuds in a filigree holder for
her. He had a good memory, then, and was anxious to make a good
impression. Would Lucas arrive tonight with more pink roses?

The Russian kissed her hand, and Addie was immediately
reminded of his other kiss Sunday night. It would not do to con-
centrate on that—no more kissing *anyone* unless it was absolutely
unavoidable. Addie had considerable practice ducking and bob-
bing before her marriage, during, and afterward, too.

"You are exquisite, my lady," the prince said. Addie wouldn't
have gone that far—her pale yellow silk dress was nice enough,
but not couture. But perhaps he was noticing the gold bangles at
her wrists and gold rope at her neck, toting them up their worth
like a jeweler.

"Thank you, Your Highness. Won't you come through into
the dining room?"

He followed her into the stylish black and white space. She'd
replaced some of the decorator's mirrors with framed photo-
graphs of the new American Radiator building in New York City

in all its black brick and gothic gold glory, and he commented immediately. "How magnified! Did you take pictures?"

"Magnificent," Addie said automatically. "Alas, no. I'm a terrible photographer. Even if the object can't move, it's always blurry when the film is developed. Isn't the building beautiful, though? It has the kind of elaborate detailing I missed being away from London." She'd longed for London's architecture more than she'd expected, even though much of New York was an imitation of the capital, even down to its social scene. Young people were untethered there too, floating away on the latest, louchest wave. She hoped they wouldn't meet the fate of the poor Bickley boy and Penelope Hardinge.

"Very true. Everywhere one looks here is feast for eyes. Like Moscow. I like countryside too, though. To ride. Hunt. Tell me about your house."

Did he plan to move in? Addie helped herself to the food, and Prince Andrei followed suit.

"Most of Compton Chase is old. Jacobean." She saw his frown. "That's early 1600s to King James the First's death in 1625."

"And it does not fall down on pretty head?"

Addie smiled. "All fixed. Mostly. The house has been in my husband's family for generations. It underwent some renovation last year." It had been worth all the mess and expense, though parts of the house were still shut up.

"It yours in full? No tail?"

"You mean entail. No. I could sell it tomorrow if I wanted." Rupert had inherited the house from his grandmother; ownership had hopscotched between members of the family. One day Addie might decide to up sticks and let another Compton move in.

Addie wondered if she was ticking all the prince's boxes as a rich widow to be conquered. Not fated to be his princess, she needed to steer the conversation back to the murders. "So, tell me, how long have you been in England?"

"Three years. Was very difficult to get out of Russia. You

have no idea of the indignitaries. The subsistence. But uncle was tireless. Though my mother..." He shrugged. "Too stubborn to come with me. Said she too old to learn new customs and language. Better to stay hiding in hovel with babushka."

"How awful for you. Can you get word to her?"

"No. I must think of her in our old dacha garden clipping the rose. She is probably shot dead."

Addie inhaled at his bluntness, but she couldn't see how his misery translated to murder of strange young English people. "You must think positively; perhaps everything is all right." She poured him more wine. "What do you think of our fair shores? I don't suppose they have places like the Thieves' Den in Moscow."

He almost laughed. "No. No fun anywhere. But perhaps is selfish to try be happy. People starve. Die on street."

Addie glanced at the spread on the sideboard, which now even in its simplicity seemed altogether too lavish. "One donates to charity the best one can." Addie's man of business, Mr. Beddoes thought her far too generous already, but perhaps she should look into Russian fundraising organizations.

"*I* am charity case. My uncle—well, not exactly uncle, he is married to my mother's second cousin—wishes for me to find employment. If I success, he will give blessing for me to marry Nadia." The prince did not sound at all enthusiastic. Did he object to the job or the bride? If he was smitten with his distant relative, would he go carting around and kissing widows anyway?

"She seems like a lovely girl," Addie said, her voice neutral.

"She is. Pretty. Smart. Her Russian is almost good. She does not like me."

"Why not?"

"She thinks I am...hoe? Shovel? A garden tool."

"Rake."

"Yes. That. But I was raised to be courtly. Is second nature."

"Perhaps you should spend less time being attentive to other women and pay more attention to her." Addie knew her advice was good, but she was far from getting any useful information out of the prince.

"I could try." The doubt was written all over his face.

"I'll help you," Addie said, wondering what she was getting herself in for. "But no more kissing."

Chapter Fifteen

Even inside the shadowy club, Freddy Rinaldi sported sunglasses and a large bandage across his nose. He squeezed Addie's gloved hand hard and brought her close. "I wanna thank you for the other day. Coming to my rescue and all. Hunter says it was you what found me."

Addie nodded and tugged herself free. All she needed was for Lucas to wonder what this was all about. He was checking her coat at the moment, grumbling that it was sure to be nicked. It had been all she could do to persuade him to come here after their dinner at Rules, and she imagined the least little thing could propel them both back into a taxi with him in high dudgeon.

"I'm glad you're feeling better, Mr. Rinaldi. Are any of my friends here tonight?"

"Trix would know. I been hiding out in my office. Don't want to scare the customers away." He grinned wolfishly; indeed, he was rather frightening in a movie villain kind of way. "She'll take you where you and your fella want to go." He snapped his fingers in the air, and Trix hurried forward.

"Good evening, Lady Adelaide. How are you this evening? Alone again?" There was no sting in the last question.

"Not tonight. My friend is seeing to our coats."

"Do you have a seating preference? Big room or back room?"

Addie felt she wasn't getting anywhere whittling down the suspect list. So far, she felt rather sorry for the four people she'd spent time with. Even if Kit and Greg were race-prejudiced idiots, the road they were on was bound to be fraught with considerable peril. The prince was at very loose ends, and Lady Lucy was just plain unhappy.

She had the list memorized, even if she hadn't eaten it. The Dean siblings, Nadia Sanborn, and Bunny Dunford were left. She asked Trix if any of them were present.

"The Deans are here. Miss Sanborn and Prince Andrei were here earlier, but..." Trix leaned forward and whispered loudly enough to be heard over the band..."I think they had a fight. Families. It's always something, isn't it?"

Addie had to agree. Her mother and sister gave her plenty of anxiety.

Lucas found her waiting at the podium and placed a territorial hand on her elbow. "Please say all the tables are taken."

"Oh, no, sir. We've got plenty of room for you. Did you want to sit with the Deans, Lady Adelaide?"

"Please. Thank you, Trix."

They followed Trix's swaying derriere through the labyrinth of tables. The hostess was wearing the red dress again, and more than a few male patrons noticed her as she moved among them. Females, too. Addie tried not to be jealous of the girl's youth and figure. Her own costume should give her sufficient confidence, a deep iris silk dress with elaborate stitching, and an amethyst parure to add her own sparkle.

"My God, you know the name of that girl. Really, Addie, you've changed since you came back from New York."

"I should hope so," Addie said. Better to go forward than back.

Once again Trix brought Addie to the quieter room. Pip and Roy Dean had just come off the dance floor and were slightly disheveled and glistening with perspiration.

"Lady Adelaide! You just missed us trying to replicate the Astaires," Roy said with a big grin.

"Little chance of that. You stepped on my foot five times, you big baboon," Pip said without rancor. "How is Lady Cecilia?"

"She's doing well. Lucas, may I introduce you to Philippa Dean and her brother Roy? This is Viscount Lucas Waring."

Pip's fingers went up immediately to her bobbed auburn hair while Roy straightened up and extended a hand. "How d'you do, my lord. Your first visit to the Thieves' Den?"

"And my last if I'm lucky," Lucas grumbled.

"Oh, it's really ever so much fun here," Pip assured him, "especially if you like to dance. The band is excellent. They're American."

"Oh, joy."

"Lucas," Addie murmured. "Be nice. Pip, would you accompany me to the loo?"

"Of course. You gentlemen behave."

Pip clutched Addie's hand once they were downstairs in the pink chintz-covered lounge. Thick smoke hung here too, with crystal ashtrays on every flat surface overflowing with cigarette butts. One young flapper seated in a cushy chair was removing a torn stocking, while another young woman added a coat of scarlet to her already-crimson lips. "Your viscount friend is absolutely divine! Is he married?"

"No. But I wouldn't get your hopes up. He's an awful snob. A stick-in-the-mud, too." Lucas would never look at a girl like Pip; she was much too middle-class, even if she was so very pretty. Lucas had long forgotten that his father had never expected to inherit, and would have been middle class himself had not his distant relatives all conveniently dropped dead.

"Why are you out with him, then?" Pip asked, fluffing her damp hair with her fingers.

"Habit, mostly. We've known each other since we were children." Addie powdered her nose, then went to use the facilities. She wouldn't mention that Lucas had proposed.

When she came out of the stall, they were alone. Pip lit a cigarette and stretched her shapely legs out in front of her. "Have you heard anything else about what happened to Lady Cecilia at the Savoy? Any one of us could have been a victim. I've been frightened to death."

Not too frightened to go out tonight, however. "You didn't see the drinks delivered, did you?" Addie asked as she washed her hands. A crumpled pile of used linen towels on the counter was most uninviting. She felt honor-bound to report her objections to Mr. Rinaldi at her earliest convenience. A proper club would have a matron stationed down here to tidy things, but then, she reminded herself, her conversation with Pip would be limited.

And this was, for all intents and purposes, an *im*proper club.

"No. I was with Millie in the loo. I wonder—this poison business—did something like that happen to Tommy Bickley? From the questions that policeman asked, I've been thinking things aren't what they appear to be."

"What do you mean?"

"People said he had a heart attack, but I can't believe it. He was only twenty, for God's sake, and didn't seem sick at all, only a little sad. He had the judgment of a not-very-bright puppy. Imagine, falling for a girl like Penelope Hardinge. She would have eaten him for breakfast if she even noticed he was alive."

Addie's comb paused in mid-air. "Excuse me?"

"Do you know her? She's so much worse than Elizabeth Ponsonby, if you can believe it. I haven't seen her around lately— her parents probably shipped her off to a secret spa to dry out. Penelope's—well, let's just say she has bad judgment, too. Tommy simply worshipped her. There's no accounting for taste, is there? Look at Bunny Dunford, always at Lucy Archibald's beck and call. I need to find a man like that. You say your viscount won't do."

"I'm afraid not," Addie said with sympathy. "You didn't tell the police about Tom Bickley and the Hardinge girl?"

"No. Why should I? It wasn't as if they were a couple. In

Tommy's dreams, perhaps. Penelope didn't give him the time of day. Poor kid."

Addie wondered what Inspector Hunter would make of this nugget of information. Pip seemed genuinely unaware that Penelope was dead. And there was nothing whatsoever in her demeanor that indicated she was a murderess, just a young woman wanting to make a good match.

Addie snapped her little beaded bag shut and followed Pip out the door and down the corridor, until she heard raised voices behind the storage room door. "You go on ahead upstairs, Pip. Gyppy tummy," Addie whispered, as if she couldn't catch her breath. "Entertain Lucas for me, will you?" The girl's eyes lit up.

Poor deluded thing.

Addie opened her bag again, pretending to search for something. Two women were arguing, one of them sounding very much like the hostess Trix. Addie leaned against the wall, wishing she had a drinking glass to help her eavesdrop.

"You need to go!"

"Why should I? …member too. Every right to…can't stop me."

"Freddy doesn't want…"

A harsh laugh. "As if Freddy matters….better watch out if he knows what's what or he'll get more of the same. You'd better warn your black boyfriend in case he sticks his nose in too."

"*Please…*"

"Don't bother. You had your chance. Go on upstairs…be charming. See if there's any dosh in *that.*"

"Just leave us alone! You have enough!"

"I'll never have enough. If you weren't such a goody-goody, you'd understand."

Addie heard the door handle turn and she sprinted back inside the ladies' loo, nearly twisting her ankle in her mad dash. Taking a deep breath, she pushed the door open an inch in time to see Trix and a young woman who could have been her double exit the storage room. They were too busy still arguing to check behind them, thank heavens. She let the door swing shut, shaking too much to leave just yet.

"So, this is where you all go to gossip. I must say, it's rather a bilious pink, isn't it? Kind of like being stuck inside someone's alimentary canal."

Rupert. "Shh!"

"It's not as if someone is going to hear me. Why don't you sit down? You look a bit dodgy. You don't really have an upset stomach, do you?"

"No. Don't tell me you've been hanging out in the ladies' loo all evening." Addie patted her upper lip with her handkerchief. Detecting made her a trifle nervous.

"What kind of a man do you take me for? Of course not—that would be disgusting. I'm dead, not depraved. I followed Trix and her cousin downstairs when it looked like things might turn interesting. I'm making myself useful in my invisible state, you know."

"Her cousin?"

"Mary Frances. Not sure what surname she's using. The girl has several aliases."

"Is she a *criminal*?" Addie asked, remembering Mr. Hunter's warnings.

Rupert nodded.

"Is Trix?"

"Not yet. The Forty Dollies have been recruiting her, however. So far, she's holding out. But she knows things."

"What kind of things?"

"Things that could get her in trouble. You'd better get upstairs before Waring sends out a search party. I sense he is not a fan of the Dean children."

Addie hoped he wasn't being too rude. Lucas had a somewhat exaggerated idea of his own consequence.

Which was why—well, it was *one* of the reasons she wasn't sure she should marry him.

Chapter Sixteen

"I have come to throw self at your mercury."

"Mercy," Addie snapped. "Do you know what time it is?"

The prince looked down at his wrist where a watch should be. "Pawned in St. Petersburg long ago. Is too early for visit? I have not at all slept." He was still wearing evening clothes, a white silk scarf around his neck, his fair hair glistening with pomade.

It wasn't even eight o'clock in the morning, and Addie had a headache. Not from overindulgence—she would never drink too much in Lucas' company—but from the scrambled bits of information gleaned at the Thieves' Den, which she had tried to make sense of before she fell asleep. She had intended to call Detective Inspector Hunter first thing this morning, but it was too early even for that.

"May I come in? You said you would help." He actually batted his platinum-tipped eyelashes.

"I am in my dressing gown with my hair loose. Is that how ladies entertain gentlemen in Russia?"

"If gentlemen very, very lucky. I shall sit quiet as mole while you sort self."

"Mouse," she corrected, still exasperated. "Do you know how to make coffee?" She couldn't depend upon Rupert to perform his magic this morning, although he was probably lurking about somewhere.

"But of course. Our life incognito was education. Can skin rabbit and boil cabbages too. Where is kitchen?"

Addie's flat was not so big that he couldn't have figured that out for himself, but she led him to the room, opened up the necessary cupboards, revealing no rabbits or cabbages, then headed off to her bathroom. Covering up her hair in a rubber shower cap, she stood under the water for two minutes to fully wake up.

Addie had a new pair of blue wide-legged trousers—well, her only pair—that Cee had talked her into in New York, and this seemed like a day for them. She topped them with a white sweater set, pinned up her hair, fastened her pearls, and swiped on coral lip rouge. Shockingly, she left her feet, still sore from dancing, bare.

After much badgering, she had persuaded Lucas to dance with her last night, and Pip, too. Once he had thawed, he'd proved to be an overly enthusiastic partner, chatting with the band on their break and making requests. Contrary to Rupert's opinion, Lucas did have some surprises left in him. He was an excellent dancer, and hapless Pip had fallen ever deeper into her crush.

The coffee smelled divine. Prince Andrei was still in the kitchen at the table, reading one of Beckett's movie magazines, and looked up as she entered.

"As fresh as daisy. You give cinema stars run for money."

Addie let herself be flattered and was grateful he didn't lecture her about the pants as Rupert might have. She poured herself a cup of coffee and added too much sugar and cream for energy. "Now, what can I do for you?"

"Is Nadia."

She expected as much. "And?"

"I worry. She not . . . Nadia."

Addie thought for a moment. "She's not behaving like herself."

"Exactly so. She worried."

"About what?"

The prince sighed. "This I do not know. Will not tell me. She has left job."

Addie had been surprised the girl had a job to begin with. "Perhaps that will make her consider matrimony more favorably."

"Pah! She speaks of going to Paris."

"I understand Paris in the springtime is lovely." Maybe Addie should go there once this was all over.

"She has friend. No, friend is not right word. There is no… warmth. I think Nadia afraid of her."

"What's her name? I know many people in society."

"Mary Something."

That wasn't helpful. "Are they acquaintances of long standing?"

From his squint, Prince Andrei appeared stumped at her question. She translated, "Have they known each other a long time?"

"I do not think so. She met this Mary at Thieves' Den when we first go. Nadia saw her there last night and ran like scolded dog. Scalded? Is hard to tell. We had just arrived! She was, how you say, caved in stone to go."

"Carved. Did she say why she needed to leave?"

His face flushed. "Woman troubles. We live in same house. Everyone knows when Nadia is ill—she is complete female dog. Was only last week she spent two days in bed yelling at everyone and asking for chocolate."

Which might account for her quitting her job—some women suffered more seriously than others during their monthlies and couldn't even stand up. Still, this was a very awkward conversation to have with a young man, no matter what language it was conducted in.

"So you left the Thieves' Den."

"Yes. I took her home, then went to gentlemen's club of my uncle. I played the billiards and won some pounds." Prince Andrei did not look quite as fresh as a daisy, but at least he'd not drunk himself into a stupor complaining about his difficult cousin all night. His skill with a cue stick might explain Addie's flowers.

"What would you like me to do?" Addie asked, anticipating the answer.

"Talk to Nadia. Find out about Mary. See if I have hope."

"You won't have hope if you go around kissing other women," Addie reminded him.

"Could not help myself. There you were in arms."

"Where I didn't want to be, if you recall."

"I sorry now. Will never happen again." The Russian gave her a dazzling smile, but Addie didn't return it.

"I'd like to get to know Nadia better, but how am I to accomplish that? She'll think it's awfully strange if I ring her up out of the blue." Addie had hardly exchanged any words with the girl the night they'd sat together at the Savoy.

"Leave to me. Be ready when I call."

As if Addie was going to sit around twiddling her thumbs waiting for Andrei's summons. She finished her coffee and eventually nudged the prince out of the flat so her day could start properly.

"That was cozy." Her dead husband was washing up the coffee cups when she reentered the kitchen.

"Oh, for heaven's sake, Rupert! Stop popping up when you're not wanted." Although she'd just as soon he get dishpan hands instead of her.

"You aren't upset because he prefers his cousin to you, are you?"

"Of course not! We have nothing in common, and he's too young for me."

"Yes, you are an ancient crone. Positively haggard." He gave her a little leer. "Those trousers suit you."

Addie had worn jodhpurs before, and had pleated sports culottes for tennis. Dressing in pajamas in public was all the rage now, too, but trousers for women were still decidedly *de trop*.

"Thank you. I'm surprised you approve after your little lecture the other day. I believe my mother would set them on fire."

"Don't be so hard on the old girl. She still likes me."

"Her one lapse in judgment."

"Everyone has their blind spots, even me. I'm sorry I didn't appreciate you more when I should have."

This was apparently the morning for apologies. What, really, was the point? It was all too late for Rupert to be sorry now.

"Never mind." Addie pulled out a pad and pen and listed the topics to discuss with Detective Inspector Hunter when she rang him up. But before she had a chance to pick up the receiver, the doorbell rang, and Mr. Hunter was on her doorstep.

"Early bird, meet worm," Rupert whispered in her ear.

Addie shoved him away with a shoulder. "Good morning! I was just about to call you."

"I hope I'm not disturbing you."

"No, as you can see, I'm dressed. Except for shoes," she added, suddenly nervous. She glanced around, but Rupert had disappeared.

"Um. Yes."

She smoothed the hem of her cardigan down. "Are you shocked?"

"Not at all. Many Indian women wear trousers under their saris. You look…very nice, but I haven't come here to discuss women's fashions."

"Of course you haven't! Please come through! May I get you coffee or tea? Have you had breakfast?"

"I know it's awfully early. But I was at the scene of a robbery just a few doors down from you, and I took a chance. Coffee would be wonderful."

Addie led him to the kitchen, which was tidy thanks to Rupert. "Anyone I know?" She set the sugar bowl and cream jug back on the table.

"I can't discuss it, but probably. Don't go hiring a new maid while Beckett is in the country. Your neighbor did and is living to regret it."

"The maid was a thief?"

Mr. Hunter shook his head. "The maid wasn't really a maid. You should have seen the ring around the tub. But definitely a thief. One of the Forty Dollies, we think. Although there are more than forty of them—I don't know why the gang cleaves to the name."

"Ali Baba and the Forty Thieves," Addie ventured.

"I expect you're right."

"Did you catch her?"

"No. We'll be checking out London's finest fences, though. Maybe we'll get lucky and retrieve some of the missing valuables."

She thought of what Rupert had said about Trix and her cousin. "These women—you say they're members of the Thieves' Den, too?"

"Some of them, yes. They clean up quite nicely in their stolen furs and jewels."

"What about Trix, the hostess?"

Mr. Hunter raised an eyebrow. "Why do you ask?"

"Something, um, someone said. I can't remember the exact details."

"We suspect the Dollies are getting information from her or Rinaldi about who's at the club. Or it's a remarkable coincidence that their houses are robbed while they're out dancing."

"Oh, dear." Addie hoped Trix wasn't cooperating voluntarily. It could explain the argument she'd overheard between the cousins. She picked up her notes from the dresser. "I'm moving down the list with your Great Eight. I was at the Thieves' Den last night, and things were *suspicious*."

"In what way?"

"Well, first I had a conversation with Philippa Dean. She doesn't know the Hardinge girl is dead. Thinks she's in a nursing home getting weaned off drink and drugs—apparently that's the *on dit* amongst the BYP to explain her absence from the social scene. But Pip's doubtful about Tommy Bickley's death. Wonders now if he was poisoned like Cee was. She told me he was in love with Penelope. Unrequited, though. The girl wouldn't have anything to do with him."

"A connection! That's the first we've heard of it! Well done, Lady Adelaide!"

Addie enjoyed the warmth of his smile. "Then as I was leaving the loo, I heard a fight between two women. Girls, really. I couldn't catch the gist of it, but one was Trix and the other her cousin, Mary Frances."

The coffee pot percolated, and Mr. Hunter rose. "I'll get the cups. Unless you've moved them from the last time I was in your kitchen."

Last August, when it was hot enough to fry an egg on the pavement. When Mr. Hunter had put her to bed, only removing her shoes. Had he chastely kissed her on the forehead? Addie wished she knew.

Chapter Seventeen

Dev felt far too comfortable in Lady Adelaide's little kitchen. Wouldn't this be a fine way to start every morning? A lovely woman, the scent of fresh coffee, congenial conversation.

Only in his dreams.

He ruthlessly quashed the fantasy. "How do you know about Mary Frances?"

"Someone mentioned something." She was vague again, and Dev wondered why. "It sounded as if she was threatening Trix. They could be twins, you know, they look so much alike."

Cousins instead of sisters. That made more sense. Trix hadn't exactly lied to him then.

"Do you know what the argument was about?"

"Not really. Mr. Rinaldi was mentioned. And I think Ollie Johnson, too. The musician. That they needed to 'watch out.'"

"You are a positive gold mine of information. Have you ruled out any of the suspects yet?" Dev trusted her instincts, even if he didn't want to subject her to any danger.

"Not really. But quite frankly, I don't think any of them that I've spoken to have the motive—or the nerve—to kill anyone. I've seen more than I've wanted to of the prince. And I did talk with Kit Wheeler and Gregory Trenton-Douglass, the night before last. They—" She paused, coloring.

"They?"

"I don't know how it could have any bearing on the case."

"Why don't you let me decide?" Dev asked.

Lady Adelaide fidgeted with her coffee cup. "I think they're relying on my discretion."

"This is a murder case, Lady Adelaide," he reminded her. "Any bit of gossip, no matter how trivial, might help."

"I know, I know." She looked pained. "They are together. In a relationship."

Ah. He didn't see how that could be pertinent either, unless Penelope Hardinge and Tom Bickley had vowed to expose them. There were still serious consequences for men like them, even as young members of society relaxed the rules and tested boundaries. He personally wouldn't want to throw them in prison, but someone might.

"They seemed to think tampering with Kit's drink was a prank," Lady Adelaide continued.

"A prank! Good lord, what kind of friends do they have?"

"That's the same question I asked them. And they've figured out about Penelope Hardinge. That she's dead, I mean."

Damn. "I hope they keep it to themselves. As you know, it's not common knowledge. So who's left?"

"Oh! I almost forgot. I had lunch with Lady Lucy Archibald on Wednesday, too."

"You certainly have been busy! And?"

Lady Adelaide bit her lip. "I don't know how to describe it. She was...on edge."

"She's the only one you knew before all this started, right?"

"Yes. Things have been very difficult for her family since the war."

Things had been very difficult for lots of families. "Her father is an earl. How bad could it be?"

Lady Adelaide's hazel eyes sparked behind her glasses. "Don't sound so dismissive. He's lost all his money. His family seat burned to the ground. And his two sons are dead."

"I beg your pardon. That does seem excessive." Dev reminded himself not to jump to conclusions—he invariably stumbled upon landing.

"It's made Lucy turn strange."

"Strange enough to murder two people and try to make a third dreadfully ill?"

"It sounds ridiculous. How would she have gotten hold of cyanide?"

It seemed unlikely that Lady Lucy had made a deal with the Dollies, but again, he was jumping to conclusions. Who was to say that Lucy and Mary Frances had not forged a fast friendship in the Thieves' Den's powder room and were busy swapping poisons and pearls? The mill theft had yielded more than bolts of cloth, and the Dollies were nothing if not entrepreneurial.

He pulled out his notebook and made some quick additions. "No clue. Yet. So by my count, Nadia Sanborn and Bernard Dunford have yet to be grilled by you."

"I'm not grilling! Really, any knowledge I have is almost accidental. I know Bunny—that is Bernard—is very fond of Lucy, so maybe things will turn out all right for her in the end. And you should add Roy Dean to your count. We danced together, but I had no opportunity to have a heart-to-heart with him."

"Don't be modest. You've been enormously helpful." She'd been right—she was able to get into places and conversations he and his men could never hope to.

"I have thought of a tidy solution, probably silly. What if poor Tommy killed Penelope because she wouldn't return his affections, then killed himself?"

Dev laughed. "Very tidy. Except for what happened to your sister."

"Maybe it *was* a prank."

"You all need better friends."

Lady Adelaide twitched. "Believe me, I wouldn't pick any of

these young people as friends. Not that there's anything wrong with them. They're just so…young."

"And you, a veritable pensioner. I'm a few years older than you are, and not ready for my pipe and slippers. Judging from my father, Hunter men want to be in the thick of things until the end."

"He sounds like mine. Papa was riding with the Beaufort Hunt when he had a heart attack. It was very unexpected. It's been almost five years, and we're still not used to the idea. "

Dev had no difficulty remembering her mother, the formidable Dowager Marchioness of Broughton, still in her blacks. "I'm sorry."

"Thank you. It was a great blow to Cee to move out of Broughton Park. She and Mama are just across the meadow in the dower house, but all 'her' horses are now our cousin Ian's. He gives her free rein of the stables, but it's the principle of the thing that's irritates her so. I wish she'd settle down. She goes from one mad idea to another."

"Do you think a husband would solve her problems?"

Lady Adelaide's lip curved upwards. "Not in my experience."

No, by all accounts, Rupert Compton had been a handful. "What does your mother have to say?"

"She's smart enough to not order Cee about, so instead she just complains to me. They both do. Oh, I'm boring to fuss! I know how lucky I am."

Dev had noticed her shadowed eyes. She might be lucky, but she was tired.

He rose. "I'll let you get on with your day. I hope you have something more entertaining planned than talking to potential murderers."

"Not really. The prince is setting up some sort of meeting between me and Nadia. He says she's been acting odd lately. But I don't know if that's today."

"Odd in what way?"

"He thinks she's frightened of someone she met at the Thieves' Den. A Mary Somebody."

Dev felt a chill. "Mary Frances, perhaps?"

"Gracious! I don't know, but I suppose it could be. She certainly was giving her own cousin an earful. And she's so pretty, too. One doesn't expect—well, that's a stupid generalization, isn't it? Not every villain twirls a mustache."

"Too right." He'd warned her that the Dollies were dangerous. Could they be behind the deaths? If so, they'd branched out into a territory that boded ill for all Londoners and beyond.

Maybe Dev had been looking at this all wrong. Mary Frances Harmon's name had not appeared on his list of suspects, but that didn't mean she wasn't one.

Chapter Eighteen

Prince Andrei had telephoned Addie just after one o'clock. She was having her fourth cup of coffee in a fruitless attempt to remain alert, along with a cheese sandwich. Somehow with all her morning visitors, she had forgotten to eat breakfast, and a cheese sandwich—no pickles—was about the limit of her culinary skill at the moment.

The prince had arranged for Nadia to take tea with him at the Lyons Corner House at the Strand and Craven Street location at three o'clock. The white and gold-fronted restaurants were ubiquitous, so Addie made a point of writing down the exact address, just in case her mind became cloudier than it already was and she wound up in Piccadilly instead. If she didn't fall asleep over her tea, she might pop into the National Gallery afterward.

She had never been to a Lyons Corner House, as they were not on the Dowager Marchioness of Broughton's list of proper ladies' luncheon establishments. Addie knew they were extremely popular and perfectly unexceptional, no matter what her mother thought. An orchestra played on each floor of the Strand restaurant, which seated over one thousand customers.

Addie wondered if she would be able to find Nadia and Andrei in the scrum without getting lost.

The company's waitresses, known as Nippies (Addie thought the name was profoundly unfortunate, but it had been voted on by the public), were renowned for their attractive appearances and speed, as they nipped around with their trays. Working at a Lyons Corner House practically guaranteed one would receive several proposals of marriage a week. Such jobs were highly sought after, and considered quite a step up from domestic service. Addie hoped Beckett wouldn't get any ideas.

She changed into a smart black and white checked suit and a black felt fedora, accessorizing with the inevitable pearls and black suede gloves. Addie had avoided anything black since the one-year anniversary of Rupert's death, but she wanted to appear serious this afternoon. If Nadia was frightened by someone or something, Addie wished to be a solid and sympathetic friend.

Prince Andrei's scheme was not the cleverest, but it was what she had to work with. She was to "bump into" them, quite by chance. A short time after her arrival, he would recall a previous engagement and hotfoot it out of the restaurant, leaving Addie and Nadia alone. They were counting on Nadia's good breeding to make the best of an awkward situation.

The porter for the mansion flats secured a taxi for Addie, only after hailing it down around the corner, so consequently she was running a little late. The day was milder, with a true promise of spring, and no fur wrap or coat was needed. Standing at the curb, Addie took a gulp of fresh air, or as fresh as it could get in Mayfair. Even in the best neighborhoods, smoke and accompanying yellow fog blighted the skies, and the buildings were streaked with soot.

She missed the country.

Though if she were at Compton Chase, there would be no reporting to Detective Inspector Devenand Hunter. She couldn't see a way to steer him into her sphere of influence in the Cotswolds without some sort of debacle occurring. Certainly anything more than the two deaths last summer should never be repeated in

Compton-under-Wood. Addie had too much respect for her neighbors to want someone killed off for her convenience.

She smiled. A good juicy robbery might lure him to the countryside, though. He seemed preoccupied with that female gang that was raising hell and blood pressures throughout Britain. Addie might misplace the diamond earrings Rupert gave her one year for Christmas—maybe her diamond bracelets too—and beg Scotland Yard for help. Request a very particular member of the force to search *everywhere*.

Oh, how foolish she was being. Addie would just have to take things as they were and make do.

She tipped the porter and settled herself in the dusty cab. Between motor and stubbornly horse-drawn vehicles, traffic was heavy, and it was well past three o'clock when the cabbie pulled up in front of Lyons. She hoped Prince Andrei had been able to find a table on the ground floor to save her from wandering up and down the stairs peering through the crowds.

She was in luck, catching his overly-enthusiastic wave as soon as she crossed the threshold. Addie hoped he wasn't being too obvious.

"I see some friends," Addie said to the hostess. "I think I'll sit with them."

She was led to their table and Andrei stood in his princely magnificence, attracting the attention of every red-blooded woman in the place, and a few of their male escorts as well. "But Lady Adelaide! How serenity! Of all people in London to run over you!"

"I think you mean serendipitous," Addie replied. "And run *into*. I'm not flattened yet, though the streets are so crowded at this time of day. I'm so glad to see you both! You've saved me from being all alone. I was just passing, and I'm simply so parched I couldn't wait until I got home for a nice cup of tea. May I join you?"

Another chair was procured and a very pretty Nippy in her black uniform with its rows of pearl buttons took Addie's order.

The cheese sandwich was still somewhat leaden in her stomach, so she asked for a dish of ice cream as well as a pot of tea. Nadia and the prince already had cups and plates in front of them and had made headway into the tiers of the tea stand.

"How delightful," Addie said, smiling warmly at Nadia. "This will give us a chance to get to know one another a little better. Your cousin has done nothing but sing your praises."

Nadia raised a skeptical plucked eyebrow. "Really?" she asked, her voice flat.

"He was so helpful after my sister's accident. If he's so thoughtful with strangers, how lucky you are to have him as family."

"No more, please. I get swallowed head." Suddenly, Prince Andrei slapped himself on his handsome brow. "I say! Is Friday, no?"

"Is Friday, yes," Nadia said, rolling her eyes. They were icy pale green, like her cousin's, and a little too acute for Addie's liking.

"Oh, I am idiot. A thousand pardons, Nadia, Lady Adelaide. I must see man about something I am completely forgot and is so important. Business, you know. I must leave *tout de suite*. My treat," he said, peeling off bills from his pocket. Billiards must be extremely profitable. "Please to stay and enjoy each other's company. You may talk now about me all you like." He gave Nadia a wink which she did not return.

In the midst of the effusive continental goodbye kisses, the waitress came with the tea and Addie's scoop of strawberry ice cream. For a moment Addie wondered if the prince was going to kiss the girl too, but he stopped himself in time and hustled out of the restaurant.

"Honestly," Nadia said, lighting up a Turkish cigarette, "how stupid does he think I am?"

Addie nearly spit out her tea. "Excuse me?"

"This meeting he claims—there is no man, is there? Business, indeed. As if Andrei has ever worked a day in his life."

"Perhaps the meeting is about a job." Addie knew Andrei had done quite a few peculiar things to keep his mother and himself alive after the revolution, but she said nothing about that.

"Nonsense. I can see you're taken in by him. I was too, in the beginning. He's very handsome. Charming. Of course, I was just a child when I first met him. If I may say so, Lady Adelaide, you are old enough to know better."

Spiteful little cat. Addie kept a smile on her face with some difficulty. "I assure you, your cousin is nothing but a friend. My affections lie...elsewhere." She paused, then decided Nadia was too sharp to be bamboozled into confidentiality. "I think he is worried about you and thought you needed a female friend."

Nadia took a long drag of her cigarette and exhaled. "Worried about me! Why?"

"He thinks you've changed lately. You quit your job. You seem nervous. Fearful."

Nadia stubbed her cigarette into the clotted cream of her scone, which seemed an awful shame to Addie. Even if it wasn't good for her figure, she was very partial to clotted cream, which had been so hard to come by during the war. "This is ridiculous! I'm leaving."

Addie covered the girl's hand. "What about Mary Frances?"

All the color left Nadia's face. "What do you know about Mary Frances?"

"Both too much and not enough. She's a dangerous young woman."

Nadia slid her hand out from under Addie's. "I have to go."

"Please don't. I'm trying to help you."

"I don't see how you—or anybody—can."

"You won't know unless you talk to me."

"What are you, some kind of do-gooding social worker? Sorry, but I don't want to wind up in jail. Or dead."

Addie went very still. "Why would that happen?" Surely Nadia wasn't confessing to the poisonings.

"Look, I know you mean well. But you're not my friend. I don't want to talk to you."

"Can you talk to Andrei?"

Nadia laughed without any mirth. "I don't trust him. Why don't you ask *him* about Mary Frances?" Nadia picked up her gloves and purse and dodged around the Nippies racing around the room.

That hadn't gone well. Instead of answers, Addie only had more questions. At least she wasn't stuck with the bill.

Chapter Nineteen

Friday night, or more accurately Saturday morning, the world was out drinking its paycheck, or trust fund, as the case may be. The young man lying in front of Dev had had one too many, the last of which had proven to be fatal.

Dev could only be grateful that Lady Adelaide had not been present to witness it, or, God forbid, be its victim. It didn't look like cyanide this time, but something else; the lab boys would figure it out.

His usual suspects were clustered in a corner, silent and white-faced. The band had stopped playing some time ago, and Trix stood rocking in Ollie Johnson's arms. Patrons of the Thieves' Den were milling around in the larger front room, waiting to be dismissed. Bob and some of the men were taking their statements. All would swear their innocence, of that Dev was sure.

Freddy Rinaldi wiped his brow with a none-too-clean hand-kerchief. His bruises hadn't faded much over the course of the week. "You gotta stop this, Inspector. I don't care what happens at the Savoy, but this is too much."

"I agree, Freddy. You didn't see anything suspicious?"

"I was in the office most of the night. Tryin' not to scare the mugs with my face. You should ask Ted—he waited on that crowd.

And Trix. She's always out and around. They tell me those kids were almost the only ones sitting in the back room. It's like their own private club lately."

"It's where the Bickley boy died, too."

"I told you, I don't know nothin' about that."

One would think with a thinner crowd, someone would have noticed something.

"Freddy, I know you have information you're not telling me."

"It has nothing to do with this!" Rinaldi waved a hand at Roy Dean's body. The boy looked for all the world as if he was asleep, no bulging eyes or protruding tongue or grimace. Unfortunately he was not pointing to his murderer, nor did he write the name on a crumpled cocktail napkin before he breathed his last.

"Where's Mary Frances tonight?"

Freddy paled beneath his mottled skin. "Who?"

"Come now. I thought you knew all your members by name."

"We got a lotta Marys. Lady Mary this and Miss Mary that."

"Freddy, at some point you'll tire of having it your way. I only hope it won't be too late. I'd like to use your office for the interviews if I may." He needed to get Roy's sister and friends away from the body so the coroner's office could do its unpleasant duty.

"The place is a rat's nest. I haven't caught up from the other day."

Dev suspected the place was always a wreck. It would discourage people from snooping. Freddy probably had everything he needed right at his fingertips and in his somewhat diabolical mind. "Set up six chairs in the hall, would you? And get someone to make some tea."

"How do you take it?"

"Not for me." Dev angled his head to the seven young people who appeared to be in shock.

All except Lady Lucy Archibald. She'd lit a gasper and was blowing smoke rings, cool as a cucumber. The victim's sister, Pip Dean, cried softly in Bernard Dunford's arms. He patted her ineffectually on the back with a hunted look, trying to catch

Lady Lucy's eye to rescue him from such naked emotion. Nadia Sanborn held fast to her cousin's hand, both of them white as chalk. Trenton-Douglass and Wheeler kept a respectable distance from each other, but looked equally shaken.

Dev walked up to them. "I'm so very sorry we are meeting again like this."

"Why haven't you stopped this madman?" Lady Lucy asked.

"Or madwoman," Dev said evenly. He thought he saw her eyelid twitch for a fraction of a second. Poison, as he reminded himself again, was often a woman's preference. "I'd like to speak to each of you individually in Mr. Rinaldi's office."

"*Now*? Why can't we do this tomorrow?" Lady Lucy asked. "We're all dead on our feet. Oops, sorry, Pip."

"Now. I'll keep it short tonight. We'll have more time tomorrow. Please follow me." He led the little group up half a flight of stairs to a narrow hallway. Rinaldi's office was at the end. Several waiters carted up chairs from below, and Dev asked his unhappy guests to make themselves comfortable.

"Miss Dean, I'd like to talk to you first. Have you spoken to your parents?"

She nodded. "They're on their way. The police are fetching them." He doubted they'd provide any useful information, but at least their daughter would have support.

Freddy's office was indeed a tip. Dev had difficulty finding clean surfaces for them to sit. The rumpled camp bed in the corner was out of the question.

He perched on a filing cabinet after setting some folders on the floor, while Miss Dean took the desk chair. She blew her nose and looked at him with watery eyes.

"Did you see anyone touch your brother's drink?"

She shook her head. "I was dancing when it happened."

"Who was at the table?"

"Everyone."

"You danced alone?"

"It was the Charleston. You don't need a partner, but I met up with a friend of R-Roy's. Howard Clark. He was sitting in the big room. You can ask him."

Dev wrote the name in his notebook, tucking the loose pages under the flap. If he kept encountering any more dead bodies, he'd need a new notebook pronto.

Or be fired pronto if he didn't solve the case.

"Tell me about your brother. Were you close?"

Pip wiped her eyes with a soggy handkerchief. "Yes. I mean, he was my *brother*. He could be annoying, but we'd always laugh about it afterwards. We had fun together."

"Can you think of anyone who might have wished him harm?"

"No, I honestly can't. He even joked around with the employees at the hotel. He was popular. Everyone liked him." She *sounded* honest. Dev would find out once he'd talked to the Brighton constabulary.

"He would have inherited the family business?"

"Yes."

"What will happen now?"

Her eyes widened. "I—I don't know."

"Was that a sore spot for you, that your brother was being groomed to take over the business and you were not?"

Pip Dean stumbled up. "You think I killed him over the bloody stupid hotel? How dare you!"

Dev rose as well. "I never said that, Miss Dean. I know you're upset. I just wondered if you have a champion that you don't know about."

"What do you mean?"

"Someone might have been upset for you. Wanted *you* to inherit."

"That's—that's *awful*." She was truly aghast.

"It is. But something to think about. Please accept my sincere condolences. I'll meet with your parents tomorrow—well, today, really—at their convenience. My sergeant, Bob Wells, can take you home."

He walked her to the door and out into the hall. "Mr. Dunford, I'll see you next."

Bernard "Bunny" Dunford looked up from his folded hands. "M-me?"

"Yes, please. It won't take long."

Dunford was of an age with the rest of them, early to mid-twenties, though shock had made him look very young tonight. He was handsome enough in a bland way, his light brown hair and grey eyes unexceptional. According to Addie, he was in love with the sharp-tongued Lucy Archibald. Dev wished him joy of her.

"What can you tell me about this evening?"

"N-nothing, really. We all met up about eleven in the b-back room. D-danced and so forth."

"What about the drinks?"

"Ted brought them. Champagne c-cocktails for the ladies. Manhattans for the gentlemen."

"Did you notice anything unusual?"

"Not a thing. I was listening to Lucy, y'see, and wasn't paying attention to the others. Then all of a sudden R-roy t-tumbled down on the floor like he'd passed out. He didn't have *that* much to drink—none of us did. We hadn't had t-time."

"Where were you sitting in relation to Mr. Dean?"

Dunford turned a lively shade of red. "Right next to him! But I swear to God I didn't do anything except give him the extra red cherries in my drink. He w-was awful fond of them, m-maraschino cherries. He ate a whole jar once on a b-bet. Every single one! Ted brought them from the bar." Dunford suddenly gave Dev a wild look. "My God! Do you suppose the cherries were poisoned and I'm the one that's supposed to be d-dead?"

"Hang on just one minute." Dev dashed downstairs and had the bartender round up all the jars of cherries, green ones too. After a word with the forensics team, he returned to the office. Dunford had recovered his normal complexion but appeared exceedingly anxious.

"Inspector, is my life in d-danger? I swear I've never d-done anything to anyone! Why is someone d-doing this?"

"I don't know, but I swear to you, I'll find out. In the meantime, it wouldn't hurt to spend a few quiet nights at home alone."

"What about Lucy? Lady Lucy, that is?"

"I'll give her the same advice. I can't tell you what to do, but until we capture the killer, nights out on the town should be strictly forbidden."

"Yes, s-sir. Is that all?"

"For now."

Dev opened the door, only to find an additional person waiting in the empty chair.

Damn it all to hell.

Chapter Twenty

"Lady Adelaide, what are you doing here?"

Oh dear. Inspector Hunter did not seem best pleased to see her.

"Told you," Rupert complained. "We could have read all about it in the newspapers a few hours from now in the comfort of your own bed, but oh, no, you had to stick your pretty powdered nose in and see for yourself. A man needs his rest, you know."

Rupert was getting nowhere near her bed, newspapers or not. "I couldn't sleep, and wanted some fun," Addie lied, ignoring Rupert entirely. She'd set her alarm clock for midnight and had quite a delightful catnap before the buzzer woke her up and Rupert told her what had happened to Roy Dean. She didn't bother asking him how he knew; it only made her more determined to get dressed and go to the Thieves' Den in person. "I thought I'd come out after all. Imagine my surprise when I was blocked at the door by a bobby!"

"How did you get in?" Inspector Hunter was practically growling.

"Your lovely Sergeant Wells was leaving with poor Pip and waved me through. Once I found out what had happened, I came up to give you all my sympathy." Addie had an idea Mr. Wells was going to get a reprimand. She tugged her midnight blue velvet skirt down and attempted to look innocent. Perhaps if she'd been wearing a longer skirt, fewer sapphires, and less lip rouge, she would have succeeded.

"I for one very glad Lady Adelaide here," Prince Andrei said. "Like mother. Or auntie," he amended, rethinking. "Perhaps big sister."

"Oh, for God's sake," Nadia said in disgust.

Addie agreed. "I'll just keep the young people company with my elderly self while you're interviewing. Oh, good! Here is some tea!" The waiter, Ted, had lumbered upstairs with an enormous tray, cups stacked precariously. There was nowhere to put it but the floor, and Rupert leaped out of the way before it landed on his lap.

Inspector Hunter shook his head and took Lucy in next. Addie bent over and poured some dodgy-looking brown liquid into thick china cups for her "children."

"Was it very awful?" she asked, passing Nadia a cup.

"No, it was a picnic in the park. Everyone likes to go out and watch their friend drop dead right before their eyes," Rupert grumbled, brushing dust off his trousers. "This portion of the club could use a thorough sweeping. You should tell that Freddy person. It's almost as bad as the loo."

"Roy was sitting there one minute and on the floor the next," Gregory Trenton-Douglass said. "Not a peep out of him. No distress. Nothing."

"I—I g-gave him my cherries," Bunny Dunford moaned. "I k-killed him!"

"Don't be a sap, Bunny. How do you know the cherries did it?" Kit Wheeler asked.

"I d-don't, of course. But I b-bet they'll hang me for it anyway." He ran his hand through his hair, causing it to stick up like half-a-dozen devil horns.

"Speaking of hanging, why are you still here?"

"L-Lucy. She may need me."

Kit snorted. "Lucy doesn't need anybody, least of all you. It's not as if you can drive her home."

"Why not?" Addie asked, passing Bunny some tea. If he was a little drunk, that might straighten him out.

"D-don't drive. Can't," Bunny said, turning red. "Well, can but d-don't." He sniffed the tea with suspicion.

"Nerves," Kit whooped rather unkindly. Bunny clenched his fist but made no move to use it.

"I don't blame you," Addie said quickly. The last thing she needed was a fight. "People are appalling drivers. I rely on my chauffeur in the country. And I'd *never* drive in London. I always take taxis."

"That's it. I'll t-take her home in a t-taxi," Bunny said.

"I drive everyone in uncle's car later," Prince Andrei offered.

"Not us. It's a nice night. We'll walk if we ever get out of here," Kit said. "We might be behind bars if we don't get our stories straight. I suppose we're all prime suspects."

Transportation sorted, everyone was quiet as they contemplated their innocence or guilt and sipped the tea, which was absolutely as vile as Addie expected. Evidently no one wanted to confess to the murder of Roy Dean while they waited in tense silence in the hall.

She checked her diamond-faced wristwatch. It was nearly two o'clock in the morning. The noise in the club below had abated, but there was a steady hum of policemen going to and fro, with the occasional raised voice. She wished she could assist Mr. Hunter with his inquiries in the club's office, but then her role and relationship with the detective would be revealed. If she had to continue to serve as a "mother," "auntie," or "big sister" to facilitate matters, so be it.

"Pip looked devastated when I ran into her outside," Addie said, trying to restart the conversation. "It's all so shocking."

No one agreed or disagreed besides sighs and low murmurs.

Her young friends were having difficulty grappling with Roy Dean's death, and were robbed of words. Unlike Tommy Bickley's, they had *seen* it.

"This lot is deader than the victim," Rupert said, wiggling his fingers in front of Bunny Dunford's pasty face. "Are they mute?"

"Stop—um, will this stop you all from going out?" Addie wished Rupert was mute himself and would go away.

"Who can think of such thing at time like this? With maniac on loose. I could be next." Prince Andrei smoldered at his cousin, but she refused to look at him. "Would you care, Nadia? Or be heartless wench?"

"Andrei, shut up! You're getting on my last nerve!"

"You and Bunny should take pill," Andrei said with a touch of malice. "I have seen worse to upset in my country, believe me."

"Russia, Russia, Russia," Kit said dismissively. "Don't be a bore, Andy, there's a good chap."

"My name not Andy! As you know. You English are so cold. Even when watching someone die, no emotion to stir blue blood. Poor Roy."

"Why would someone want to kill him?" Addie asked, pleased with the opening. "Did he have enemies? It seems ridiculous to think so—he was so very genial."

"Only his sister. N-now she can get her hands on the family b-business," Bunny replied.

Nadia glared at him. "Bunny! What an awful thing to say! Pip's not like that at all! She wants to get married, not run a hotel."

Bunny shrugged. "I'm j-just saying some m-might find it r-relevant."

Was that an angle worth looking at by the police? Pip had seemed very fond of her brother, but one really never knew what went on inside someone's head. Addie barely knew what went on in her own half the time, especially when Rupert was nearby.

"Are you and Pip great friends, Nadia?" Addie asked.

"Well, yes, I do have friends, contrary to what *some* people have told you. Millie Avery and Pip and I are quite chummy. Millie was meant to come out with us tonight. She'll be glad she didn't."

Addie was grateful there was one less suspect. "So, what do you all think happened?"

"Isn't it obvious? I mean, the man confessed. It was Bunny with his bloody cherries." Kit smirked.

Bunny Dunford stood up and took a step forward. "N-not funny, Kit!" This time, both fists were clenched.

"Oh, put a sock in it, Dunford. I'm not going to waste my time with you as a punching bag. I'll leave that to your lady-love."

"Stop it, Kit. Don't be cruel." Nadia rose, putting her cup down on the chair. "I need some air. Do you suppose the coppers will let me cadge a cigarette outside? I'll promise not to run away."

Andrei hopped up. "I come with you."

"Please, no. I want to be alone."

"Suit self. Now who is cruel?"

Rupert chuckled. "Ah. Young love. Were we ever this stupid, Addie? They know as well as we do they'll end up marrying. Nadia's father will find some innocuous outpost for the prince to exercise his limited diplomatic skills, and Nadia will throw killer parties. Perhaps not killer—that was an unfortunate choice of words."

Addie wasn't as sure as Rupert, but this was neither the time nor the place for an argument. Andrei slumped back down in the uncomfortable chair with a dramatic expression worthy of one of Beckett's cinema actors, and Nadia flounced off.

Lucy emerged from the office, her somewhat mangy fox jacket draped over her shoulders. "Greg, he wants to see you next. I'm dying for a gasper."

Bunny leaped up and brought out his cigarette case. He gave Kit a black look after lighting Lucy's cigarette. "I'll see you home, L-Lucy."

"All right. But you can't come in. The parents will be beside themselves at this hour. Night, all. Good luck at the Inquisition."

She sauntered away, appearing to have not a care in the world. Bunny followed behind her like a puppy.

"Good riddance," Kit muttered.

"Do you dislike them?" Addie asked.

He shrugged, and checked to see if Andrei was listening, keeping his voice soft. "Lucy's all right. She's as mean as a snake and all the more interesting for it. But Bunny is a nitwit. Fellow doesn't have any bal—I mean, spine. Lets Lucy call all the shots. I'd never put up with it if Greg treated me that way."

"No indeed. Successful relationships should be in balance." Addie wondered if Rupert would agree, now that he was on the straight and narrow.

Chapter Twenty-One

Saturday

Addie woke up to the insistent ringing of the telephone. Pushing up her eye mask, she answered in a none-too-friendly tone. She had definitely not gotten enough sleep.

"What in hell were you playing at?"

Evidently he'd woken up on the wrong side of the bed, and wanted her to join him. Figuratively speaking, of course. "Good morning to you too, Inspector." She hadn't said goodnight to him, intuiting she'd better escape before he finished questioning everyone.

"I'm serious. This isn't a game but a murder inquiry. There was no reason for you to be there last night."

"This morning, but who's counting the hours? I kept the children company. Acted as a calming influence," Addie replied, stung. She'd done her best to coax them to have confidence in her. To confess, but that hadn't worked.

"And who's to say being calm is a good thing? Someone might have revealed something in their distress."

"They did! Bunny Dunford seems to think the cherries were poisoned. And that Pip might have wanted to kill her brother so she could get her hands on the hotel."

"I know this already. What else?"

There really wasn't anything else. The inspector was right to be annoyed. "Bunny is not very popular with Greg and Kit—they think he's awfully wet, and that Lucy runs roughshod over him. Prince Andrei is courting Nadia, but it's not going well."

"So, they're all at daggers-drawn. Good. That might lead someone to finally tell the truth."

"I'm sorry I'm not more helpful."

"It's not your fault, Lady Adelaide." He paused. "*I'm* sorry I was short with you. This case is making me demented. There's something else going on at the Thieves' Den apart from the murders, too."

"You mean with the Dolly-people?"

"Forget I ever mentioned them! Those women are criminals you don't want to consort with."

"Are they responsible for Mr. Rinaldi's beating?"

She heard Mr. Hunter's world-weary sigh. "As if he'd tell me. And no, the women usually are not violent. Their male friends— that's another story."

"What can I do to help?" After she had some coffee, of course.

"What? No, no, no. You've done enough, and I release you from your informal assistance with our inquiries. You should go back to the country. If I can find the link between obtaining the poisons and our perpetrator, I'll have the case solved."

"What about the cherries?"

"Ah. Interesting. According to the autopsy, the cherries were just cherries. None of the jars of cherries I confiscated from the bar were tampered with either."

"So Bunny Dunford *wasn't* the intended victim!"

"Probably not. He seems too harmless to kill, anyway."

"And doesn't fit in with the other victims. His family has been here since the Conqueror, and are richer than the king. Very respectable. But Penelope Hardinge was the daughter of a shady businessman. Tommy Bickley's father made his fortune in beer. Some people might believe Kit Wheeler is defying the laws of God and man. The Deans are first-generation money through trade. Sour grapes."

"What do you mean?"

Addie plumped the pillows behind her. "We don't always reward self-made or 'different' people in Britain, do we? There's always a stigma. As though 'good birth' and toeing the line mean everything."

"You'd know more about that than I."

Addie's cheeks pinked, even though he couldn't see her. "I don't say it's fair. It just *is.*"

"I'll take your opinion under advisement. So, which of our suspects is a disgruntled, jealous, heartless murderer out to avenge the rules of society?"

Addie couldn't utter her suspicion. It was just too awful to contemplate. "I don't know. The numbers are at least going down with Roy Dean's death."

"And causing me no end of trouble. Deputy Commissioner Olive wants my head."

"You really haven't had much of a chance to make sense of things!"

"It's three deaths, Lady Adelaide. My time is up. Theirs is."

She could hear the frustration and regret in his voice. "I'm sure something will turn up soon." She cleared her throat. "If it's all right with you, I thought I'd pay a condolence call on Pip."

"I was on my way there myself to speak to her parents."

Addie leaped out of bed. "Right now?" A quick shower, a slap of lipstick, one of her leftover mourning dresses—it wouldn't take her too long.

"Within the hour. I have some paperwork to finish up."

"Goodness, did you ever get home last night?"

"No."

"They have a flat on Curzon Street, right?" She and the Deans had shared a taxi the other night.

"Number 44."

Addie felt shy suddenly. "Would you—will you come back to my flat for breakfast after? Or lunch, rather."

There was another silence on the line. "I'm not sure that's a good idea."

"Well, a man once told me one has to eat sometime. We don't have to talk about the case."

"Let me think about it."

Addie decided to think positively. Although, really, she should be in a panic. There was barely a crust of bread left in the house if he decided to come.

"See you shortly." She hung the phone up, far too happy for the circumstances.

"What in hell *are* you playing at?" Rupert blocked the door to the bathroom, looking as fresh as a skilled undertaker could make him.

"Get out of my way, Rupert. I have to get ready."

"You like the detective inspector, don't you? I mean, *like* him."

"What if I do?"

"I don't want to see you hurt again." He sounded sincere.

This kind, sincere Rupert was very hard for her to deal with.

"I won't get hurt. And I won't hurt anyone."

"What about your little speech on British class problems? You don't see the difficulty?"

"Why can't Mr. Hunter be my friend?"

Rupert raised an eyebrow that she longed to tug down. "Don't be naïve, pet. Imagine telling the dowager marchioness you had lunch alone in your flat with a policeman. This particular policeman."

Addie didn't want to hear another word and said so. She was distracted by a noise at the door, and went down the hall to investigate, leaving Rupert to stew in his prejudiced juices.

The opening door practically smacked her in the face.

"Beckett! Fitz!" She hardly knew which to hug first, but her dog decided for her as he knocked her down and began to thoroughly lick her face. The slobber mixed with happy tears. "What are you doing here?"

Beckett grinned. "Thought you might be missing me, Lady A. And they told me this little fiend has been moping around for months. Everyone's well and all settled into Compton Chase. Your sister wanted to come back with me, but your ma put the kibosh on that."

"What about Jack?"

"Oh, he's busy in the garden."

"I mean, how are things between you?" Addie asked, struggling to her feet with the wriggling dog in her arms.

"It won't do him no harm to miss me some more."

"No more worries about Jane?"

Beckett snapped her fingers. "Poof! Gone!"

Addie's heart sank. "You don't mean she's quit service?" It was hell trying to staff Compton Chase, despite generous blandishments. There were many more professional opportunities for young women nowadays, and Addie didn't begrudge the girls one bit for trying to advance themselves. But the huge house didn't run itself. Addie could wield a duster if she had to, but it was not something she aspired to.

"Oh, no. She's still there. She's walking out with Fred Johnson from the Home Farm. He and that Josie quarreled and she's got herself engaged to Phil Baird whose pa owns the new garage in the village."

"There's a new garage?" She knew about the old one. How many cars did her neighbors own now? Addie had been away too long.

If Inspector Hunter didn't want her help, would she go home soon?

"I have to go out, Beckett, but I expect to be back shortly. Do you think you could throw something simple together for lunch for Mr. Hunter and me? You may have to order in some groceries."

At least she wouldn't be having lunch alone in her flat with a man—Beckett and Fitz would be there to chaperone.

And possibly Rupert too, damn him.

Chapter Twenty-Two

Mr. Dean looked so much like Roy that Addie was temporarily robbed of the comforting words she'd planned to say. He opened the door himself, as the Dean siblings had shared a service flat while they were in Town with no live-in servants. A small cluster of people were seated in the blandly-decorated narrow parlor, including Detective Inspector Hunter, who appeared weary to the bone as he rose at her entrance. His sergeant Bob Wells was with him, still alive after what Addie presumed had been a severe dressing-down about his conduct last night. She gave him an especially warm smile to make up for it.

Pip and her mother were in black, both pale. Addie was used to seeing Pip painted, but she wasn't wearing a speck of makeup, and her short copper hair was flat and tucked behind her ears with bobby pins.

"I am so very sorry for your loss, Mr. and Mrs. Dean, Pip." She sat and grasped Pip's hand. Mrs. Dean shot her daughter a questioning look. "Let me introduce myself. I'm Lady Adelaide Compton. My younger sister Lady Cecilia Merrill and I have befriended your children recently, and she sends her condolences as well." Or would, if she knew. So far, nothing had been in the papers, at least not in the first editions. Addie definitely didn't need Cee back in town sniffing around and putting herself in danger.

Mr. Dean frowned. "Compton. Is your husband the famous flying ace?"

"He was, yes. He passed on a year ago." But didn't pass on quite far enough.

"Of course, that's right. Terrible business, all this. The Detective Inspector over there is just finishing up. He tells us he has no idea who'd do such a thing to our boy."

"He was always so full of life," Mrs. Dean said in a weak voice. "I can't believe he's gone."

"Nor can any of us. He was a lovely young man," Addie said, hoping she wasn't laying it on too thick. But under the circumstances, mourners didn't want to hear anything negative about their loved ones. She'd heard a lot of happy lies when Rupert died, and hadn't minded the prevarications. And really, she had nothing bad to say about Roy; she'd barely known him.

"I came by to offer Pip the use of my flat if she doesn't want to be alone. I have a guest bedroom I'd be happy to have her stay in for as long as she likes." This idea had come upon her in the taxi ride over, and on the whole, Addie didn't think it was a bad one.

"That's very kind of you," Mr. Dean said. "But we're taking her home to Brighton once our boy's body is released and the police say we can leave. Some sea air will put roses back on those cheeks. And my wife can use the company."

"Of course. I understand. I do hope you'll stay in touch, Pip."

The girl nodded. "I'd like that. But who knows when I'll be back in London. Perhaps you and Viscount Waring can come to Brighton for a weekend when the weather is warmer."

"Nothing but the best at our hotel," Mr. Dean said. "You won't be slumming, I assure you. We cater to an exclusive clientele such as yourselves. Lots of lords and ladies. A prince or two, too."

Addie was embarrassed for a number of reasons. "It sounds

delightful. Is there anything I can arrange in Town for you before you go home?"

"We'll muddle along. There's a restaurant in the building for the tenants—we'll get something sent up."

Addie rose. "I'll leave you to make your plans. Again, let me know if there's anything I can do."

"Thank you, Lady Adelaide. We're touched by your concern."

Mr. Hunter and Bob Wells stood up too. "Please know your son's death is a priority at the Yard. We'll be in touch if there's any news."

"See if you can kill any stories in the rags. Bad for business, don't you know. *'Hotelier's heir poisoned.'* The punters will get it all mixed up and never come to the Seaside for fear the fish is off."

Pip had shut her eyes at this bald statement, and Addie felt truly sorry for her. But everyone dealt with grief in their own way; who was she to judge?

Mr. Dean escorted them to the lift, his booming goodbyes echoing in the hallway. Addie stepped into the cage, and the policemen followed.

"I'm sorry if I got you into trouble last night, Sergeant Wells."

"The guv'nor wasn't happy, but I'm still here, my lady." The man gave her a cheeky grin.

"Don't count on my good nature again, Bob. Lady Adelaide, may I take you home? I have a squad car downstairs. You don't mind, do you, Bob? Go home and get some sleep."

"Not likely with little Joan teething twenty-five hours of the day. But I'll try my best."

"I'll see you at nine sharp tomorrow."

Bob saluted and ambled off.

"But it's Sunday tomorrow!" Addie said.

"And until we solve this crime, just another day of the week for us."

"I'll say a prayer for you." While Addie might be bored to near death at Compton St. Cuthbert's with the annoying Reverend

Rivers, the rector of the Grosvenor Chapel in South Audley Street was vastly more efficient in his sermonizing.

"Here we are." Mr. Hunter guided her around the converted Crossley tender and opened the door. Addie slid in, holding fast to her skirt.

"What did you think of the Deans?" she asked as they motored down Curzon Street.

"It hasn't really hit them yet. I expect once they get back to Brighton, things will fall apart, for Mr. Dean in particular."

"I don't know. His business may preoccupy him. He seems very…keen."

"One can hope. To lose a son—to lose *any* child—is a terrible tragedy."

Addie and Rupert had not been blessed with children, which she'd convinced herself was a lucky thing. But there were times— well, best not to dwell on what was never to be. She was quiet as they drove through Saturday shopping traffic, Mr. Hunter driving skillfully despite his exhaustion.

"You aren't too tired for lunch, are you? Beckett got back this morning and she's putting together something for us. Nothing fancy." Beckett really wasn't capable of fancy, but Addie valued her nonetheless.

"I'd kill for a good cup of coffee. The stuff at my office is rubbish."

"I'm sure we can accommodate. You really were up all night?"

"Yes. When I called you, I was with the coroner. The Deans gave us permission by phone to perform the autopsy as quickly as possible."

Addie shuddered. "I don't know how you do it."

"Someone has to." He turned onto Mount Street and parked not too far from the entrance to her flat. Addie waited until he opened the door, not that she was some helpless female. But she knew Mr. Hunter liked to do everything by the book.

Beckett must have been waiting by the front window. She

opened it, and Fitz escaped into the black and white marble hall-way, turning in circles and yipping. Mr. Hunter bent to scratch him behind the ears, which earned him total devotion.

"This little fellow will cheer you up. Who's a good boy, eh?"

Not really Fitz. But he hadn't been here in Town long enough to cause mischief yet. "Do you have a dog, Mr. Hunter?"

"No. With my irregular schedule, it would be impossible. I don't have access to a back garden like yours, either."

"There's the Mount Street Gardens down the street, too. Fitz is spoiled for choice."

"Fitz is spoiled, period," Beckett said fondly, joining in the ear-scratching.

"I trust you've managed to get lunch for us?"

"Of course, Lady A. Everything's in the dining room. Help yourselves. I have silver to polish."

So she had found Addie's list. Nothing on it was too onerous. Addie was also grateful Beckett was giving them their privacy.

"Could you bring in a pot of coffee too?"

"*Strong* coffee, please. I need to get back to my office after lunch." He gave Beckett a smile which rather weakened Addie's knees.

"You won't take the afternoon off?"

Mr. Hunter gave her a look which told her how foolish her idea was.

Beckett had set the table with Addie's best china and crystal, but a large platter of thick roast beef sandwiches brought lunch back down to earth. Several bottles of beer were in the champagne cooler, and a pitcher of lemonade was on the sideboard.

"This looks perfect," Mr. Hunter said. "I can't remember the last time I ate real food."

"At least you haven't been forced to taste what passes for the Thieves' Den midnight supper. Most undistinguished."

"The whole place is undistinguished. I'd love to shut it down."

Addie took a sip of lemonade and was gratified to see the

inspector flip open the stopper from a bottle of beer. The man needed to unwind a little. She could apply powder under her eyes to diminish the dark smidges, but Mr. Hunter was not so fortunate. "Maybe you should until the murders get solved."

"There are drawbacks. We feel the activity is pretty much contained to one location, apart from the anomaly at the Savoy. I have men undercover there now every night as well—quite an eye-opening experience for those innocent young lads who thought they were so street-savvy. And the press is cooperating so far, keeping the sensationalism down to a manageable level."

"It's still the same small group of revelers, isn't it?" The Deans— well, now dead or almost gone—the prince and his cousin, Kit and Greg, Bunny Dunford and Lucy.

"Getting smaller by the week. The murderer must be pretty spooked by now, and perhaps that will lead to a mistake."

They both chewed thoughtfully on what was excellent roast beef.

Addie carefully blotted her lips. "Is it at all possible that it's someone outside that circle?"

"Becoming attached, are you? That could prove fatal, you know." Mr. Hunter reached for another sandwich.

"No! It's nothing like that." It was exactly like that. Though she'd known most of these young people only a week, it was dreadful to believe one of them was a killer.

And as for Lucy—

Addie shut her eyes, wishing she could shut her mind as well.

Chapter Twenty-Three

Saturday evening

Addie had to admit that she was thrilled to bits that Beckett had returned and brought Fitz with her. She shouldn't be so attached to a dog—or a killer—but Addie had truly missed him while she was away, and relieved that the little fellow seemed to remember her after so many months. Or at least associated her with food, as he begged for treats from her dinner plate, his brown eyes bright.

It was nice having someone else fix meals, too. Beckett wasn't much of a cook, although those roast beef sandwiches had hit the spot earlier. Addie had gotten very tired of what passed for a "midnight supper" at the Thieves' Den, and was ridiculously pleased with tinned tomato soup and toasted cheese from her own kitchen.

She was staying in tonight, not only because Deven and Hunter had told her to. Roy Dean's death had cast a pall on the little group, and all of Addie's efforts to meet them this evening, together or separately, came to naught. She'd have to tell the inspector she wasn't much use in the information gathering department, not that he wanted her to be involved anymore.

She couldn't blame the young people for being frightened.

Or suspicious of one another. It was clear to them that they'd all been present during the poisonings. One of them—or perhaps two—was likely guilty. As much as they wanted to blame the waiter Ted Boyce, or the bartender, or even Freddy Rinaldi himself, they were grasping at straws.

Addie took her dishes into the kitchen. The door to Beckett's room was open, and she looked in to see the maid fiddling with her wireless.

"You may not be going out, Lady A, but we can always push the table away and dance right here!" The BBC broadcast entertainment from the Savoy nightly, not that Addie needed a reminder of that. It had only been a week since Cee had been poisoned there, and quite a lot had happened.

Too much, really.

"I'm much too lazy to foxtrot with you, Beckett." Addie had changed into her trousers and a loose sweater and was nearly as comfortable in them as she would be in pajamas.

"I'll dance as I do the dishes. It makes the time go faster, don't it? Do you want me to put the dog out after I wash up?"

"No. I really should take him for a quick walk. He needs his exercise after all the treats he's been slipped today." In addition, Fitz had been the recipient of an entire leftover roast beef sandwich, stolen from the kitchen table before Beckett had a chance to wrap it. Addie grabbed her tam, camel hair coat, and Fitz's leash from their hooks by the service door. The dog did his own dance as she snapped the leash on his collar.

The sky was already dark, but the streetlights were bright enough. There were a fair number of people out on a Saturday night, some dressed to the nines, others as casual as she was, with their own pets in tow. She headed for the Mount Street Gardens, in her opinion one of the loveliest little parks in London. Nothing was quite as good as tramping over her own green fields, but this came close.

"Beautiful night, isn't it?"

Addie tripped, and she could feel the chill of the hand that caught her through the fine wool of her coat. "Don't you get tired of jumping out of the bushes?"

"I'm jumping on the pavement, my dear. Not a bush to be seen yet. You shouldn't be out alone, you know. It's not safe. Anything might happen," Rupert chided.

"Anything has already happened. This area is perfectly safe." Mayfair was as sought-after as it was in Regency days.

"One might think so, at the exorbitant property prices. But even in the smartest postcodes, one never knows about one's neighbors. There was a rumor, you know, that one of Edward the VII's sons was Jack the Ripper, and you can't do better than Buckingham Palace."

"Poppycock."

"Please allow me to be chivalrous. You're too beautiful to be out wandering the streets alone. As beautiful as the night."

Addie felt her cheeks warm, and immediately was annoyed with herself. Bad enough to fall for Rupert's charm while he was alive, but now? "Do not cozen me."

Rupert shrugged. "Well, it's true. We already know a madman's on the loose. I would so hate to have you become his next victim."

She wouldn't like it much either. "Is it a man then?"

"Ah. Slip of the tongue. Alas, as usual, I am not privy to the specifics. Just know when it is time to become your champion again, I stand at the ready."

"How very noble of you," Addie murmured, hoping any passersby would think she was speaking to Fitz.

They entered the park through the pillars. Several people were enjoying the cool spring evening on the benches placed throughout the winding path. Sitting down on one of them, Addie let Fitz off his lead, and he promptly went to lubricate the shrubbery.

"I say, don't we know those girls over there under the lamppost?" Rupert asked. Addie squinted in the dark, but could make out nothing more than two female forms engaged in a quiet yet lively discussion, judging from their hand gestures. "Stay right where you are. Back in a tick."

Fritz trotted behind Rupert, stubby tail wagging. Could the dog see him, or was it a coincidence? Ignoring Rupert's instruction, Addie hopped off the bench to get her dog under control before he licked someone to death.

She approached the young women, who fell suddenly silent. Gracious! "Nadia? Trix?"

No. Not Trix. Upon closer inspection, it was her conniving cousin Mary Frances.

Oh dear.

Rupert put his finger over his mouth in warning, as if Addie didn't know how to hold her tongue. Five years of marriage to the man was a good education.

Obviously flustered, Nadia leaped off the bench. "Lady Adelaide! What are you doing here?"

"Walking this disreputable little beast. I didn't know you lived in the neighborhood." Addie had called the girl this afternoon, ostensibly to see how she was faring after their horrible night. Nadia had claimed she planned on staying home. No mention had been made of clandestine meetings.

"Oh, not too far. My parents live in Grosvenor Square."

Then why wasn't she sitting in *that* park?

"It's a wonderful night for a walk, isn't it? So clear and fresh." Except for an occasional whiff of the Thames on the breeze.

"Um. Yes."

Addie turned to Mary Frances, who was clad in a mink jacket with something white and shimmery underneath. She pretended she didn't recognize the girl's true identity, which was easy—Trix and Mary Frances were remarkably alike. "Do you have the night off from the Thieves' Den, Trix? I imagine everyone there is just gutted about poor Roy Dean."

"Sure. But I gotta ankle. Nadia, you have my—uh—letter? "

Under the streetlight, Nadia flushed, but fished an envelope out of her purse. Mary Frances put it in hers, then rose. "Everything's jake now. Toodles, ladies."

Addie waited for the young woman to disappear down the path. "That wasn't Trix."

Nadia slumped back on the bench. "No."

"Is she the reason Prince Andrei is so upset with you?"

"He's always upset. He's Russian. Haven't you read the classics? Dostoevsky? Tolstoy? Gloom and doom from page one to The End. It's required."

An education from Cheltenham Ladies College only went so far. No, Addie had not read either of them and wasn't apt to. They didn't sound at all appealing. "Why were you meeting Mary Frances?"

"She helped me out with something."

Addie wondered what had been in the envelope. Surely not a love letter. "Did she supply the poison?"

Nadia gasped, then jerked up from the bench. "What? What do you mean?"

"Sit down." Addie was a little surprised when the girl did without an argument. "The poison that was used to contaminate the drinks. Don't be a Dumb Dora. It doesn't suit you."

Over on the next bench, Rupert buried his face in his hands. It was a shame he couldn't interrogate her himself. If he didn't care for Addie's methods, too bad. The sooner she got to the bottom of all this, the faster she could get back to Compton Chase.

Of course, that meant leaving a certain detective inspector behind, but maybe Rupert too.

"No! Of course not. I haven't poisoned anyone. I have to go."

Addie grabbed her arm. "Not yet. I'm trying to help, Nadia. You ran off on me once; don't do it again."

"I don't know what you want me to say!"

Addie sat down next to her, and Fitz jumped into her lap. "The truth would be nice. The police are interested in Mary Frances, you know."

"How do *you* know?"

How much should Addie reveal? "I met Mr. Hunter last summer at...at another case. Naturally when my sister was poisoned, he remembered me and warned me about some of the people that frequent the Thieves' Den."

"Why hasn't he arrested her then? What's she supposed to have done?"

"I think the better question is, what hasn't she? The women she 'works' with have robbed countless homes and stores. Blackmail, drugs, nothing is beyond them."

Nadia kept her plush lips sealed.

"You're afraid, aren't you?"

At last, she nodded. "I did something stupid. It's finished now."

"I can't help you if you won't tell me," Addie said, frustrated.

"I don't need your help. I'll be fine."

Addie knew when to give up. "Please yourself. But if you decide you do need a friend, I'm here."

Nadia stood up. "I really have to go. Andrei is dropping by."

"I thought he lived with your family."

"Um, what I meant is, he's coming home. I know you mean well, Lady Adelaide, but...butt out, won't you? This doesn't concern you." She moved swiftly down the walkway through the stone pillars.

"Well, you can lead a horse to water, but you can't make him—or her—drink." Rupert took Nadia's place, stretching his legs out in front of him onto the path. Addie wondered idly if pedestrians could trip over them, or if he was somehow protected in his ghostly invisibility and they'd simply walk through.

"What do you think Mary Frances has over Nadia?"

"The usual, I expect. Drugs. Sexual indiscretions. Maybe even something at Whitehall. I don't think the Dollies are into international intrigue yet, but one never knows with young women nowadays. They're almost as incorrigible as young men."

"You sound like my mother. Andrei said Nadia quit her job. Maybe that's why she said 'it was finished.'"

"Hm. Well, we're not going to find out anymore sitting around here, and I confess my cold bottom is becoming a touch chillier. Say, what did you do with my new Chesterfield coat, my dear?"

"It went in the church jumble sale. I didn't think you'd have need of it where you were supposed to go." She'd given away everything of Rupert's before she left for America, much as one does with a baby crib when one thinks one's family is complete. Trust the Fellow Upstairs to have the last laugh.

"That was bespoke," Rupert said peevishly. "Now some farmer is probably shearing his sheep in it."

"How was I to know you'd return? After last August, I thought I had truly seen the back of you."

"No such luck. Now we're partners in crime." Rupert gave her a brilliant smile and she kept her fists firmly in her lap.

Chapter Twenty-Four

Sunday

Dev's mother had been scandalized when he told her he was going in to work at Scotland Yard instead of accompany her to church, as he often did as a dutiful son. Chandani Hunter took her Commandments seriously; as a convert, she could out-Anglican an archbishop. Dev sometimes wondered if his mother missed her original faith, but was too smart to ask.

His own faith—what there was of it—was being sorely tried. Human nature being what it was, and police work engaged with the worst of it, meant he was constantly disappointed in his fellow man. All the philosophy and religious texts he studied for his own edification did not fully explain why men—and women too—so often chose the wrong path.

But if they didn't, Dev wouldn't have job security, now, would he?

Although that was being called into question. Deputy Commissioner Olive had stated in no uncertain terms that he expected the department to solve this case before others decided there were no consequences to killing off Bright Young People, and moved on to the middle-aged and elderly.

"Leave the boy alone," his father said, raising his eyes briefly from his newspaper. "If he's to make anything of himself, it doesn't matter whether it's the Sabbath or St. Swithin's Day. Murderers don't check the calendar and wait for it to be convenient."

"Thank you, Father." He didn't bother objecting to the "boy" appellation—his father used it for anyone younger than fifty.

"I still cannot like it. What is the expression…all work and no play makes Jack a dull dog? You need a personal life. Look at Bobby." Dev's mother had taken quite a shine to his sergeant and his family, particularly baby Joan. A colorful afghan and been knitted and presented.

"*Bob* doesn't shoulder the ultimate responsibility," Dev said. Besides, this case did have a unique twist. He hadn't enlightened either of his parents about Lady Adelaide Compton's involvement. He could imagine their opinions well enough.

"Will you come tonight for supper at least?"

"I don't want to promise anything, Ma." He planned a visit to the Thieves' Den before things got too lively. It might be the Sabbath, but that meant absolutely nothing to its thrill-seeking patrons. Freddy Rinaldi had had plenty of time to consider Dev's words. Maybe he was ready to spill. If his membership kept dropping dead, it would be an incentive.

Harry Hunter poured himself another cup of strong tea from a Rockingham Brown Betty. "You'll figure it out. I have every confidence in you. Why, once…" His father proceeded to share a story from his own days with the Metropolitan Police that Dev had heard many times. An impossible case. A full complement of suspects, red herrings galore. Dev waited patiently as he always did until the miscreant was hanged, then bid his parents good-bye.

He was behind his desk at eight, equipped with a bacon roll and a flask of coffee his mother had pressed upon him. The floor was nearly deserted, and Bob wasn't due for another hour. Dev spread the contents of the relevant folders across his blotter, waiting for something to leap out at him. His instincts told him the Dollies were up to their pretty necks somehow in all this; he needed to find where they and his suspects intersected. It would be a feather in the department's cap if he could reduce their crimes. They were a nuisance to the business community, but thus far they had not committed murder directly as far as Dev was aware.

But if he could prove they had provided the cyanide for the first two killings, he'd finally be getting somewhere. The nicotine used on poor Roy Dean was easily obtainable from a variety of sources, but cyanide was a different matter altogether.

He studied the abandoned mill robbery information. Impossible to know when it had been committed. But bolts of fine worsted fabric had turned up with several fences only recently, so the theft of the cyanide fit the time frame. The former manager of the mill seemed to think most of the chemicals had been binned, but apparently enough had been left to do their evil work.

If Dev couldn't get anywhere with Freddy Rinaldi tonight, maybe Trix would be more cooperative. He knew blood was thicker than water, but Trix seemed like a smart girl. Winding up in jail was probably not on her agenda.

He looked up at Bob's knock on the doorframe. He was early—he must want to make something of himself, too.

Or little Joan's crying had driven him to the comparative calm of Scotland Yard.

"Morning, guv. There's a chap downstairs to see you. Ollie Whatsis, the trumpet player with the band at the Thieves' Den."

"It's his band, Bob. Don't demote him." Ollie Johnson's All American Band had gotten rave reviews from Those in the Know. Dev didn't count himself as all that much of a jazz fan, and it was obvious Bob wasn't.

"Call down and have them send him up." It was mighty early for a fellow who'd likely been playing all night long. Maybe Ollie Johnson had never even gone to bed.

But instead of showing up in his white tie and tails, Johnson was in a sharp checked suit, his wiry hair tamed by hair oil. He looked far fresher than Dev felt. "Please be seated. Would you like some coffee?"

"No, thank you."

"Wise choice. It's pretty vile here. What can I do for you, Mr. Johnson?"

"You told me to come any time if I had any news. I wasn't sure you'd be here." He looked around Dev's semi-shabby office, obviously unimpressed.

"Well, I am. No rest for the wicked."

"I'm leavin' for Paris tomorrow night, and I'm taking Trix Harmon with me."

Dev felt a stab of disappointment. If he had expected Johnson to present the murderer on a silver platter, he was out of luck. "This is sudden."

The man shrugged his shoulders. "The French love their jazz. I've had a better offer for the band, and anyway, I can't stay here. People are dyin', ain't they? I don't want Trix mixed up in it anymore. That Rinaldi has no backbone. He's runnin' scared. Me, I'm just runnin' with my girl. Getting' out of the way. But I wanted to make sure me and my boys are off your suspect list. Trix, too. Wouldn't do for the *gendarmes* to come knockin'."

"As I told you, we've ruled out any involvement of your band." Dev paused, choosing his words carefully. "We believe Miss Harmon might be a person of interest in a very tangential way."

Johnson's sculpted lips flattened. "What do you mean by that?"

"Has she spoken to you about her cousin?"

"She's got too many cousins to count. Don't have much truck with 'em."

"She was seen with this one just the other night at the club. Mary Frances." Dev did not imagine the light of recognition in Johnson's eyes at the mention of the name.

"Oh. Her."

"She's mixed up with a girl gang called the Forty Dollies. You've heard of them?"

"Trix has nothin' to do with that bunch. They're one reason she wants to get away."

"They're very persuasive, recruiting family members and neighbors in the Elephant and Castle district."

"They ain't gonna persuade Trix. We're gettin' married tomorrow before we leave."

"My felicitations." Were the French less race-conscious than the British? Young Mr. and Mrs. Johnson had a difficult road ahead of them. Dev was reminded of his mother's efforts to assimilate. It was a shame she had had to give up so much; she was very brave.

Braver in some ways than her son.

"I'll want to interview her again before you leave," Dev continued. "I had planned on dropping by the club tonight. You'll both be there?"

"Last show. Rinaldi don't know it yet, though." Johnson drew a breath. "I won't let you bully her." He looked ready to tangle with him, inside Scotland Yard or out.

"I wouldn't dream of it. You can be present if you wish." Dev wasn't sure that was a wise tactic; Trix might be less than forthcoming if she was trying to impress her future husband with her virtue. But she'd been so prickly with him the other day— Johnson's support might be beneficial.

The musician leaned forward. "Look. Trix is just a kid. You can't blame her for her family. We all got skeletons in our closets."

Dev had cousins on another continent—who knew what they were up to? He nodded. "Fair enough. Tell her I'll stop in before the Thieves' Den opens. Freddy too."

Johnson snorted. "Good luck with him. Man's afraid of his own shadow."

"The beating can't have helped."

"Something funny's goin' on there for sure. Good luck findin' out what." Johnson rose, and Dev extended his hand across the desk. After a second, Johnson shook it.

"Good luck to you, too," Dev said.

Johnson probably knew a lot more than he was telling, but Dev didn't blame the man for getting out while the getting was possible. He had a feeling the Thieves' Den's days were numbered. There were a dozen other private clubs the Bright Young People could indulge themselves in, so the pointless party wouldn't stop.

Bob popped his head in. "Any news?"

"Not really. The Thieves' Den is about to lose its band and hostess, neither of which should affect us much."

"You're sure Trix Harmon's not involved in the murders in some way?"

"Oh, she's involved in something, but not necessarily the murders. She's a bright girl and taking her chance before things go too far south. Any new information about the Bergeron robbery?"

Bob pulled up Johnson's chair and was about to expound when Dev's phone rang.

His day was about to get more interesting and it wasn't even nine o'clock yet.

Chapter Twenty-Five

Addie had been here before—gosh, just seven days ago. This week had had more twists and turns than a carnival ride, and she felt much too old for one of those. She supposed she might have called the inspector at his office to report on running into Nadia and Mary Frances Harmon last night, but it was a fine morning, and she craved fresh air. She had a new suit, too—heather-gray, and a matching cunning veil with one curled dusty rose feather. Beckett had thought she looked very smart, although had wrinkled her nose when Addie disclosed where she was going. In Beckett's unwanted opinion, ladies did not visit policemen on their premises unless they were under arrest.

"Good morning, Inspector! I called your flat, but got no answer. Then I remembered you were slave-driving poor Sergeant Wells this morning, and here I am!" Bob Wells turned scarlet, a fairly normal color for him every time he encountered Addie, she noted.

"Bob, please fetch me another cup. I guess I could do with a break. You'll share some of my mother's coffee with me, yes? It's excellent."

"I'd love to. And I didn't think you'd mind, me coming here so early. I barely slept. I have a clue! Or what I hope will be. You'll have to sort it out."

"Thanks for your confidence. I hope I can recognize a clue as well as you do."

Was he poking fun at her? Gracious, he looked tired, and was that a strand of silver in his glossy dark hair? Addie was busy pulling out white hair every day. Beckett warned her she'd soon be bald.

She watched as Bob returned with a surprisingly pretty tea cup without a matching saucer. Mr. Hunter waved him away, then unscrewed the cap of a flask he pulled from his bottom desk drawer.

"It might not be as hot as it should be. Do you want half my bacon roll too?"

"Oh, no. I had a bowl of Irish oatmeal, the one dish Beckett is genius at. Loads of double cream and golden syrup. Bad for one's figure, but so very delicious. But please, have your breakfast. I know how hard you've been working. Um...perhaps you'd like to come to supper tonight? I promise more than roast beef sandwiches." Addie had not planned to issue that invitation, but somehow she had.

"Sorry, I can't. I have a few interviews to conduct at the Thieves' Den."

"Could I come too?" She could wear her gold striped evening gown. She had lovely turquoise jewelry she usually wore with it, and a feathered bandeau.

"Best not. So, what is this clue?" He took a bite of his roll.

"Well, I took Fitz for a walk last night—"

He swallowed hurriedly. "Alone?"

Addie couldn't very well mention Rupert. "Yes, of course."

Mr. Hunter looked grim. "That's not wise, Lady Adelaide. You could be a target yourself. An attractive woman on a dark street— why, it's an invitation to all the mischief-makers in Mayfair."

Men. Always telling one what one should or shouldn't do. Annoyed, she concentrated on the word *attractive* and took a sip of coffee. As he'd said, it was very good.

She set her cup down. "Nevertheless, I persisted and here I am, safe and sound. I only went as far as the Mount Street Gardens and had Fitz to protect me." Mr. Hunter probably knew just how useless Fitz was as a guard dog, but he said nothing.

"Anyway, who do you think I bumped into?"

"I haven't the foggiest. Lady Adelaide, need I remind you that I'm very busy? Please get to the point." He was clearly at his wits' end—three murders and an attempted murder would do that to one, and probably accounted for his grumpy mood.

"Nadia Sanborn and Mary Frances Harmon were having a *tête-à-tête* on a bench. They were not happy to see me. I pretended I thought Mary Frances was her cousin Trix, and they didn't tell me otherwise. Nadia gave Mary Frances a rather thick envelope—for services rendered, I presume. Nadia told me she had done something stupid but was finished. I asked her if she'd bought poison from Mary Frances—"

"*What*? Lady Adelaide, I know you think you're helping, but leave the questions to the police! Do you see what you've done?" His face was flushed in anger, and for the first time, Addie could imagine what being a criminal under his black gaze felt like.

"I didn't do anything!"

"Nothing but tip our hand, if we can ever find their hideout. If the Dollies are involved in passing out poisons, you can bet they'll clean up all traces. Destroy all evidence, or transfer it to a new safe place."

"I don't think Nadia plans to see Mary Frances again to tell her anything," Addie said in a small voice.

"*She* may not want to, but Mary Frances may have other ideas. If Nadia is being blackmailed, Mary Frances will be expecting another thick envelope, and you were a witness. These women are relentless, Lady Adelaide, and now you're in their gunsights."

"But I didn't say or do anything suspicious!" Addie protested. She wasn't about to raid their hideout. If the police didn't know where it was—

A dreadful and intriguing idea flashed across her mind.

"So you think. Curiosity killed the cat, you know. I want you to go back to the Cotswolds and forget this past week. I don't know what I was thinking, letting someone like you get involved. Again! I should have my head examined."

Someone like you? He sounded so dreadfully dismissive. "Dr. Bergman is acquainted with Sigmund Freud. Do you want a referral?" Addie asked tartly. She knew she'd been useful in the investigation so far. She was not some helpless creature to be kept buried in the country away from the big bad city. An empty-headed twit who only lived for fashion and folly, and was about to inform the detective of just that.

"Calm down," Rupert said. He was sitting cross-legged on an oak filing cabinet like a swami again, but didn't look a bit uncomfortable. Why was he here? He was the most annoying, aggravating—

"I will *not*..." Addie began, then realized to whom she was speaking. Mr. Hunter already thought she was not quite in her right mind. "Um, I will not cause problems, I promise."

"You certainly won't. If I have to put you on a train myself, I will."

"You can't boss me around, Inspector Hunter! I'm not poor Bob."

"Poor Bob? I'll have you know he loves his job. And is good at it. You need to withdraw. Now."

Addie was fairly sure she'd be good at a job if she had one; she was intelligent enough, even if she didn't know Russian literature. It wasn't her fault that society expected her to be festive, philanthropic yet fundamentally idle.

"Now, children," Rupert murmured, smoothing down his ridiculous moustache, "no fighting."

"I'll do as I please!" Addie said to both men.

"That's fine," Mr. Hunter growled, "as long as you do as you please in the country."

"You forget yourself." Addie was alarmed by the ice in her voice. It was as if her mother had joined them and had taken over her vocal chords. Rupert hissed and disappeared as unexpectedly as he'd appeared.

He'd always hated confrontation. Usually because he was guilty.

Mr. Hunter stood up. "My apologies, my lady. I don't know what's come over me." He didn't sound one jot sorry as he picked up the telephone receiver. "Sergeant Wells, could you please escort Lady Adelaide downstairs and procure a taxi for her? Thanks." He hung up and glared at her. "Or would you prefer 'poor Bob' drive you home so you can lecture him on my slave-driving ways? Perhaps you can infiltrate the policemen's union and call another strike. But no doubt you think police are unnecessary when it comes to detecting. After all, anyone can blunder about and ask questions, can't they?"

Sergeant Wells opened the office door, a shy smile on his face. "Ready, Lady Adelaide?"

"Beyond ready. Good day, Inspector." Without waiting for his reply, she walked out with spectacular deportment, chin pointed to the rather cobwebby ceiling, and headed for the lift. "You needn't come down with me, Sergeant Wells. I know my way, and I promise to leave the building."

"Um, uh, are you all right, Lady Adelaide?"

"Of course! It will take more than one pig-headed man to discompose me. I've had a great deal of practice over the years."

"Tut tut." Rupert was back at her elbow. She gave him a satisfactory little shove.

"There's no need to resort to violence."

"How is your little girl, Sergeant Wells?" Addie asked, poking Rupert once more. Could she trip him? Though Sergeant Wells might think she was under the influence if her foot went astray and she tumbled to the linoleum.

"She's got a tooth coming in already and is a little crab-pot. But bonny just the same."

"How lovely," Addie said, distracted. "Really, you don't need to go down to the street with me."

"Guv's orders. Doesn't do to cross Inspector Hunter."

"I bet not. He's an ogre, isn't he?"

Sergeant Wells looked shocked. "Oh, no, ma'am. You couldn't find a fairer boss. And he's smart as a whip, too. Sees the trees *and* the forest. He's going places, and I hope he takes me with him."

Addie had an idea where to send him, but that wouldn't be kind to Bob. She and Rupert slipped into the lift, and Sergeant Wells maneuvered them to the ground floor. Once outside, he flagged down a cab and directed the driver to Mount Street.

Once they were underway, Addie leaned forward. "I've changed my mind." She gave a new address and Rupert moaned, much like a clanking ghost in a ruined abbey in a gothic novel.

Chapter Twenty-Six

"Don't touch anything," Rupert warned. Addie was grateful she wore gloves, and had no intention of leaning against anything or, perish the thought, sitting down. The club did not show to advantage in daylight or sobriety. The combined sharp smells of alcohol and perspiration permeated the vestibule. Beyond, tables and chairs had been pushed to the side, white tablecloths trailing on the floor, dirty glasses littering every surface. Whoever came in to clean after Saturday night's frivolity hadn't been in yet.

"Jeez, can't a guy get any sleep around here?" Freddy Rinaldi tried to further smooth down his brilliantined dark hair. He was barefoot, wearing a dressing gown of an indeterminate color, and looked none too pleased to see her after she and Rupert took turns beating on the door for a full five minutes.

Mr. Rinaldi was a brave man eschewing shoes in such a place. Her own left gray suede shoe was stuck to a mysterious sticky patch on the floor, and the muck could only get worse the further they entered the club's rooms. Somehow the grime wasn't so visible at night.

"You must be frightfully distressed after all the fuss," Addie said, oozing faux sympathy. He did look a wreck, nearly as bad as the Thieves' Den itself.

"I'll be even more distressed if I can't get some sleep. Hunter was in my office most of the night before last—it doubles as my bedroom. I like to be on top of things here, so I live in."

"How very convenient. Or inconvenient, since you say Inspector Hunter commandeered your space. Did he bully you terribly?"

"Hell, no. Nobody bullies Fredo Rinaldi." The fading bruises on his face told a different story. "I managed to talk him into keeping the club open, didn't I? What the he—um, why are you here so early? We don't open till eight. At night," he emphasized.

"Well, I wondered if you could tell me where to find Patricia Harmon. Trix."

"What do you want her for?"

"She's such a nice girl, isn't she?" Addie said, avoiding the question. "So very pretty. Smart, too."

"Sorry to disappoint, your ladyship, but Trix isn't like that. She has a boyfriend."

It took Addie a few seconds to figure out what Rinaldi inferred. Every day was an education.

"Oh! You misunderstand. I have a message for her. From… uh, from Nadia Sanborn."

"Why don't you write it down, and I'll see she gets it tonight."

"I'm afraid it's rather urgent."

Rinaldi gave her a knowing look. "Are you sure it isn't her cousin Miss Sanborn wants?"

Addie played dumb, which wasn't all that difficult at the moment. "Her cousin?"

"Mary Frances. She's around here sometimes. Miss Sanborn and she are thick as, well, thieves." He chuckled at his own little joke.

"No, I'm quite sure she mentioned Trix. Along with the message—" she patted her handbag—"I have something to give her, too. Something quite, um, valuable. If I could have her address so I could pay her a quick visit, I'd be eternally grateful." Addie batted her lashes behind her eyeglasses in an attempt to seal the deal.

"Ugh. Don't give the man any ideas," Rupert said in disgust. "I know his type. Give him and inch and he'll be all over you like a bad rash."

"Sounds familiar," Addie muttered into her glove.

"I object to being classified with this rotter. Really, Addie, I do hope you can see the difference."

Pomaded hair. Tick. Weaselly moustache. Tick. Slender yet strong build. Tick. Rinaldi could be Rupert's lower-class twin.

"I was a war hero while this guy claimed he had flat feet! Stop thinking like that!"

For once, she enjoyed the fact that Rupert could sometimes read her mind. It was amusing to torture him the teeniest bit. It almost made up for the years of unfaithfulness.

Almost.

"I'm a reformed character. Reform*ing*, anyhow. Everybody Upstairs thinks so. I don't know why you can't see that," Rupert grumbled, smoothing his own hair down. Addie had to admit that he was still ridiculously attractive, even if he *was* dead.

"The address, Mr. Rinaldi? And then you can get back to bed," Addie said firmly.

"She ain't, uh, isn't at home with her parents any more. Taken up with Ollie Johnson, the band leader, she has."

Addie had suspected as much from the girl's blushes. "And where might I find them?"

"They're in a residential hotel down the street. The Albert. Caters to the Covent Garden crowd. Actors, musicians, and such. Nobody cares what time they come in, or their condition when they do."

"That will save me taxi fare! Thank you so much for your help, Mr. Rinaldi. Trix will thank you too!" Addie allowed the manager to open the door to the street for her, then slam it shut, only just avoiding catching Rupert's sleeve.

The sunshine caused her to pause and blink. "Lay on, Macduff. Which direction shall we go in?"

"Turn left. What would you do without me?" Rupert asked.

"You really don't want an answer."

Was he to be at her heels for the rest of her life? It was one thing to promise "as long as we both shall live." He'd already reneged by dying and certainly hadn't forsaken all others when he was alive. While they were getting along remarkably well at the moment, the situation was, to say the very least, odd.

In less than two minutes, they were at the Albert, once a small private mansion. It appeared to have fallen on challenging times, the gold letters on its glass sign over the front door peeling. Addie turned the handle and was overwhelmed with the scent of Brasso, which had been used to polish the sconces in the reception area. Efforts at civilization were being made with an imitation Persian carpet on the floor and a vase of paper flowers between two mismatched chairs. A harried-looking young man presided over a dinged mahogany countertop, sorting papers in front of him. He cringed briefly at a piercing shriek coming from upstairs, then turned his attention to Addie.

"Good morning, madam. How may I help you?"

The fellow was exceptionally handsome, with curly fair hair, his modulated voice mellow and accentless. "Actor," whispered Rupert. "Works here for his room and board. First big break. He's in the chorus of *No No Nanette*, and his feet hurt like the devil."

Rupert was an amazing font of knowledge on occasion. "Good morning. I am Lady Adelaide Compton." She handed him a calling card and paused while the fellow's cerulean blue eyes goggled. Such long eyelashes. Beckett would be beside herself. In Addie's opinion, the young man might go far if his feet recovered, perhaps even all the way to Hollywood.

"I would like to speak to Miss Patricia Harmon if I may. I believe she is a guest of Mr. Ollie Johnson."

"Shacking up, as it were. Living in sin," Rupert added, leaning on the counter. Thankfully the actor-clerk couldn't see or hear him.

"Let me go upstairs and see if they're in. I know Mr. Johnson left earlier this morning, but I believe he returned."

"Thank you. I'll wait." Addie slid gracefully into one of the lobby chairs and crossed her ankles. Rupert went behind the front desk as soon as the young man left and disarranged the papers he had been so meticulously stacking.

"Rupert! Don't be naughty!"

"I can't help it—I get so bored. *You'll* find out."

Addie hoped not—she intended to be on a direct path to Heaven with no detours once she kicked the bucket. Laughter floated down from upstairs, and somewhere someone was playing an oboe.

The young man came downstairs alone. "They will be along shortly. Do you require privacy? I can let you into the breakfast room. Service is over."

"Thank you. That's very kind," Addie replied. The "they" bothered her a little; she had hoped to speak to Trix by herself.

He unlocked double doors that once must have opened to a rather majestic dining room. The high ceiling was elaborately decorated, and two floor to ceiling windows looked out onto the street. A massive carved marble fireplace contained ashes and, disgustingly, dozens of cigarette butts.

Addie could still smell burnt toast, although the small tables crowded together had been cleared and were set for the next meal. A hamper of soiled linen stood in a corner, and a tray of dirty coffee cups and eggy plates was on the sideboard awaiting attention.

"Let me get rid of these dishes. May I get you a cup of tea? I believe the cook is still in the kitchen."

"Oh, no thank you! The Albert serves breakfast only?"

"Yes, my lady. We find our guests shift very well for themselves the rest of the day. Should you have any friends interested in staying with us, breakfast is six to eight on weekdays, eight to ten on weekends. Sunday mornings are usually lightly attended, as you can imagine. We cater to a creative crowd that doesn't necessarily keep track of time. Please take a seat anywhere." He heaved up the tray and pushed through a baize door at the rear of the room.

The room was relatively cheerful, with movie and play posters as a nod to the hotel's clientele on the flocked walls. Beckett would approve. Addie sat down at a table, careful not to disturb anything. Rupert poked about the sideboard, dusting it with his handkerchief. Then he climbed atop it, resuming his favorite swami-snake charmer position.

He'd always been flexible, Addie recalled, climbing in and out of planes and cars and beds with impunity.

Addie reapplied the pink lipstick that matched the feather on her veil and tried to be patient. Trix seemed like a reasonable sort of person, and Addie was confident she could make headway with her in ways that Scotland Yard couldn't.

For example, Addie had several five pound notes in her handbag.

Chapter Twenty-Seven

The couple entered, Ollie Johnson gripping Trix's hand. She wore a brown twinset and tweed skirt, a far cry from her usual evening attire, looking almost like an innocent school girl. Addie attempted a reassuring smile.

"What's this about then?" the trumpeter asked, sounding none too friendly.

"Good morning, Trix, Mr. Johnson. Thank you so much for seeing me. Won't you both sit down?"

"Why?"

"Well, if you sit, sir, I'll tell you," Addie replied. Actually, she hadn't thought through exactly what she was going to say. "I'll make it worth your while."

Trix shook her head. "I have nothing to tell *you*, Lady Adelaide, except this. Oliver and me, we're leaving tomorrow on the night train to Paris. We're getting married, and we'll be done with the Thieves' Den for good."

"And the Dollies too?"

Trix opened her mouth, then shut it.

"She has nothin' to do with them," Mr. Johnson said. "Nothin' to do with the murders, either."

"I believe you." The expression on both their faces was almost comical. "I heard your cousin threaten you the other night. Mr. Johnson, too."

"*What?* You never told me that!" He was thunderous.

Trix gave Addie a look. "She's all talk, Oliver."

"Tell that to Freddy and his ribs." Mr. Johnson tucked Trix against him. "The sooner we get outta here, the better. Tell the lady what she wants to know."

"I agree," Addie replied. "I think you're a very intelligent young woman to jump at your chance for happiness. Unfortunately, Penelope Hardinge, Tommy Bickley, and Roy Dean will never have that chance. My sister was almost a victim as well, but thanks to God's grace and excellent medical care, she survived."

"I might have had something to do with it too," Rupert said, preening from the sideboard.

"I don't know who killed them, and that's a fact!" Trix cried.

"But I imagine you do know where the Dollies keep their ill-gotten goods. It's somewhere in your old neighborhood, isn't it? And you know your attendance records at the club have been used to break in to empty houses while members are enjoying themselves on a night out. I don't believe you meant to help, but it only took a second for your cousin to read a list and dispatch her clever friends to rob silly young rich people. No real harm done, right? They're all careless and a bit stupid. They deserve it, don't they?"

"Don't say anything, honey. She don't know what she's talkin' about."

"I don't suppose I could get you to leave us alone, Mr. Johnson."

"You suppose right."

Addie sighed. "I don't want to get you in trouble, Trix. Truly. I wish you nothing but joy, and I'd be glad to give you a substantial wedding present to help get you both settled in Paris. Ah, Paris in the spring. I envy you."

"How substantial?"

Addie wondered if Ollie Johnson knew just how tough his pretty young fiancée was. "Five pounds?"

"Ten."

"Done." Addie opened her purse. "But first, we need to deal with Mary Frances. What hold does she have over Nadia Sanborn?"

"Drugs," Trix said promptly. "Cocaine. Nadia was dabbling, and Mary Frances sold it to her. She's stopped now, but afraid her father will find out. The prince, too."

"So Mary Frances is blackmailing her?"

Trix nodded. "She's not very nice, my cousin."

An understatement. "Do you think she sold poison to someone who used it on Penelope Hardinge and Tommy Bickley?"

The girl shrugged. "She might have. With no questions asked. As long as she got her money, she wouldn't have cared who got what at first. And maybe she didn't know how it would be used, or the end result. But I know she's nervous as a cat now. She thinks the police will pin it all on her. And who knows? Maybe she did kill them all for kicks—I wouldn't put anything past her. She wants to get away too and needs some quick money."

"Where can I find her?"

Rupert materialized at her elbow. "Oh, no. Oh, *hell* no. You are not going to some slum to beard the lioness in her den. What does that mean, anyway? Lions don't even have beards. Your Inspector Hunter would have a conniption. He'll kill you if you're not dead already. I can only do so much to protect you, Addie. Don't test my resources."

Trix frowned. "You can't go there alone, Lady Adelaide. You'd stick out like a sore thumb, and I wouldn't vouch for your safety."

"Ah! A voice of reason! Listen to the child, Addie."

"Can you two leave for Paris today instead?" Addie counted out three five pound notes. "No one will know that you told me the address." She slid a coral bracelet from her wrist, unclipped the matching earrings, and placed them atop her bribe. Trix turned to Mr. Johnson. After what felt like an hour, he nodded.

"Freddy will be pis—put out, but he'll have one last night with the rest of the band. My boys can follow tomorrow as planned. We'll just have to get married in Paris."

Addie thought that might be easier said than done—as American and British citizens, there might be more red tape than anyone bargained for—the French were known for their croissants and convoluted paperwork. With a sigh, she withdrew another five pound note.

"Do you have a piece of paper and a pencil? I'll write down where Mary Frances stays most of the time. The Dollies move around some and split up their stash, but there's a lot at her flat right now—jewelry, furs, the odd silver tea set before it goes to the fence."

Addie found the receipt from Lyons Corner House—that benighted tea seemed like a lifetime ago. She watched as Trix printed the address on the back. "Thank you! You've been very helpful. I wish you both a long and happy marriage."

"You're not going there now, are you?" Trix stuffed the money and jewelry in the pocket of her skirt.

"She certainly isn't," Rupert said firmly.

Addie knew when to throw in the towel. "I'll leave that to the police. And don't worry—I'll never tell where I got the information." Or how. Addie had a feeling Mr. Hunter would not be impressed with her cavalier attitude towards bribery.

If the Metropolitan Police Force had access to funds to pay off informants, that would change everything, wouldn't it? Life would be way easier for them.

The young lovers went upstairs to pack. Addie sat back, thinking she should feel more triumphant. She was about to break up a robbery ring—and possibly identify a murderer.

"I should call Lucas."

"Whatever for? My God, you're not going to enlist him in hunting down Mary Frances Harmon, are you?"

"Of course not. As I told the future Mr. and Mrs. Johnson, the police can handle all that. I should tell him about Roy Dean."

Rupert sniffed. "He won't care."

"He might care for Pip's sake. He unwound some as the evening wore on and was rather kind to her the other night."

"Waring kind? I think you're addled, Addie."

"Ha ha. Very funny. Let's go see if we can persuade that dancing desk clerk if we may borrow his phone."

The young man fell all over himself to assist her. Mr. Hunter's card between her fingers was well-thumbed, the writing in pencil on the back a little smudged.

In her most "daughter of a marquess" voice, she asked to be put through to him, and got Bob on the line first. After identifying herself in a much warmer tone, she waited for Mr. Hunter to pick up.

Which he didn't. Bob came back, his embarrassment obvious by a slight stutter. Addie was sure the man was blushing as he said he'd relay her information to his boss.

Fine. Let Hunter be sorry later. She'd make him *grovel*. But after a brief war with herself, justice won out. She gave Mary Frances's address to Sergeant Wells, enjoying his little gasp of surprise, then hung the receiver back in its cradle.

It was time to go home to Mount Street.

Both Fitz and Beckett were pleased to see her, Fitz more demonstrably as he ran around her feet in circles. Addie had lost Rupert somewhere on South Audley Street, which was perfectly all right with her. She changed from her suit to a pair of Japanese lounging pajamas, removing the diamond and sapphire wedding and engagement rings she still had on. The coral set wasn't all that valuable, and would look good with Trix's peachy complexion. If Addie wanted another, she had the funds to buy one.

After a light lunch, she phoned Lucas at his club. He wasn't in, but she left a message inviting him round for cocktails later. She really had ignored him since she came back from the States. He'd been enormously patient with her about his marriage proposal—other men would have given up by now. Called her fickle or a tease. She was none of those things, just indecisive. Marriage was not for everyone, contrary to what most people believed. Addie had tried it once, with negative results.

If, Heaven forfend, she was widowed again, would she have two dead husbands haunting her? It didn't bode well for future matrimonial plans, did it?

Chapter Twenty-Eight

Addie kissed Lucas's cheek once Beckett ushered him into her drawing room. The sun's brightness was waning at this hour of the day, but Addie had positioned herself in a lingering ray. "Sorry I haven't called—" they both said at the exact same time.

"Ladies first," Lucas said, with a smile. It really was a lovely smile, causing deep creases in his perennially-tanned cheeks. No one could say that Lord Lucas Waring was not a handsome man.

Of course, handsome men were dangerous to one's heart, if one still had one.

"It's only been since Thursday, but quite a lot has happened. Come. Sit down. Beckett, I think martinis are in order."

Beckett bobbed and left for the kitchen. She'd already prepared a tray of nibbles, and soon the sound of the cocktail shaker was heard.

"Martinis, eh? Sounds serious. So, what's up?"

"You know the young people you met the other night—Philippa and Roy Dean?"

"Yes. The hotel siblings. Brighton, wasn't it? The boy's a bit of a dolt, but the sister was quite charming."

Addie nodded. "Poor doltish Roy was murdered Friday night. His drink was poisoned."

"*What*?"

Anything else he might have said was stopped as Beckett came in bearing their refreshments. Lucas was old-fashioned, never speaking anything of consequence in front of servants. He'd be horrified to know that Beckett was one of Addie's closest confidantes.

The maid withdrew, and Lucas took a large gulp of his drink. "Tell me what happened."

"Now, don't say you told me so, but it happened at the Thieves' Den. The police believe he ingested nicotine."

"That's it! I forbid you from going there again!"

Addie took a sip of her martini to calm herself before she tore Lucas's head off. He was not entitled to forbid her anything, nor was any man. Never, ever again.

"You needn't worry. I'm thinking about going to Compton Chase soon." Since Inspector Hunter seemed unwilling to accept her assistance or advice, or even her phone calls, there was no point in staying in Town.

"I'm glad to hear it. We can go down on the train together tomorrow. I planned to leave—I have some estate matters that can't wait while I kick up my heels here."

The implication was that he'd been waiting for Addie to say yes to his proposal.

That was not going to happen today.

"I'm not quite ready—there are few loose ends I need to take care of. Shopping, you know," Addie lied.

"You women and your shopping! So, what's become of the Dean girl? Should I go and pay my respects?"

"Her parents are taking her back to Brighton in a day or two— once the police finish whatever it is they do—but I'm sure she'd love a visit. They're devastated, as you can imagine. I can give you the address."

"Poor kid. What the hell is happening lately? Cee gets poisoned, Dean dies. This sort of thing shouldn't be happening out in the open."

"Is murder best a private affair then?" Addie asked with a raised eyebrow. Last summer, someone died very privately in her tithe barn.

"You know what I mean. There's obviously a crazy person on the loose in good society. What are the police saying?"

"Not much. There's a limited list of suspects, but an additional complication. There's a women's crime syndicate involved somehow, the Forty Dollies."

"Good heavens. Their reputation has even reached the Cotswolds. Don't they go into stores and steal merchandise?"

"Yes, that and a lot more. Their vile grip might be coming to an end, though." If Mr. Hunter used her information. Addie hoped he wouldn't ignore it, thinking she was just some foolish fantasist. For a moment she thought she might excuse herself to try to talk to him again. But that would be rude, with Lucas sitting across from her.

Should she ask him to stay for dinner? Or maybe they could go out. *Not* to the Thieves' Den. She hadn't really given him a fair shake. Addie and Beckett had their usual signal ready—if Addie wanted to get rid of Lucas, Beckett would come in and announce she would be late to Lady Grimes's party if she didn't get dressed soon. There was no Lady Grimes as far as Addie knew, and she was grateful Lucas was too trusting to open up his Debrett's.

She crunched on a nut thoughtfully. What if she told Lucas that she *was* ready to accept his proposal? They could have a long engagement. Addie was in no hurry to marry again—or ever, really, if she was honest with herself. She had no interest in being forbidden or managed or hemmed in. And while she had known Lucas forever, she wasn't certain they had all that much in common anymore.

He wasn't pressing her, which was a relief. In fact, right now he was standing and asking for Pip's address so he could drop in and deliver his condolences before it got too late.

"Her parents are staying with her, I believe. Number 44, Curzon Street."

"Maybe I'll take them all out to dinner if they're up to it. Thanks for the drink, Addie. I'll look forward to seeing you in the country soon."

Well. It seemed there was no need of Lady Grimes. Beckett poked her head in. "Did I hear the door close?"

"You did. Lord Waring is gone."

"He didn't even finish his martini! Aren't they any good?"

Addie expected Beckett had taken a taste for herself in the kitchen. "They're delicious," she said topping hers off. "Just right. You really have a knack."

"Thank you, Lady A." Beckett grinned. "So, no wedding bells yet?"

"Not for me." Addie wondered what Lucas would make of Mr. Dean.

The doorbell buzzed. "Maybe his lordship forgot something," Beckett said, going to the front hall.

"Good afternoon, Miss Beckett. Is your mistress in?"

That voice. He was absolutely the last person Addie expected to darken her door. If he'd come to be grumpy, he could just go grump somewhere else.

Beckett stepped into the drawing room. "Detective Inspector Hunter from Scotland Yard is here to see you, Lady A. Are you receiving?"

The man was only a few feet away in the hall and had heard every word. Addie should say no. Mr. Hunter hadn't even shown her the courtesy of answering his phone earlier.

Had he come to apologize? She could endure that. Or had he come to quiz her about how she obtained Mary Frances's address—maybe he'd arrest her until she confessed. She picked up her martini, fishing the olive out of it.

Just as Bunny Dunford must have fished out his cherries to give to Roy Dean. Somehow the little green globe was no longer appealing. Addie plopped it back into the glass with a splash. "Of course I'm receiving, Beckett. Show him in."

In the hours since she had last seen him, he had become more crumpled and weary. Her first urge was to fix him a drink, but she kept her hands still. "What can I do for you, Inspector?" She did not invite him to sit.

"I won't keep you long. How did you find out Mary Frances Harmon's address?"

"I asked the right person." She felt under no obligation to peach on Trix, and hoped she was bound for France right this minute.

"Did you visit her yourself?"

"No, of course not. That would have spooked her, wouldn't it? Given her the opportunity to destroy evidence, as you were so worried about. Did you get what you were looking for?"

"And a bit more. Mary Frances Harmon is dead. Strangled. What do you know about it?"

Oh dear. Those spots danced before her eyes again. At least in her pajamas, she wouldn't give Mr. Hunter a show when she slipped to the floor. No view of her lace knickers for him.

Chapter Twenty-Nine

Dev had seen Lady Adelaide faint a few times before, so he wasn't as distressed as he might have been. He shouted out to Beckett, then lifted the woman back to the sofa. Sitting beside her, he arranged her silk-clad limbs, and removed her spectacles. He should feel some shame for shocking her like that, but that wasn't quite the emotion that roiled through him at present.

She smelled delicious—Chanel No 5, if his nose was functioning. Her pale lashes fluttered, but her eyes remained closed. A small "v" of worry was etched between her neat eyebrows, and her lips were parted.

Snow White waiting for a kiss.

But not from him.

"A cold washcloth, please, and strong, sweet tea, I think," he told the maid. She rushed off, and he smoothed Lady Adelaide's soft golden hair from her forehead. At this distance, Dev could have counted her freckles had he wanted to.

He hoped she wasn't ill. Or drunk—he seemed to remember she had difficulty holding her liquor. A frosted cocktail shaker rested on a tray on the table along with two half-full glasses, a bowl of nuts, and crackers topped with tiny shrimp in some kind of sauce. After the day he'd had, he was starving, so he ate one.

"I'll take care of her now, Inspector," Miss Beckett said, wielding a dripping washcloth. "The kettle's on in the kitchen. Would you be so kind as to make the tea?"

Disappointed, Dev went to the small white tiled kitchen and waited for the whistle. Beckett had already shoved tea leaves in a flowered tea pot, and a matching mug with several spoons of sugar added sat on the enamel table.

All very homely, quite a change from the last flat he'd visited. Mary Frances Harmon had been found sprawled out amongst her glittery ill-gotten goods. Robbery had apparently not been the motive, though it would be hard to tell what could possibly be missing from her vast share of the Dollies' booty strewn throughout. There were coats made of every type of animal fur and clothes in the very latest fashion crammed in the closets, boxes of jewelry tipsily stacked on tables, some spilling their contents to the floor.

Plenty of ammunition to play dress up. The Dollies were known for their good looks and sense of style—it was why they were able to get away with so much—male clerks were easily duped and distracted, poor saps. What she had planned to keep or to fence would always be a mystery.

Her bathroom had been a veritable chemist's shop. Whether she partook personally, Dev had found cocaine and morphia vials in her effects, as well as other drugs—of most interest to him, nicotine and digitalis. He'd ordered the lot taken off the premises to be stored under lock and key. However, there were no conveniently-labeled bottles of cyanide.

He'd lost the opportunity to question her, not that he'd have gotten any straight answers. Brazen lies, especially before judges, often got the girls off with a mere warning. The Dollies worked in cells, and Dev did not know who had been in hers, although his men were looking for any records she might have kept.

Had she made someone jealous? Perhaps she'd not divided the spoils equally. The finger marks at her throat had looked like those of a man, though. They'd have to round up as many of the Dollies' male compatriots as they could find for a little chat.

The kettle boiled, and Dev poured the scalding water in the pot. He felt at home in this spotless kitchen, even if he'd only been here two or three times. It was fully stocked with every amenity, a luxury few people could afford. Lady Adelaide kept two posh residences, both near perfect. As a hard-working stiff, he should feel some resentment, but was too tired to muster much feeling at all.

He strained the tea and carried the mug into the drawing room. Lady Adelaide was sitting up, Beckett beside her, her face very pale.

More opportunity to count those freckles.

She licked her lips and took a sip of tea, then put it down. Her hands, he noticed, were shaking. "She's really dead?"

"Yes."

"Wh-when?"

"The medical examiner thinks it happened somewhere between midnight and four a.m."

She suddenly looked more relaxed. "So it wasn't because of me."

"Pardon?"

"I didn't know where she was then. I only told Bob. Sergeant Wells. And that was just before noon."

Yes. And Dev had moved immediately with his men, despite their doubt about Lady Adelaide's reliability.

No one in the neighborhood had seen or heard anything, or so they said. No one seemed particularly sorry that Mary Frances Harmon was dead, either. For so young a woman, she had been ruthless.

One reaps what one sows.

"Drink your tea, Lady A," Beckett said soothingly.

Lady Adelaide made a face, but did as instructed. She set the mug down again with the cocktail paraphernalia. "Did you think *I* killed her?" she asked.

"Of course not," Dev replied. Lady Adelaide was capable of a great many things, but he was sure murder wasn't one of them.

"I saw her last night. Spoke to her."

"And you pretended she was her cousin Trix?"

Lady Adelaide nodded. "It seemed safer."

"Tell me again what transpired when you met in the park." He'd been upset this morning, perhaps not paying total attention. Annoyed. Tired. Angry that she'd interfered. There was no excuse for how he'd treated her, however. Bob had given him a respectful amount of hell, and if Dev's mother ever found out—

He'd been raised to be a gentleman.

Lady Adelaide put her glasses back on. "It was about nine or nine-thirty. I walked the dog. Let him off the lead for a bit while I sat down on a bench. Perhaps a dozen people were sitting and wandering about—it was a nice night, and I felt perfectly safe. There was a full moon and lots of stars, plus of course, the park is well-lit. I saw two young women a few benches away. I recognized Nadia immediately, and thought at first she was talking to Trix. I should have known Trix would be at work at that hour." She took another sip of tea.

"I walked up to them, since Fitz was being a nuisance. Nadia jumped up. She was very nervous, and seemed 'caught in the act,' if you will. I said something to Mary Frances about Roy Dean's death, how everyone at the Thieves' Den must be so upset, and she didn't enlighten me as to who she really was. We hardly exchanged a handful of words. She asked Nadia for her 'letter,' and off she went."

"What was she wearing?"

"A blond mink jacket with a white sequined dress beneath it. White silk shoes with a strap and a diamante buckle. Quite a lot of paste diamonds. But maybe they were real—she was a thief, wasn't she? She positively gleamed under the lamplight. Like an angel. Ironic, isn't it?"

She was still wearing the dress when she was discovered,

minus the fur coat and footwear. The police had found the shoes kicked off in a corner; presumably the coat was hanging in the closet with all the others. "Did she say where she was going?"

"No. I spoke to Nadia for a few minutes after she left, and told her I knew that she hadn't been meeting Trix but Mary Frances. Nadia said she was finished dealing with the girl, and that I should mind my own business."

Fat chance of that, which so far had worked in Dev's favor, no matter where he thought Lady Adelaide should really be. Her observations had been astute, and somehow she had gotten Trix—for he was sure it was she—to divulge her cousin's address.

"You came straight home after you walked the dog?"

"Yes. It had been a long day. I'd called all around earlier, trying to talk to the group of young people. Everyone said they were staying in out of respect for Roy. I went to bed before eleven— Beckett can vouch for me."

"I'm a light sleeper, sir. I'd know if Lady A left the flat and went out to murder some tart."

Dev almost laughed. "It looks like a visit to Miss Sanborn is in order. Just what this case needs—to offend some diplomat. Likely I'll be shipped off to Australia." Which might make for a pleasant change.

"Surely not!" Lady Adelaide cried. "I'll speak to someone in authority."

"That might cause more harm than good. Our relationship— our *professional* relationship—has been very unorthodox. While I'm grateful for your assistance, I really do have to insist that you step back. It's gotten much more dangerous now. One can be choosy about where and what one drinks, but one cannot avoid a strangler."

"I have a gun, and I know how to use it. My papa taught me."

Dev stopped himself from rolling his eyes. Of course she did, and of course she would. "Again, more harm than good. It's one thing to shoot at a tin can target, another at a human being, no matter how vile. I cannot tell a grown woman what to do, but I implore you to forget about all this and go home. I'll somehow muddle on without you." He gave her a rueful smile.

"I'll—I'll think about it. I still have some shopping to do."

"I'd hate to think of you dying over a new dress." He checked his watch. "I'd better stop by the Sanborns. Wish me luck."

"Can we get you anything before you go? Tea? Coffee?"

"No, thank you. But I wouldn't mind snaffling some of these shrimp things. That bacon roll was a long time ago." And he'd never had a chance to finish it.

"Of course." She looked down at her ringless hands. "I have a confession to make."

He braced himself. "Oh, yes?"

"After I left the Yard, I visited Freddy Rinaldi very briefly to ask where Trix was living. I found her at the Albert Hotel with the band leader, Ollie Johnson."

"Yes, I know. They're getting married tomorrow, and leaving for Paris on the night train. I sent some men to bring them in for questioning a little while ago."

"You won't find them. They decided to go this afternoon." She drew a deep breath. "What if they killed Mary Frances?"

Dev sighed. "You *have* been busy." Trix had protected her cousin. Why would she kill her? But Johnson would probably do anything to protect Trix. Was the man cold-blooded enough to strangle a woman and then go chat up a detective inspector at Scotland Yard a few hours later? Dev would have to cable the *Préfecture*.

Perhaps the poisonings and the murder of Mary Frances Harmon were unrelated. Dev felt a headache coming on, and it wasn't only because he was hungry.

Chapter Thirty

Monday

Addie had slept poorly, and was awake lying in her bed and staring at the Georgian medallion on the ceiling when the doorbell rang at seven-thirty. She heard Fitz's defensive bark and Beckett's footsteps hurtling down the hallway.

She had an urge to put the blanket over her head. Anything at this hour couldn't be good.

The maid entered without knocking. "It's Miss Sanborn, Lady A. She's a right mess. Says the police have taken the prince away and it's an emergency. Shall I tell her to go home? *I'm* barely awake."

"No! Give me five minutes. Fix her some breakfast or tea or something. When *you* wake up sufficiently." Addie slid out of bed. She'd changed from her pretty silk lounging pajamas last night to the real thing, a cheerful yellow cotton top and drawstring pants which would have to do to greet her unexpected visitor in. After splashing cold water on her face and running a brush through her hair, Addie cleaned her teeth, put on her glasses, and joined her guest in the drawing room.

Nadia sat on the couch, a cup of coffee and a plate of untouched toast before her. She had cried off any makeup she might have been wearing, and looked as if she'd gotten dressed in the dark. Wearing a striped jumper over a floral chiffon skirt, with knee socks and oxfords, she was not her usual elegant, composed self. "I didn't know where else to turn. My father—oh! He's so angry, and my mother has locked herself in her room, ruing the day she ever left Russia." She blew her nose into one of Addie's embroidered linen napkins. "You said you wanted to help."

"I will help, if I can. What has happened? Why don't you start from the beginning? Everything, this time."

"Do you know that Mary Frances Harmon is dead?"

Addie nodded.

"The police think Andrei killed her."

Absurd. Addie had developed a tentative fondness for the young man. In his own stumbling way, he meant well. "Why?"

"Because the idiot said he did! They came yesterday in the early evening to ask questions, and he confessed before they got very far. He insisted—*insisted*—that they arrest him. Inspector Hunter tried to reason with him, but it did no good. Then he said he poisoned Roy Dean and tried to kill your sister, too. It isn't true! I know it isn't! He was dancing with you when Lady Cecilia's drink came. And it wasn't even hers anyway. It was Kit's, wasn't it?"

"Why would he confess if he wasn't guilty?"

Nadia wiped the tears from her cheeks with the palm of her hand. "Because he thinks I am. At least for killing Mary Frances. He knows things. We had an argument about her."

"I think I know things, too, Nadia. She sold you drugs and was blackmailing you, wasn't she?" Addie asked softly.

The girl nodded. "But I told you Saturday night, I was done. I told her, too. There would be no more money from me. I would have told my parents everything, but I didn't get the chance before the police came."

"Are you all right?"

"What do you mean?"

"The after-effects when one weans oneself from drugs can be difficult and painful." Addie had reason to know. Her friend Barbara had had a devil of a time, requiring professional nursing.

"It was never like that. I only used a little cocaine, like everybody does, which made me happy while it lasted. God forbid I should be happy," she said, bitter.

"That's not real happiness and you know it, Nadia. Have you told your parents?"

"Yes. Everything. They are furious with me."

"Do they think Andrei is guilty?"

"No. They blame me for his stupidity. If I had treated him right, blah blah blah."

Addie put a hand on the girl's shoulder. "He loves you, Nadia."

"But why? I'm really awful to him sometimes. He drives me crazy."

"Who knows why we fall in love? It's quite the mystery when we give our hearts up to hope. Do you object because it seems like an arranged marriage?"

"It *is* an arranged marriage! My mother and her cousin cooked it up when we were both in the cradle. Of course, Russia was not supposed to fall. I was going to be a princess there."

Addie smiled, picturing Nadia in a tiara without the unfortunate argyle knee socks. "You'll still be a princess."

"Only if we get Andrei out of jail."

"Let me see what I can do."

"You said you knew Inspector Hunter. Can you talk to him? I'm sure he'd listen to you."

Perhaps. "I can try."

"And do you know a good solicitor? Or do we need a barrister? I never can remember which is which."

Addie had excellent legal representation, but even better, she did have Devenand Hunter's telephone numbers. This time she would make sure he answered her call.

"Do your parents know where you are?"

"No. I couldn't sleep and have been walking around until I thought you might be awake."

"I want you to call them and tell them you are safe. Then you are going to drink that coffee and eat that toast. I will put you in a taxi once you're done."

"Thank you, Lady Adelaide." There was no trace of the cool, sophisticated young woman Addie was used to seeing.

"Don't thank me yet. Go on. The phone is right over there. I'll give you privacy."

Addie went into the kitchen, where Beckett was reading one of the morning's papers. A stack was under her elbow. Both she and Addie liked to be well-informed, so they had several delivered daily.

"'Death of a Dolly!'" Beckett read the headline with some relish. "It's all over the news, and there's even a photograph of handsome Mr. Hunter coming out of her criminal lair! Gosh, he takes a good picture."

Addie exercised some control by not asking to see it. She knew he would hate the attention.

"Do any of the articles mention an arrest?"

"Nope. Not even one of those 'assisting with inquiries' thingies. Mum's the word."

Addie wondered how long that would last when a Russian prince was involved. He must love Nadia a great deal if he was willing to sacrifice his hard-won freedom.

And be really stupid. Or at least massively confused.

Unless he knew something about Nadia that Addie and the police didn't.

That was the trouble—Addie couldn't see any of the remaining group involved in pre-meditated murder. The cunning to secure poison, the sleight-of-hand to contaminate the drinks, the ability to appear shocked and sick at the results—all of it described an evil stranger.

Addie poured her own cup of coffee from the pot and added too much sugar and cream. She needed a jolt after the sleepless night she'd had, although one cup of coffee was not apt to be enough. She grabbed a paper and skimmed the front page. The Dollies had made such an impression on the British populace that the reporters were having a field day.

A mug shot of Mary Frances from a few years ago had been printed. Instead of looking contrite, she smiled hugely at the camera. She hadn't been convicted, though—some technicality had prevented her from seeing the inside of a prison.

Addie left the paper on the kitchen table and went back to the drawing room. Nadia was glum, chewing her toast with little enthusiasm. "My father is going to Scotland Yard this afternoon with his solicitor. He says heads will roll if they don't release Andrei."

Poor Mr. Hunter's fears were being confirmed. Addie opened the credenza drawer and raided her pound note stash. "Here's cab fare, Nadia. Please go straight home and don't talk to anyone. So far, the press has not caught wind of Andrei's arrest, or at least it didn't make the morning papers. Chin up—it will be all right."

"Maybe. I can't see how unless Andrei comes to his senses." She brushed some crumbs from her skirt and rose.

Addie walked her to the door and then jumped into the shower. She dressed and primped in record time, choosing a sober long-sleeved navy wool dress and twisting her damp hair up under a matching broad-brimmed hat. It was mild enough outside to forgo a coat, but she took a fur scarf.

The building's porter waved a taxi down for her, and Addie was soon creeping through early morning traffic between horse carts and omnibuses. Time might have been of the essence, but one couldn't rush Monday in London.

She gave her name at reception desk at Scotland Yard, then cooled her heels waiting to be allowed up. The waxed linoleum floor was so shiny, one could probably see her knickers as she paced, so she sat down on a hard oak bench. Addie was sure the inspector was at his desk even at this hour—he probably had not gone home for very long. Her suspicions were confirmed as he walked toward her, in the same suit he wore yesterday.

"You need to go on vacation," Addie whispered.

He shook his head. "Not anytime soon. Why are you here, Lady Adelaide?" To her surprise, he steered her out of the lobby onto the street, keeping a hand on her elbow until they came to a tiny café, its windows steamy. He opened the door for her, and the scent of cooking bacon made her mouth water. The waitress pointed to an empty booth, and they slid in across from each other.

She appeared immediately with a pot of coffee. "G'mornin', Mr. Hunter," she said. "What's yours and the lady's pleasure?"

"Two coffees," he ordered, and the waitress obligingly filled the thick white mugs on the table. "Have you had breakfast?"

Addie realized she hadn't.

"Two full English. Thanks, Susie. Now, I'll repeat—why are you here?"

Addie picked up a spoon and briefly examined her reflection. She was not bright-eyed and bushy-tailed. "I'm sorry. I should have called first. I meant to, but Nadia was desperate, and I didn't know if you would talk to me after you telling me to leave everything alone." Addie rather enjoyed the dig. "She dragged me out of bed at seven-thirty, she's so worried about Prince Andrei."

"Is she going to confess too?"

"No, and she swears Andrei is innocent. Her father is in a state and is about to come after you. I thought I should warn you."

"Very kind. Already taken care of." He poured a dollop of milk into his cup and drank half of it in one go.

"What do you mean?"

"The prince is on his way home. I made sure of it, since I sent Bob with him. There should really be a law regarding false confessions. Wasting our time. Then I could lock him up all over again."

"You sent him home? Why?"

"Because the young moron couldn't tell me *where* he'd murdered Mary Frances, how he'd done it, or what she was wearing when he killed her. 'At her flat,' 'the usual way,' and 'clothes' were a bit vague for us. Your description of her dress was most helpful, by the way."

"Oh!"

"Once we established he didn't kill Mary Frances, he withdrew his assertion that he was the St. Petersburg Poisoner. And yes, he called himself that. The fellow is unstable. He actually kissed my hands when I released him. Almost slobbered. Said he was sorry for the bother, but he wanted to save Nadia, whom he knew to be innocent, but he didn't trust us to see that for ourselves because, apparently, we are British. Ah! Breakfast! Thank you, Susie."

Addie looked at the plate overflowing with an ungodly amount of greasy goodness. "Do you come here often?"

"It's close. The food is fast and cheap and plentiful. Everything a poor, tired copper could ask for." Mr. Hunter tucked in.

Addie could manage eggs and toast and bacon in the morning. The tomatoes and mushrooms were somewhat acceptable, but she was wary of the sausage, black pudding, and beans. She asked Mr. Hunter if he'd like her portions, to which he readily agreed.

She carefully spooned the excess onto his plate. "Did you sleep at all?"

"For about an hour. We have a bunk room, but the cots are left over from the war and are just as comfortable as you can imagine. At least there were no incoming bombs or flooding. I wanted young Andropov to get the full Scotland Yard experience, you know, the harsh hanging lightbulb, the ghastly coffee, endless cigarette smoke blown in his face, me barking questions at him for hours. He'll think twice before he decides to be chivalrous again."

"You seem awfully cheerful." And hungry.

"Why not? I'm having breakfast with a beautiful woman,

even if I'm making no headway on this bloo—uh, blasted case.

Beautiful, eh? Addie knew she was blushing, and hid behind her hat brim. "I'm sure it will be over soon."

"I hope so. Are you going to eat your fried bread?"

Chapter Thirty-One

Tuesday

Addie woke up, for once, at a delightfully decadent hour. Ten o'clock. She'd slept a solid twelve hours. No one had arrived desperate at her doorstep. Better yet, no one had died.

That she knew of.

She stretched, washed up, and padded out into the flat. Fitz was snoozing on the white couch and didn't even snuffle in greeting. So much for loyalty. "Beckett?"

"In here, Lady A."

Addie entered the kitchen to find her maid arranging pink roses in a shiny silver vase. "Oh, my. Do you have an admirer?"

"You do, Lady A." She passed over the accompanying card. "Two of 'em. Three if you want to be technical."

"'With all thanks, Nadia and Andrei.' But I really didn't do anything."

"You *would* have, if Mr. Hunter hadn't done it first. And there's more flowers in the dining room from Lord Waring. White lilies. Here's *his* card."

Thinking of you at this difficult time. Waring.

How very odd. Lucas knew nothing of her recent police

escapades. And they weren't difficult so much as frustrating.

"Where did Lord Waring's flowers come from?"

"I threw the box down the chute, but I remember. Mayfair Posies. This lot came from Florals by Frederick."

Addie flipped through the directory tucked under the phone on the credenza and dialed the number for Mayfair Posies. After several rings, a breathless voice answered.

"Good morning. This is Lady Adelaide Compton on Mount Street. I received a delivery from you earlier today. White lilies from Lord Waring."

"Yes, of course, Lady Adelaide. But there's some mistake. I remember pink roses were ordered. I answered the phone myself. The lilies were meant for—oh dear! We're understaffed this morning and the addresses must have gotten mixed up. I would be happy to send someone to make an exchange."

"That won't be necessary. But perhaps you should resend some lilies to Miss Dean in Curzon Street."

There was an uncomfortable silence on the line. The poor florist probably thought Lucas was a two-timing Casanova, which might actually do something for his sterling reputation. Sterling reputations were somewhat overrated, weren't they?

"Just out of curiosity, what did he intend to say on my card?"

"One minute. I'll look it up in the order book." Addie heard the phone clunk onto the counter, as well as some muffled curses. After a short while, the woman came back. "I do apologize, my lady. Yours was to read, *Miss you already. See you soon! Lucas.* That's with an exclamation point at the end of the second sentence. As I said, I'd be happy to correct the deliveries immediately."

"On second thought, never mind about the lilies. Leave everything as it is. I sense the hand of God." Or was Rupert playing matchmaker? Addie supposed he could enter a flower shop as easily as anybody and shuffle order slips around. Who knew where he was most of the day? "Thank you for your help. Good-bye."

"Honestly, Addie. Next you'll accuse me of having a heart."

Rupert stood before her, pale and somewhat perplexed, as if he'd been interrupted from something more important. Addie wished she could discover where Rupert went when he was not bothering her, as long as it did not require a visit to any intemperate region.

"Did you do it?"

He held up a hand. "You can't blame me for everything! I did not! I swear on my mother's grave."

"Your mother isn't dead, only in Cornwall."

Rupert tapped his chin in contemplation. "Isn't Waring a dark horse, stringing along the Dean girl."

"He's not stringing her along. *He* does have a heart, and feels sympathy for her loss. He sent her flowers, which was very nice of him." Lucas was always nice.

"Bah. Aren't you jealous?"

Addie thought for a moment. "Not in the least. Lucas routinely does the appropriate thing."

"That's what you think."

"Honestly, Rupert, you keep hinting darkly about Lucas' faults, but you never specify. I think you're the one who's jealous."

"Maybe," he said, surprising her.

"Too late. I'm going to visit Nadia and Andrei, and I'd appreciate it if you stayed home."

"Oh, all right. I suppose I could do some reading on the psychology of the criminal mind. If there is such a thing. I'll probably be fobbed off with Arthur Conan Doyle."

Exactly what library was he going to visit? She hoped he wouldn't tamper with the card catalog and mis-shelve books. "That sounds most worthy. I'm going to have breakfast now. Enjoy your day."

"Bah," Rupert repeated as he faded away.

"Who were you talking to?" Beckett asked when Addie went back into the kitchen.

"The florist. There was a mistake with the lilies, but it's cleared up now."

What if Lucas married Pip? She was bright, young, pretty, and probably biddable, just the sort of wife he *should* have. She'd be so grateful to be a viscountess, she'd probably never put a foot wrong. The more Addie thought about it, the happier she was that the flowers had been misdelivered. Now all she had to do was steer Lucas toward Pip.

But men were, by and large, unsteerable. Addie would have to make him think courting Pip was all his idea. Lucas was so proper, he'd probably go through with a marriage to Addie even if he was wildly in love with Pip. He wouldn't want to go back on his word. So Addie must—

Yes. She really must put him out of his not-very-miserable misery. She'd stalled long enough. Her mother would be broken-hearted, but Addie's mother was bound to be annoyed by much of what this decade promised.

She made her own coffee and her own toast, even though Beckett was right there at the kitchen table working on a cross-word puzzle. She fixed a cup for the maid, too, and they discussed the day ahead. Addie planned to visit the Deans first, who would be leaving London any day.

She'd pass the baton to Pip.

Addie bathed and dressed. A light rain was falling, so she chose a flowered silk print dress to cheer herself up. Armed with a plain canvas hat, raincoat, and umbrella, she taxied to Curzon Street, after calling first to see if her presence was welcome.

Pip was alone in the flat. Her parents were having lunch with old friends, and Pip confided that she was relieved to have the place to herself. A huge bouquet of sweetly-scented pink roses rested on the mantel, Lucas' card leaning against the glass vase.

"I'm so tired of it all, Lady Adelaide. My parents mean well, but they're after me now that I'm their only chick. My father decides when I should go to bed, as if I'm a little girl all over again. My mother wants to know if I had enough to eat at breakfast. They're both full of suggestions. Perhaps I'd be more comfortable in other shoes. Maybe I should put on lip rouge. I don't know how I'm going to bear it when I go back to Brighton and go under the microscope."

Pip wasn't wearing any lip rouge at all. In a black dress that sucked the life right out of her, she appeared unhappier today than she did on Saturday. Her glorious auburn hair was in need of a good shampoo, too.

"I'm so sorry, Pip. My offer of the guest room still stands."

"If only I could come to stay with you! But there's the funeral on Friday. My father has been arranging everything by phone. We're leaving tomorrow. I don't suppose you can come."

Addie avoided funerals when she could. "I'm afraid not. But suppose I ask Lord Waring to go in my place. I'm sure he wouldn't mind a trip to Brighton." She wasn't sure of any such thing, but would do her best to convince him it was his duty to support Pip "at this difficult time."

Pip blushed, a welcome adjustment to her pale face. "He sent me roses. That was very kind of him."

"He's a kind man," Addie agreed. "Did your parents like him? He *did* come here Sunday evening, didn't he?"

"Yes. For a little while. He invited us out to supper, but my mother didn't think going out was decent."

"But they're out now!"

"Not in public. Their friends have a house in Marylebone and they're having lunch there. But we did order some food to be sent up from the building's restaurant. I don't think it was up to Lord Waring's standards, but he was very nice about it."

"He would be—he's very nice on almost all occasions. I have a confession to make, but please don't tell anyone, not even your parents. Lord Waring asked me to marry him last year."

"Oh!" There was a lot of regret in that one syllable.

"But I'm not going to. I don't want to marry anyone, not even a man as nice as Lucas. I've known him all my life, you see. It would be like marrying my brother. Um, that was tactless—I'm sure Roy would laugh about it, though. He was so jolly, wasn't he? Anyhow, I wanted to tell you the field is clear. If you like him—and I think you do—I'll do everything in my power to help you make a match of it."

The girl's face had transformed with careful joy. "Lady Adelaide! Are you sure?"

"Quite. Lucas deserves someone as nice as he is. I think I told you he's a little stiff, somewhat old-fashioned. You are just the girl to liven him up. I watched you two dance last week and I could tell he liked you."

"I *thought* he did, even after you told me it was hopeless. And then he sent me flowers with this message. Here—read it!"

Addie knew what the card said, but took it anyway. "'Miss you already. See you soon!' Well, that certainly sounds encouraging." Maybe she would be joining Rupert in hell after this good intention.

"He's frightfully handsome, don't you think?"

He was, but he did not make Addie's heart go pitter-pat anymore. That ship had sailed.

Chapter Thirty-Two

The Sanborns' house in Grosvenor Square reminded Addie of a museum. The front hall ceiling was tall and gilded, and large portraits of what Addie presumed were Sanborn ancestors stared down in disapproval from the walls. She was told by an extremely dignified butler that the family was at lunch, but if she wished to wait, he would escort her into the Blue Room.

Which was very blue, walls covered in blue damask, furniture upholstered in blue velvet. Russian triptychs of a religious nature hung on the walls, and a thick floral carpet was at her feet. Silver and enameled *objets* littered every surface. It must be a chore to dust—Beckett would have boxed up half of it in protest.

Addie picked up a leather-bound volume, but found it was printed in Russian. The alphabet was interesting in itself, so she studied it, trying to make sense of anything that looked familiar. She spoke schoolgirl French, though she was very rusty, not having gone abroad in quite a while. Languages were not really her forte.

She sometimes wondered what was.

She didn't have too long to wait. The door opened, and Nadia, Andrei and a distinguished-looking gentleman entered, all wreathed in smiles.

"Lady Adelaide! We planned to visit *you*!" Nadia said, her smile broadening even more. "Thank you so much!" Nadia kissed her on both cheeks, Continental-style, and Andrei followed suit.

"Really," Addie said, speaking directly to Nadia's father, "I didn't do anything. By the time I got to Scotland Yard, Prince Andrei had already been released. Detective Inspector Hunter is an excellent judge of character, you know. It would be unusual to be able to fool him." Addie hoped this praise might somehow go from Sanborn's ears to someone else's, like the commissioner's.

"Oh! Where are my manners? Lady Adelaide, may I present my father, Sir Digby Sanborn. Papa, this is the wonderful Lady Adelaide Compton."

"Wonderful indeed. The children have been singing your praises, Lady Adelaide. Thank you for taking the trouble to aid them. Young people are so rackety nowadays, aren't they? That place they like to go dancing? The Fox Den or whatever it's called? I can't approve of it, I'm afraid. Full of unsavory characters. Even the Prince of Wales has been warned to stay away, not that he always obeys his elders. My little girl and my nephew need a steady guiding hand in their circle, someone mature enough to recognize life's pitfalls."

"Yes, that is I in a nutshell," Addie said, keeping a straight face with difficulty. Soon she'd be plucking whiskers from her chin and tucking heating pads behind her back. Buying canes and orthopedic shoes.

"May we offer you some lunch? We've just finished, but I'm sure Cook can whip something up."

"No, no, I had a late breakfast, but thank you. I wonder if I might speak to Nadia and the prince alone, Sir Digby."

"Of course! I need to get back to Whitehall anyhow. No rest for the wicked, eh? One thing after the other. Cyprus, you know. Lots to do before the first of May. Well, I'm off. You two behave." Sir Digby gave Addie a wink and left them alone.

"Please to sit," the prince said. "I feel such shame I must grovel at feet."

Addie dropped into one of the velvet chairs, hoping Andrei wouldn't fall down on the rug. She was relieved when the cousins settled on the sofa. "Don't be silly. You were only trying to protect Nadia."

"I told him I can take care of myself."

"Ha! If so, that witch Mary Frances would not have gotten fingers in you."

"Well, that's over now. Unless she comes back to haunt me."

Uh oh. Stranger things had happened, as Addie well knew. "I must ask you questions, and you must be truthful. Did you know where Mary Frances lived?"

Nadia shook her head. "We always met at the Thieves' Den, and then that once in the park where you saw us."

"No," Andrei said. "Was not my type."

"But you like blondes," Nadia teased, fluffing her own pale hair.

"I like *you*. And Lady Adelaide. But not in that way," Andrei said to Addie quickly. "No offense."

"None taken. Did you know any of her friends, Nadia?"

"I saw her with a big table of girls at the club regularly, but never met any of them."

Inspector Hunter could quiz Mr. Rinaldi about that, if he'd answer. Maybe one of them decided Mary Frances had to go. Addie had not decided whether she thought the girl's death had anything to do with the poisonings—it was all terribly complicated. She didn't know how the police kept everything straight.

"Will you be going back to the Thieves' Den? I know your father doesn't approve."

Nadia clasped Andrei's hand. "No. We'll be spending our nights right here, playing cards or something."

"I teach her how to play *Svoyi Koziri*. No luck, all strategy." Andrei beat his chest with his free hand. "There is something wrong with friends. I feel it."

"What do you mean?"

"Your sister. Roy. That boy Tommy. Is prank? Too—what is word—coincidence. We all there, every time. I do not wish to sit with Kit or Greg or Bunny or Lucy. Maybe even Pip. One is killer."

"Andrei! How can you say such a thing?"

"I say because is true. Is not me. Is not you. Is one of them."

"But not Pip! She wouldn't kill her own brother! I've known her since we were at school together."

"People change. Countries change. One cannot depend on anything."

Such a bleak outlook, but more or less true, thought Addie. If Andrei was trying to cast suspicion on the others, he was doing a damn good job.

But maybe that's what he meant to do. He might not have been involved with Mary Frances, but it didn't mean he wasn't the St. Petersburg Poisoner.

"I saw Pip earlier. They're going home tomorrow. The funeral is on Friday."

"We should go, Andrei. How is she?"

"Tired. Sad." *Infatuated.* Addie rose, and Andrei hopped up like the gentleman he was supposed to be, and brought Nadia with him. "Well, I came to check up on you both, and thank you for the roses. They're lovely."

"Pink. See? I remember." Andrei grinned.

"Andrei starts his new job on Monday," Nadia said with a note of pride in her voice. "At the RRRA. The Russian Refugees Relief Association," she clarified.

"Oh?"

"Finally I have something worthy. To work with my people. Raise money. There is still much to be done after all these years. Nadia will help too."

"That sounds excellent! Congratulations."

"For three years, I drug my feet at finding work. Princes do not work in my country, you know. But I want Nadia to be proud of me." The two exchanged a look.

More wedding bells. Addie felt a bit like a fairy godmother.

The rain was coming down harder, but Addie decided the short walk from Grosvenor Square to Mount Street would do her good. She avoided most puddles and managed not to get into an umbrella war with the other pedestrians. London rain smelled different from country rain—sharper, far less wholesome—and she felt a deep longing for Compton Chase.

She let herself into the flat, endured Fitz's jumping, and took off her wet shoes while Beckett gave her a phone call report from a little notepad. The florist again, Millie Avery wondering how Cee was, her personal shopper at Harrods, Angela Shipman next door, an appeal from the Red Cross, and Lord Marbury, Lucy's father.

"The Earl of Marbury? What does he want?"

"He didn't say, Lady A. He was calling from a public place— there was so much noise I could barely understand him. I told him you'd be back by teatime—I hope that was all right."

"Of course. I hope Lady Lucy is all right." She had not spoken to the girl since she strutted out of the police station early Saturday morning. Addie couldn't call the earl back; he'd not left a number.

She changed into another pair of silk pajamas and helped Beckett assemble and eat a quick late lunch. Then she methodically called everyone back. The florist was still worried that Addie would inform Lord Waring of the mix-up. He was a valued customer, whether he stopped in when he was in Town or telephoned from the country. Addie assured the woman her lips were zipped, and happily accepted a future bribe of free flowers of her choice. Addie gave Millie Compton Chase's telephone exchange so she could find out how Cee was for herself. She agreed to look over the clothing that her shopper would be sending over—not that she needed another stitch—and rang Angela, who wasn't in, thank goodness, for Addie was rather tired of hearing how annoyed Angela was with her husband Ernest. She pledged fifty pounds to the Red Cross, and sent Beckett to the post box with a check.

"Alone at last," Addie said to Fitz, as she flopped down on the couch, wondering where Rupert was.

And then the doorbell rang.

Chapter Thirty-Three

The Earl of Marbury might once have stood taller, but he was stooped now, shorter than his daughter. Shriveled. Wizened. And all sorts of other diminishing words Dev could think of without a thesaurus handy. One good gust of wind, and he looked like he might be blown over.

Dev could understand why, after now knowing the history of the family. Considering his heirs were dead, his wife in permanent mourning, his estate razed, and his fortune sadly depleted, standing up straight was the least of the man's concerns.

"Please, my lord, sit down," Dev said, after shaking the man's trembling hand. "Tell me how I can help you."

Lady Adelaide had been insistent that he come right over to Mount Street as quickly as he could. It was now nearing six o'clock, and Dev had been looking forward to finally going home.

A full complement of tea things were on the low drawing room table, but nothing had been touched. Dev's stomach rebelled in protest, but he couldn't help himself to sustenance until he knew what the current crisis was.

"Maybe I'm being foolish," the earl began, his voice as reedy as his body. "I didn't think to call the authorities in, but Lady Adelaide persuaded me to at least talk to you."

"She can be very persuasive. Tell me what's wrong."

Lady Adelaide had been brief and to the point on the phone: Lady Lucy Archibald was missing.

"I know young people today do as they please, but my Lucy has been devoted to her mother since her brothers died. I don't think she'd elope or any such thing without telling us."

Dev's impression of Lady Lucy was a little different. She had been cold and cutting during their interviews, as if no mortal had any right to question her about anything. Alas, Dev was altogether too mortal, and had too many questions. Her answers had been evasive and sly, and it would not surprise him at all to discover she was at the heart of this mess.

All the arrows pointed to her.

"How long has she been missing?"

The earl raked a hand through his thinning gray hair. "This will sound dreadful, but I'm not sure. She told her mother Sunday after church that she was feeling ill, and didn't want any lunch or dinner. With so many late nights, it wasn't a surprise—she's been burning the candle at both ends. She taped a note to her door, asking that she not be disturbed as she wanted to sleep in on Monday. We of course obeyed her wishes. She'd been looking a touch peaky, my wife thought, and if *she* noticed, it must have been true."

"Does your wife have vision problems?"

"No, no, nothing like that. Marian—that's my wife—isn't well herself. Is...is a bit of a hypochondriac, if I may be so bald. Her doctor gives her pills for her nerves. A quack, in my opinion, though the pills do seem to work most of the time. But they make her somewhat vague. She loses track of thoughts. Time. She sleeps a great deal, and has turned to God when she is awake. Lucy is very good with her and manages the household as best she can. She reads the Bible to Marian for hours on end."

No wonder Lady Lucy wanted to go out dancing and drinking every night. Dev busily rearranged his previous opinion, though the arrows remained stubbornly pointed.

"Anyway, yesterday morning I went to a rare book auction in Bath by train. Not as a buyer, mind, but as a seller. I had two lots up, and they did very well, praise God, to borrow my wife's words. I stayed at the Abbey Hotel and had dinner with some friends, other collectors. It's a sort of fraternity, though I don't participate much anymore."

Marbury rose and shuffled to the drawing room window, where rain continued to splatter. "I had a famous library at one point—fortunately the most valuable books were housed in Town rather than in Gloucestershire, or they would have been lost in the fire. Don't let anyone tell you that you can't eat books—they've been our mainstay for years. Bless my father and his father before him for having such a discerning eye." His finger traced a racing raindrop. "I got home at midday. We have a girl who comes in for a few hours Tuesdays and Fridays to do some cooking and light housekeeping. She went in to check on Lucy—the note was still on the door, you see—and found the bed made and no trace of my daughter."

"Your wife didn't realize she left the house?" Dev asked.

The earl's face mottled. "No, Inspector. Marian didn't leave her bed. If she wondered where Lucy was, it was only fleeting. The cleaning girl thinks my wife had gone without lunch or dinner yesterday. Marian was so hungry she ate two breakfasts."

"There was no other note? Any suitcases missing?"

"Nothing like that. Everything seemed to be in order in her room—I asked the girl before she left, not that she knows every pair of shoes or dress Lucy owns. Her suitcase is still in the closet. Once I realized what happened, I tried to call around to some of Lucy's friends." He reached into his pocket and passed a scribbled note card to Dev.

It was a very short list. There were rings around some names, presumably those he was unable to reach. "I wondered if she'd gone out dancing and then spent the night with one of them. It wouldn't be like her, but then if she had too much giggle water, as you young people say, I could understand it. She's still young, too young to be bogged down with the care of her mother. I couldn't reach half of them, and then I thought of Lady Adelaide."

"But for all you know, she may have left Sunday."

The earl covered his eyes. "Oh, God, that's true. She could have left the flat by way of the kitchen service door. We would have seen her otherwise."

Dev wrote a few key phrases in his notebook, and tucked the card in the back. "Did she know you were going to Bath?"

"I think so. I mean, I told her last week, but she doesn't always pay full attention. Like her mother," he said with some bitterness.

Dev felt a well of sympathy for the man. He was the pater-familias of what, exactly? His sons were dead. His wife was a difficult invalid and his daughter had finally rebelled. "Do you know if Lady Lucy had any money tucked away?"

"Ha. What an amusing question. No, and she didn't have any ancestral jewels to pawn. I did that long ago."

"What about Bunny?" Lady Adelaide asked.

"Who?"

"Bernard Dunford. Do you know him, my lord?"

"Lucy doesn't bring her friends around much. But she has mentioned him. Marian thought she might like him."

Dev was sure that would be news to young Dunford.

The earl turned to Lady Adelaide. "This Dunford—is he our sort?" There was too much hope in his voice. Dev, being definitely not their "sort," said nothing.

"Yes, Lord Marbury. His father isn't titled, but he is quite well-to-do. A very old family. I know nothing objectionable about them or him, and I believe he is fond of *her*."

"A light at the end of the tunnel, perhaps." He sighed. "We couldn't afford a splashy come-out for Lucy five years ago, you know. It wouldn't have looked right anyhow, with so many dead or ill. Marian's sister helped, but the girl didn't take. Lucy's not

one for suffering fools gladly and developed a reputation. She's…
blunt. It will take a special fellow to appreciate her."

Or someone deaf and desperate.

"Did you call Mr. Dunford?"

"Of course not!" the earl spluttered. "I didn't imagine Lucy
to be with some man. She's not like that."

Dev had everyone's telephone numbers in his notebook. He
headed to the phone on the sideboard.

"What are you doing?"

"Don't worry, sir. I won't announce to Dunford that Lady
Lucy's run off. I'll be discreet."

"Maybe she's been kidnapped," the earl mumbled. "That would
make more sense than her just up and leaving."

After Marbury's grim description of his daughter's life, Dev
thought it was a wonder she hadn't disappeared before.

Dunford, like many young men of means before him, had
a suite at the Albany. The phone trilled endlessly, but no one
picked up.

"He's not answering. Lady Adelaide, do you know if he has
a manservant?"

She looked apologetic. "I don't. I've really not had a chance to
talk to him. We spoke a little early Saturday morning after—" She
glanced at Lord Marbury, who was no doubt in ignorance about
Roy Dean's death—"the dancing party, and the only unusual
thing I know is that he doesn't like to drive."

Odd, that. Most young men of Dev's acquaintance were keen
to get behind the wheel.

Lord Marbury returned to the sofa. "I'll take a whisky if you
have it, Lady Adelaide. My nerves are shot."

"Of course. Inspector, please help yourself to some tea and
sandwiches."

Dev didn't have to be asked twice. He was absolutely starving,
although he did feel some guilt eating in front of the earl, who
resembled a morose basset hound at the moment.

Lady Adelaide went to the drinks cart and came back with a glass full of deeply brown liquid. She poured her own tea, and nibbled on a cucumber sandwich.

"What would you like us to do, my lord? If you file a formal complaint, we can report your daughter as a missing person, assuming she left on Sunday."

"No. No official police involvement. Nothing public. I don't want her name in the newspapers and her picture hanging in every precinct. She'll never find a husband then."

Dev had an idea she was going to have quite a lot of trouble in that department anyway.

The earl was agitated. "You must swear to me that you'll keep all this confidential. You—you're a gentleman, aren't you, even if you are a...policeman."

"My word of honor, for what it's worth," Dev said quietly, wondering what word Archibald was really reaching for.

"We can speak quietly to her friends and see if they know anything," Addie said. "How she was feeling. What she was thinking. Maybe she just needed to get away by herself for a little while to clear her head."

Dev said, "You mentioned an aunt. Could she have gone to her?"

"Charlotte died last year. Left Marian nothing, when she knew it could have helped." Archibald was more than halfway through with his drink already. Dev knew people of his "sort" never discussed money. They usually didn't need to.

"Does Lady Lucy have any interests or hobbies?" he asked.

"Doesn't really have time for 'em now. Devoted to the care of her mother, which, believe me, is a full-time job. She used to like to paint when she was a girl. Water colors. We even had them framed, but they're gone. Burnt. She goes to the National Gallery every now and then."

It was unlikely that Lady Lucy had holed up there overnight amongst the Rembrandts.

"And she used to ride. Remember, Lady Adelaide? No one could beat her—she was the best rider in the county even when she was still in pigtails. A natural seat, and firm hands that could tame anything. It broke her heart—and mine too—when I sold the last of the horses."

"I'm sure she'll be home soon," Lady Adelaide said. "May I fix you a plate?"

Marbury swallowed the rest of his whisky. "I need to get home. Marian will be wondering what's become of me." He pointed to the tray. "Would it be too much trouble to wrap some of this up so I can take it with me? Marian does have a sweet tooth."

"Of course not! I'll have Beckett do it right now." She bent forward but Dev stopped her.

"Here, I'll carry it in to the kitchen." It was the only way he could guarantee himself a few more sandwiches and a piece of cake.

Chapter Thirty-Four

"Well. What do you think? I wouldn't want to trade places with Lucy."

"I wouldn't want to trade places with the earl," Inspector Hunter said. He was on his second cup of tea and had eaten every bit of what Beckett hadn't bagged up for Lord Marbury. Dark outside now, he really should go home, but Addie was grateful for his company.

She found she was not hungry at all. Lucy was missing.

Was it possible she was dead too?

He put his cup down. "You said when you had lunch with her last week that she was on edge. Did she seem worried or troubled over something specific?"

"I wish I knew. She was…brittle, you know? Arch. But underneath, oh, the poor thing. What a life she's been leading. I had no idea, and I don't think anyone else did either."

He pulled out the index card the earl had given him from his notebook and passed it to her. "You know all these young women on the list, don't you?"

There were only five names. Millicent Avery, Nadia Sanborn, Philippa Dean, Lady Cecilia Merrill, and Clover Crosby. The last three names had a circle around them. "I know Clover is in New

York, so she'd be of no help. I can't see Lucy booking a transatlantic passage if she has no funds."

"Would Dunford loan her money?"

"Gosh! That would be so very inappropriate. Compromising. I can't imagine Lucy asking or accepting. She has so much pride."

"If she's anxious to get away, and he's anxious to prove his affection, it wouldn't be completely out of the question."

Addie frowned. "I just can't see it. But..."

"But?"

"Maybe they ran away together. Eloped. Even though her father thinks she wouldn't. Lucy knows her parents are in no position to give her a proper wedding. She might have thought she was doing them a kindness."

Was Lucy a married woman already? They were both of age, and Bunny was definitely smitten, poor fellow. Or perhaps—

"Oh! I've just thought of something else. Maybe she went to visit my sister. I invited her down to keep Cee company when we were at Claridge's. She refused—I know why now—but maybe she changed her mind."

"Why don't you call Compton Chase?"

Addie did so. Both her mother and her sister got on the line together, and Addie could barely get a word in. After what seemed like forever, she asked about Lucy.

She was not there. Cee hadn't heard a word from her since she'd gotten out of the hospital. Addie asked them both to call her if Lucy tried to get in touch. And not to gossip all over Gloucestershire that Lucy had done a bunk.

She gave them a lame excuse to get off the phone as quickly as possible before their curiosity totally overtook them. Lady Grimes to the rescue again. Addie really needed to get dressed. A dinner party. What was she wearing? The blush chiffon she'd bought in New York. Was she going to wear the pink diamond ring Rupert had given her for their fifth anniversary? Yes.

More questions. "Who is this Lady Grimes? I don't think

we've met." Lady Broughton believed she knew everyone worth knowing.

"She's American, Mama. Her late husband was Irish." Addie would have to remember these details, for her mother would. She glanced over at Mr. Hunter, who was leaning back in his chair, eyes closed.

"Grimes. Grimes. The name is not ringing any bells."

"It is a very recent title. A knighthood, actually." Which might explain his missing Debrett's page.

"I thought you said her husband is dead."

"He was knighted. Then he died almost immediately afterward. It was very sudden."

"But she's out of mourning and entertaining already? I hope she waited a decent interval. Not like you last year with that awful house party. If you'd waited another six months, no one would have died."

Addie really should know better not to lie to her mother. It never went well.

Somehow she managed to get off the phone, and tiptoed to the seating area. Mr. Hunter appeared to be asleep. Addie sat down on the couch, and took the opportunity to stare at him shamelessly.

Shiny dark hair, not from pomade, in need of a cut. Unconscionably long eyelashes. Sharp cheekbones. A formidable nose that he once said was like his grandfather's. A truly beautiful mouth. He'd loosened his tie, and the column of his throat was—

"Delicious, isn't he? Even I can see his appeal." Rupert was next to her on the couch, staring along.

"Shh!"

"You'll be the one waking him up with your shushing. He's overworked, you know. Much too dedicated. I confess I admire him. He has not let his background impede his ambition. If anything, he works twice as hard. Maybe even thrice."

Addie was in no mood for Rupert, even if he was praising the police detective. She shook her finger fiercely at him, but that only made him smile. "You can't get rid of me so easily. I have news."

What, she mouthed.

"All of your Great Eight suspects are dying or disappearing. Guess who's gone to the south of France? Those madcap young lovers, that's who."

"Lucy and Bunny?" Addie whispered. Mr. Hunter twitched but his eyes remained shut.

"No, not them. Young Greg and Kit. Kit fancies himself a novelist, you know. Thinks if he rubs shoulders with Hemingway and Fitzgerald, it will do him some good. Doubtful, though, even if his grasp of grammar is passable. I'm sure they will find other diversions to fill the hours."

"Does Mr. Hunter know they've left England?" Everyone had been warned to inform the police of any travel.

"He should get their letter in tomorrow's post. I don't imagine he'll be pleased. His case is falling apart."

Mr. Hunter was already under so much pressure. Why, look, he'd fallen asleep in her drawing room!

"*You* should go to the south of France when this is all over. Stop in Paris to hear Ollie Johnson's All American Band on the way and check up on Trix."

Addie didn't give a fig about Trix or France. "I just want to go home. Have a quiet summer with no one dropping dead."

"That would be delightful. It would also mean that my services were no longer needed, and I could move...on."

Nothing sounded better to Addie. No more Rupert! She could move...on...as well.

He nodded toward the chair. "Are you going to wake him up?"

It seemed a shame to do so. One didn't fall asleep in chairs unless one was exhausted. She wondered if Mr. Hunter would get a stiff neck, but he looked fairly comfortable. She shook her head.

"I think you should. What will the neighbors say?"

Addie didn't give a fig for the neighbors, either. The only ones she knew really well were Ernest and Angela Shipman next door, and they had enough skeletons in their own closet to prevent them from being judgmental.

She stood up, put her fingers to her lips, and waved Rupert on to follow her. She could hear Beckett's radio, and stopped in to tell the maid she needn't bother with anything else for the day. If Addie got hungry later, she'd make herself a midnight snack. And also, there was a very handsome man sleeping in the drawing room who shouldn't be disturbed.

Fitz was snoozing in the center of Addie's bed and had rolled over to reveal his tummy for rubbing. She complied, then asked Rupert to sit down.

"How do you know about Kit and Greg? The usual way— that you can't tell me?"

Rupert adjusted his cuff. "I've been doing some digging on my own, going out and about. Making myself useful. Can't be a dewdropper all day, can I? I overheard them talking to their landlady."

"You trespassed into their flat?"

"Don't sound so horrified. It was the least I could do—you weren't making progress with them."

"So, did they do it?" Addie decided to stay in her silk pajamas, but she did unpin her hair and brush it. It wasn't close to bedtime, and Fitz still needed his last romp in the back garden, but it felt divine to free her hair. "Tell me they did. I don't like them much. And not for the reason you're thinking."

"Do what in particular?"

"Any of it."

Rupert rolled his eyes heavenward. "I only wish I knew. You know how it is."

Unfortunately, Addie did. "Give me an educated guess."

"All right. I don't think so. They might be snobs, but that's not a crime. Remember, that cocktail was intended for Kit at the Savoy."

"A perfect way for him to throw us off the scent! And not as dangerous as the other ones. If he had to drink it, it would only have made him sick."

"Frankly, my dear, he's not all that clever, even if he thinks he is. And he's much too squeamish to strangle anyone."

Addie was tempted to toss her hairbrush in frustration. "How is this going to end?"

Rupert was prevented from answering by a knock on the bedroom door.

Chapter Thirty-Five

She was talking to herself again; she must be under some stress too. The apologetic words on Dev's lips vanished when she opened the door. Lady Adelaide had let her hair down, and it was as if temptation itself stood before him. Her hair skimmed her silk-encased shoulders and fell to the middle of her back in golden and bronze waves. The tiny strands above her forehead were curled into little corkscrews.

Dev knew it was just hair. Hell, he had hair of his own, some of which was probably sticking up every which way after his unplanned nap. His hand went to his head to assure he didn't look like a hedgehog.

Lady Adelaide looked like a Siren, ready to cast sailors adrift in the nicest way.

She was a very nice woman.

When he woke up, he should have just let himself out of the flat and gone straight home.

"Um…"

"Well, if it isn't Sleeping Beauty!" she teased, smiling up at him. "I didn't have the heart to wake you."

"I'm so sorry. I don't usually fall unconscious in a lady's flat." *Damn*. That sounded all wrong.

"Let me fix you tea or coffee before you go. It won't be any trouble."

Dev should leave. He should leave now. "All right. That's very kind. Coffee would be wonderful. I could fall asleep again on the Tube and miss my stop."

"Have you been getting any rest at all?" Lady Adelaide asked, as he followed her down the hall to the kitchen.

"Not much. What did you find out when you called home?" Dev really couldn't believe he'd slept through the conversation.

"No one's heard from Lucy. They'll call if they do." He watched as she measured coffee grounds into the pot, her hair shimmering in the harsh overhead light.

This was all so...unprofessional. Maybe he *should* turn in his warrant card. Quit the Yard and take up...what exactly? He'd been careful with his savings, and had a tidy sum put away for a rainy day.

Dev felt like he was in the middle of a deluge.

He'd enjoyed the country, what little of it he'd seen last year when he stayed in Compton-Under-Wood. Of course, that might have had something to do with his favorite resident. Maybe he could buy a small shop somewhere. Become a fixture in the village, doling out sweets to the kiddies and drinking a pint or two at the local pub.

Who was he kidding? He'd never be accepted. He'd felt the suspicious stares last summer when he'd left the city. He received nearly as many of them in London, where there was a healthy-sized Anglo-Indian community.

His mouth twisted. A great many young Indian princes had chosen to study at Cambridge and Oxford. Perhaps he could pass himself off as one of them.

Lady Adelaide set the coffee things in front of him. "Just milk, yes?"

She remembered. Well, she was a bright woman. An experienced hostess. He shouldn't make anything of it.

Back to business to make up for his unforgivable lapse. "So, have we decided? An elopement or a trip of some kind. I agree with her father—I don't think the entire police force should be involved."

Unless she was his murderer, which was looking more and more likely.

"You warned everyone not to continue to go out. Maybe that was too much for her. She needed the escape."

"It's possible."

You also told her not to go anywhere without notifying you."

"I did."

"And yet she has."

"I admit, I don't like it." He didn't like anything about this case.

"Do you think she left Sunday or Monday?"

"Sunday seems more likely, if her mother wasn't taken care of on Monday. It does seem out of character after listening to the earl sing her praises, though. If Lady Lucy was the sole caregiver—"

"Perhaps she forgot her father would be out of town." The coffee pot had finished percolating, and Lady Adelaide poured a stream of steaming liquid into his cup. He added his milk and stirred.

Could the girl be guilty? She had reason to be resentful of all those whose lives she thought were easier than hers.

And was she capable of strangling someone? Dev had initially thought the marks left on Mary Frances Harmon's throat had been made by a man, but Lady Lucy was built along Valkyrie lines. And if she'd been a skilled horsewoman, she'd be strong enough.

"How long have you known the family?"

Lady Adelaide sipped her own coffee. "Really, forever. Their country house is—or was—midway between Compton Chase and Broughton Park. Our parents were friendly, as one is amongst the big houses. Hunts and balls and such. Cee is a couple of years older, but she and Lucy played together as children. I knew her brothers quite well."

"Do you think she's capable of killing?"

Lady Adelaide briefly shut her beautiful hazel eyes. "I wouldn't have thought so. She's not an easy person to like nowadays, but she was a very normal little girl."

Dev finished his coffee. "I think I'll drop by the Thieves' Den on my way home. Perhaps Dunford is there and knows something. At any rate, it won't hurt to have a look in. See how Freddy is coping with the loss of his band."

"I know Nadia and the Prince have sworn off the place, so you won't see them. I saw them earlier today, and love is in the air."

"Good, although that doesn't mean they're not still suspects. What about Trenton-Douglass and Wheeler?"

Lady Adelaide's cheeks turned pink. "Um. Th-there's a rumor that they've gone to France. I meant to tell you when you woke up, but it slipped my mind."

"France!" Dev bit back another "f" word. "Where did you hear that?"

"Someone called when you were asleep. My old friend Lady Grimes. She knows the boys, and someone told her."

"I told them not to leave without notifying me!" That village shop was looking more likely by the minute. He'd never experienced this level of frustration in the dozen years he'd been at the Yard. More names to send off to his counterpart in Paris.

"I am sorry," Lady Adelaide said in a small voice.

"It's not your fault," Dev said, reining in his temper. "You've been more than helpful. A brick. I apologize for being dismissive of your help the other day. It's just that—"

He wanted to protect her. Because he—

"—we discourage members of the public from getting involved in police business. After last summer, you already know the risks, and I do too. Deputy Commissioner Olive would have my head on a platter if anything happened to you."

Lady Adelaide smiled at him. "I like your head where it is."

"Me, too, though it doesn't seem to be working very efficiently."

He pushed himself away from the table. "It's late. I'd better go. Thank you so much for your hospitality."

"Any time."

"You will call me if you hear anything? Or think of anything? I admit I need all the help I can get at this point."

Lady Adelaide nodded. "I'll walk you to the door."

It wasn't very far. He followed, her silk pajamas fluttering with each step. He was so very weary, that all the coffee in the world would not help.

He looked down on her, wishing he could think of something witty to say. Wishing that he wasn't thinking about bending to kiss her soft, smiling mouth. This hadn't been a social call, and Lady Adelaide was not a woman to be trifled with.

"Good night," he said, and listened on the other side in the hallway as she turned locks and slid bolts. She was safe. For tonight.

From him, at least.

Chapter Thirty-Six

Wednesday

Lucy's disappearance had plagued Addie all night. Was it a sign of her guilt? Did she simply decide she'd had enough misery and sought to end it all? Or did she have a secret admirer who had whisked her away to France?

She wondered how Inspector Hunter's visit to the Thieves' Den had gone. If she never stepped inside its dark recesses again, that would be fine with her.

She'd forgotten to ring up Lucas yesterday to tell him about Roy's funeral. She should thank him for the flowers, too, not breathing a word of the mistake. Addie knew he was used to rising early; he was very involved with the farming side of his estate. No absentee ownership for him. When his father had unexpectedly inherited Waring Hall and the viscountcy, the man didn't have the first clue how to manage his acreage. Addie's father had taken Lucas' father under his wing, and little Lucas had trotted behind, picking up as much information as the Marquess of Broughton could provide.

Lucas was now the man whose advice everyone in the area asked for. He was a proponent of the most modern farming methods, and had even taken courses at the agricultural college in

Cirencester to add to his Oxford degree. He'd worked for the government during the war, designing better practices for the production and transport of food that were so necessary for the troops and those left at home.

It had not been dangerous work, and Lucas was always a little embarrassed about getting off so easy. At the time Addie had just been grateful that he hadn't been blown to bits like so many of their friends.

She placed the trunk call to Gloucestershire and waited patiently for the operator to connect them. Lucas' butler Davis answered, and asked her to hold. Addie pictured him fetching Lucas out of his dining room while he was having his daily round of deviled kidneys.

"Hallo? Addie?"

"Good morning, Lucas. Yes, it's I."

"You're up bright and early."

"I've been having trouble sleeping lately. There's been so much going on."

"Time for you to come home where you belong."

He sounded very bossy, but Addie couldn't really argue with him. "Listen, I have a great favor to ask of you. You've been so kind to Philippa Dean. Her brother's funeral is on Friday. I wonder if you want to go to it in my place."

The line was silent, save for a crackle. Then, "Is it in Brighton? Why can't you go? We could go together."

Addie sighed, hoping he could hear it. "I just can't. I find funerals much too upsetting. They—they stir up so many bad memories. After Rupert's—and Kathleen's—I'm swearing off them for a while. I'm sure you understand."

"Well," he chuckled, "I hope if I die you make an exception."

"Don't even think it! The world would be a sadder place without you." Oh, dear. She didn't want to lead him on, but she certainly wished he'd reach a fine old age.

Preferably with Pip Dean by his side spooning oatmeal into his toothless mouth.

"Do you have the details? Time, place, etcetera?"

"I don't, but I'm sure you could call the Seaside Hotel and find out the arrangements. I saw Pip yesterday and she needs her friends around her. Oh! And thank you for the flowers. They're my favorites," she lied.

"You're very welcome. Speaking of friends, I hear that Lady Lucy Archibald is in the neighborhood again."

"*What*?"

"My steward saw her get off the train at Marbury Halt the other day. They never stop there anymore, of course, what with the house gone, so he made particular note of it. I wonder who she's gone to visit. Maybe an old nanny or something."

"Lucas! When was this?"

"Sunday evening, I think. He was coming back from a weekend in London. He mentioned it Monday when I got home from Town myself."

"Oh, Lucas! I love you! I mean, how lovely—that is, never mind. I've been worried about Lucy too, and you've just relieved my mind. I have to go. You *will* go to the funeral, won't you? It would be *lovely*." If she said the word one more time, he would think she was deranged.

"I'll try."

"Thank you so much! It's been lovely speaking with you. Have a lovely day!" Addie hung up and made a call to Scotland Yard immediately.

She was put right through to Inspector Hunter this time. "Guess what?"

"It's either too early or too late for games. What is it, Lady Adelaide?"

"I know where Lucy is! Or at least I know where she was Sunday night."

"Not at home in bed?"

"It seems not. She took a train from London and got off at her old stop. Marbury Halt. She must have had to ask specially, for they don't routinely stop there. It's just a lean-to with a bench, not a station, and I'm not even sure that's still standing now that their home burned down."

"Where do you suppose she went?"

"Lucas—that is Lord Waring—suggested she might be visiting a nanny or a former servant. But I don't think there are occupied cottages on the land, and in any event the earl doesn't have the money to support old retainers."

"Did Lord Waring see her?"

"No. His steward was on the same train and told him."

She could hear him shuffling papers. "Was she alone? I haven't been able to track down Dunford."

"I don't know. I didn't think to ask, and I'm not sure Lucas would have known anyway."

"Well, thank you."

Addie was surprised. "That's it? Don't you want to call the Cirencester constabulary to check up on her?"

"What would you have me do, Lady Adelaide? I swore to her father—on my dubious honor—that I would not make his daughter's disappearance public. She's probably just gone home for a few days to reminisce."

"There is no home! Just a falling-down gatehouse!" Addie cried.

"There? You see? She's got a roof over her head."

"Detective Inspector Hunter," Addie said, summoning the freezing tones of the Dowager Marchioness of Broughton, "you cannot allow a suspect in three murders— no, possibly four—to play house in the Cotswolds. If you won't go get her, I will."

"Oh, for heaven's sake. Of course I'm going there. I just have to clear it with my superiors. See if I can requisition a car."

Addie grinned. She should have known better. Inspector Hunter was nothing if not thorough. And honorable. "The train would be faster."

"It would. But having the convenience of a car in the country—"

"I know! We'll go down to Compton-Under-Wood on the train together, then take one of Rupert's cars to Marbury. You'll be spoiled for choice—I haven't sold any of them yet, although I really should."

"You are *not* coming with me!"

Applesauce! He *couldn't* go without her. Not when they were so close to perhaps finally figuring everything out.

"It's rather remote. I know where the place is, and the fastest backroads to get there. And if Lucy is hesitant to see you, I can convince her as an old friend." Surely he would appreciate her logic.

It was so quiet she wondered if he'd hung the receiver up. Finally, she heard a resigned sigh. "All right."

Addie kept her hands from clapping, which would be hard to do anyway when she was holding a phone. "Are you going to tell her parents before we leave?"

"No. It would be cruel to get their hopes up if she's not there... or, uh, injured. It's Wednesday, and a lot could have happened since Sunday."

Addie swallowed. "You don't think she's taken her own life, do you?"

"I hope not. I plan to arrest her. But if she has, I hope she left a signed confession."

"Dev!" Addie said, shocked. The thought was too dreadful to contemplate.

Chapter Thirty-Seven

They had met a little past eleven in Paddington Station and changed trains at Kemble. The weather was better than yesterday, yet overcast. The further they got from London, the darker the clouds overhead. Addie hoped it wouldn't rain for Lucy's sake. While Mr. Hunter might think she had a roof over her head in the gatehouse, Addie wasn't so sure. Lucy had mentioned pigeons roosting, after all.

Once the plans had been finalized, Addie had called home to have someone leave a car at Compton-Under-Wood's train station, so they could motor at once to Marbury without having to answer what were bound to be endless questions coming from the temporary residents of Compton Chase.

Addie had told her mother to expect two guests tonight—Lucy and Inspector Hunter. The dowager marchioness had been exceptionally quiet at the news, which made Addie exceptionally nervous. Sometimes her mother's lack of conversation was more frightening than any words she could utter. Addie didn't want her mother to try to bully the inspector—although she had every confidence that he could hold his own. There was something steady and centered about him that even her mother would find impenetrable.

Constance Merrill, Dowager Marchioness of Broughton, had

not yet forgiven Mr. Hunter for involving Addie in last August's murder investigation. It really wasn't his fault—or anyone's—that things had almost been so disastrous.

Addie was better prepared today, although she doubted she would need the small revolver she carried in her purse. She said nothing about it to Mr. Hunter, not wanting to earn his disapproval. He would probably think she'd accidentally shoot herself, or worse, him, but her aim was excellent. In the absence of any sons, her father had made it his business to teach both his daughters how to handle a gun. It was loaded with precisely one bullet, for that's all she'd need to make her point.

The inspector had bought them rather dry sandwiches and weak tea from the trolley that came through the train car—"on my expense account"—but Addie had no appetite. She wouldn't feel at ease until she knew Lucy was safe.

And innocent.

"Are you going to eat that half?" Mr. Hunter asked.

Addie handed the sandwich over in its waxed paper wrapper. "I have butterflies," she confessed.

"I want you to wait in the car while I check out the gatehouse," he said for the fifth or sixth time.

She knew he meant to spare her anything gruesome. "I know."

"You need to promise me, Lady Adelaide."

"I—I promise."

He raised an eyebrow but said nothing, his strong white teeth biting into ham and cheese. Once he'd swallowed, he began a severe lecture about interfering with the police, which Addie nodded along to. She had a feeling she was not fooling him at all.

But she was not going to sit idly by if the situation warranted her aid.

The train pulled into Compton-Under-Wood's familiar station in good time. The rain had held off, though the day was gloomy. But it was almost impossible for any village in the Cotswolds to not show to advantage, and Compton-Under-Wood was no exception. Baskets of multi-colored pansies and vinca hung from the station's roof overhang, and tubs of bright yellow daffodils lined the platform. In a month, they'd be replaced with tulips, and Addie looked forward to seeing them when she took occasional trips into Town.

She took a deep breath, inadvertently inhaling some smoke from the engine, but nothing could dampen her spirits. How glad she was to almost be home! Tonight she'd sleep in her own bed, and wake up to the gentle hills outside her window. She could touch base with Forbes and the rest of her staff, whom she had missed during her months away. They were practically family, and had rallied around her when Rupert died.

She recognized his red Lagonda in the small parking area. Despite the iffy weather, her chauffeur had left the top down, and there was a picnic basket in the back seat. Whatever was in there was bound to be better than railroad sandwiches.

"Do you know how to start it?" Mr. Hunter asked.

"Of course." Rupert had been very proud of his fleet of cars, and was eager to show anyone with a modicum of interest all the nuts and bolts. They were cared for now by a young chauffeur and two ancient grooms, who had made the unlikely transition from horses to automobiles.

If Addie sold the extra cars, she'd have to think of some way for the old men to occupy themselves. By rights, they should both have retired, but they'd been at Compton Chase since they were boys. It was the only home they knew.

Much to her father's disappointment, Addie was no equestrienne. No riding to the hounds or hurtling over fences for her. But she did like to drive in the country. She hoped Mr. Hunter was suitably impressed with her mechanical skills as she coaxed the engine to life.

"Hop in!"

"I can drive if you direct me."

"The braking system is very tricky." It was almost exactly the opposite of most cars.

He remained on the pavement. "I'm sure I can figure it out."

"Why, Mr. Hunter, never tell me you're afraid to drive with a woman."

The flush on his dark cheeks was hard to spot, but she managed. "Oh! You are! Really, I thought you were a modern man. Equal opportunities for all."

"Equal opportunities to crash and become crippled for life," he mumbled. "I've ridden with your sister. It's a wonder I'm standing here."

"Oh, Cee's a terrible driver. She doesn't wear her eyeglasses. Too vain. But what's on my nose, Inspector?"

"Your spectacles. And she *was* wearing glasses. Blue-tinted ones."

"Plain glass. Really, I'll have a talk with her as soon as I can and tell her she traumatized a big, strong policeman." She checked to see if he was still blushing. On the whole, it was a rather charming trait.

"You're sure I can't drive?" Addie heard the resignation in his voice.

"Very. The property is not far as the crow flies, though we're not crows, are we. But I know the best back roads. Some of them are little better than grass tracks, though. It's been a while since I've visited, but I doubt the lanes have improved."

"Great." Mr. Hunter folded himself into the passenger seat, looking as if he were about to be hanged.

"It will be all right, I promise," Addie said airily, driving through the outskirts of Compton-Under-Wood. The houses gradually thinned out, and after ten minutes, Addie made a right turn at a fork in the road.

"Hold on to your hat. It will be bumpy."

They drove over a cattle grate, and the road ahead narrowed. Overgrown hedgerows lined both sides, and Addie could have stuck her hand out the window and plucked a leaf without any trouble.

"Who lives around here?" Mr. Hunter asked. "And are they going to hit us head-on?"

"There are several large farms. Lots more cows and sheep than people, though. They don't drive." Addie cleared the dark natural tunnel, and Mr. Hunter appeared slightly more relaxed.

"Look. Civilization," Addie cracked. Up ahead was an abandoned pub, its faded sign swinging in the breeze. There wasn't a cottage to be seen, just more hedgerows, open fields beyond them, and the odd sheep.

"I can see why they went out of business. This is probably the most…rural place I've ever been."

"Well, I did tell you we were taking a short cut. I wish the day were brighter. When it's clear, you can see the Painswick Beacon."

"How much longer?"

"You aren't getting nervous, are you?"

"Not at all." He cleared his throat. "Your driving is unexceptional."

"Faint praise, sir."

"All right. You show considerable skill behind the wheel. I'm impressed."

"That's better. We're about three or four miles away, I think. We have to pass a tiny village a little ways from the gatehouse, although I imagine it might be as abandoned as that pub back there. Once the family left the area, there wasn't much point. People need work, and likely scattered."

"I'd like to stop there first and get the lay of the land. Perhaps someone has seen Lady Lucy and will know where she is. We'll have a better idea of what to expect."

"That sounds reasonable."

They drove on in companionable silence, Addie avoiding a runaway pheasant and a decent-sized hole in the road. It wouldn't do to puncture a tire, although if pressed, she could probably change it—Rupert had been insistent in his instruction. But in her green-striped frock with its matching jacket, she wasn't dressed for it.

A signpost directed them to Marbury, and within minutes, Addie and Mr. Hunter rolled through a larger crossroad to the village.

"See, if we'd come the long way, this is how we'd come in. Oh! There's someone up ahead working in their front garden. I'll stop."

There were half-a-dozen cottages, but this one was the only one that showed signs of habitation. Smoke drifted from the chimney, and the fellow who had been raking paused to look them over.

Mr. Hunter climbed out of the car, and Addie followed. She noted he made a point to smile broadly—to appear as unthreatening as possible.

"Good afternoon, sir. My name is Devenand Hunter. I—I'm a friend of the Earl of Marbury. And this is Lady Adelaide Compton. We've come to see Lady Lucy."

"*You're* a friend of the earl's?" the man asked doubtfully.

"Well, an acquaintance, anyhow. He's charged me with Lady Lucy's well-being. Have you seen her recently?"

The man wiped a streak of dirt from his forehead. "I don't know as I should tell you."

Addie stepped forward. "Please. The earl and the countess are worried. There was a misunderstanding—you know how it is between children and parents sometimes."

"No, I don't. My missus and I weren't so blessed."

"Neither were my late husband and I," Addie confided. "But as a human being, I can understand and empathize. I'm sure you can too."

"It's none of my business."

Addie opened up her purse. It was much heavier than usual because of the gun, but she was able to pull out two pound notes. "Will this help?"

"Lady Adelaide," Mr. Hunter warned.

"It's my lucky week," the man said, pocketing the money. "They're at the gatehouse, what's left of it. Came down Monday to buy food from me. I shared what I could. I guess they're still there. Don't know any different."

"Thank you!" Addie beamed at the fellow, but he didn't beam back.

"They?" Mr. Hunter asked.

"Lady Lucy and her boyfriend. As I said, it's none of my business what they're getting up to. I've known her since she was a little kid, coming to my old shop for sweets with her big brothers. Well, the shop's closed, and her brothers are dead. Let her have her fun. Life's short."

Chapter Thirty-Eight

"Do you think she's with Bunny?" Addie asked once they were back in the Lagonda.

"Who else could it be?"

"I don't know. I've only ever seen Lucy with him, and she's never mentioned anyone else. But Bunny! I would not have thought he was the type to have a fling with. He's so...*earnest*." Ordinary.

"There's no accounting for taste."

No, there wasn't. Addie had had a few chances for flings before, during, and after her marriage. Now that she was a widow, the coast was clear, so to speak, providing Rupert didn't leap out of the wardrobe at an inopportune moment. But she hadn't met anyone—with one exception—who appealed to her.

And that one person—well, it would be nothing short of a miracle if her feelings were returned. And then she couldn't work her mind around the barriers that society, and both their mothers, would erect.

For heaven's sake! She was almost thirty-two years old. She should be able to do as she pleased.

But first, she had to help Mr. Hunter solve these crimes.

"Here we are."

The gatehouse had once been a small castle-like building of

mellow Cotswold stone, but now it was missing windows. It had been a miniature of the big house that was lost to the fire, and still had some charm. There was a turret, and crumbling crenellations decorated the roof. Ivy covered most of the walls, growing into the interior through empty window frames. The iron gate with the Marbury crest it guarded was shut and securely padlocked. Grass had taken over the drive as far as the eye could see.

Mr. Hunter poked a finger in her face. "You are to stay here."

"Yes, sir."

"Do not move. I mean it."

Mr. Hunter certainly seemed authoritative and forceful. She could see why Bob admired him so. She sat back, ready to listen for his commands.

But as it happened, Mr. Hunter didn't even get out of the Lagonda before Lucy's head popped out of an empty window.

"Addie! Is that you?"

The relief Addie felt robbed her of speech. Mr. Hunter made up for it. "Lady Lucy, are you all right? I spoke with your father yesterday, and your parents are worried sick."

"Never better. I suppose if you've come all this way you'll have to come in to see for yourself though." She sounded less than enthusiastic. "Don't expect tea. We're on short rations."

"Then it's a good thing we brought a picnic basket. Inspector Hunter, can you reach it and bring it in?" Addie got out of the car and smoothed down her wrinkled skirt. A solitary raindrop landed on her nose.

Lucy didn't sound remorseful or guilty. That was a good sign, wasn't it?

The girl opened the door. She was wearing jodhpurs and an old sweater, her light brown hair covered by a paisley scarf. This was the Lucy that Addie had known, a country girl to her toes, fresh-faced and horse-mad. There was no horse available, but long-faced Bunny Dunford stood in the background, rubbing his hands together in nervousness.

She gave Lucy a kiss on her cheek. "Hello, Lucy, Bunny. I'm so glad we found you."

"Were we misplaced?"

"Don't joke. Your father is really distressed."

"Oh, I doubt that. I'm not a rare book gone missing, and my mother doesn't even know I'm there half the time. What's in the basket? We're starving to death. Come on back to the kitchen. I have a fire going in the stove to take the damp out."

"We were g-going b-back tomorrow," Bunny said. "It's b-been very chilly at n-night." He turned scarlet. Addie wondered where they both had slept, but as the ex-shopkeeper said, it was none of her business.

"Yes, my little escape was very poorly planned. I'd forgotten the shop in the village is closed. Poor Mr. Runyon gave us some of his own tins to tide us over. We couldn't go further afield without a car."

"F-fish paste," Bunny added, making a face.

He seemed very anxious, and so he should be. Eloping with a girl and then not marrying her! Well, Addie supposed, Mr. Runyon was not an ordained minister, and there didn't seem to be another soul about.

"I believe I asked both of you to inform me of any travel," Mr. Hunter interjected.

"I'm afraid this was a very last-minute decision," Lucy said. "I...forgot."

"You are very forgetful, Lady Lucy."

Addie would have shrunk at the inspector's withering stare, but it didn't affect Lucy one bit. She simply shrugged and began to unpack the basket on a warped refectory table. The room was, as promised, warm, and dry enough. As opposed to the parlor they'd passed, the ceiling and windows were intact, and the floor looked as if it had been recently swept.

"Where were you Saturday night between midnight and four o'clock Sunday morning?"

"In my bed!" Lucy snapped. "After what happened to Roy Dean, I decided never to go out again with those people. Apparently, they're capable of anything. In fact, that's why I had to leave London. It was too, too depressing." She paused. "But it's depressing here. I wonder if I'll ever find a place to be happy in again. Oh, look, Bunny, fresh bread. Cheese. No fish paste in sight." She tore off a piece from the loaf and chewed.

"L-Lucy came to see me Sunday afternoon. I t-tried to talk her out of coming here, but she w-was d-determined. So I f-felt it was my d-duty to come with her. T-to protect her." Lucy rolled her eyes but said nothing to the contrary.

"And Mr. Dunford, where were you Saturday night?"

"Home. L-like L-Lucy."

"Can anyone corroborate that? A valet, for example? The porter of your building?"

"My man d-doesn't sleep in. The p-porter d-drinks. I d-don't know if he saw me or d-didn't see me. Or m-maybe he s-saw two of m-me!" The joke fell flat.

"Why are you asking us about Saturday night? Roy Dean died Friday night, and you know where we were—getting hounded by *you.*"

"There's been another…incident." Addie expected the detective to say more, but he didn't.

"D-did somebody else d-die?" Bunny asked.

"Yes."

"Who?"

"I doubt you knew her, Lady Lucy."

"Then why are you asking if I have an alibi?"

"Force of habit, I suppose."

There was an awkward silence. Addie put her handbag down. "Let me help you with the food." She took the top off the flask. "Lemonade. If you give me a knife and a cutting board, I can slice things up. There are apples, too. Some fruitcake. "

"Ha. If only there was a knife. Anything that was useful was taken by thieves. We have nothing but chipped mugs, this awful old table, and two mice-infested mattresses upstairs. You should have seen the state of things when we arrived Sunday night."

"Speaking of which, my mother is expecting you at Compton Chase this evening if you're tired of camping out. Bunny, you're more than welcome, too."

"No. We'll have one more night in our little love nest. Right, Bunny?"

Bunny Dunford's sputtering words were indecipherable.

"Oh, I'm teasing. He was a perfect gentleman, weren't you, Bunny? But I know what you two must be thinking. He *has* offered to make an honest woman of me. I'm considering it."

Poor, poor Bunny Dunford.

Mr. Hunter reached into his pocket and brought out a folding knife. "Courtesy of His Majesty's Army. It's been with me through thick and thin."

Spreading a napkin from the basket on the table, Addie took it and hacked away at the bread, cheese and apples. "There's not enough lemonade for everyone. Lucy, is there a well anywhere about?"

"In the back garden. The water is still good, surprisingly enough. Bunny, why don't you make yourself useful and bring us some water in those mugs?"

He shot out the kitchen door like a faithful hound.

"Are you really going to marry him?" Addie asked softly.

"I'll have to now, won't I? I'm a compromised virgin, just like in one of those silly romance novels my mother used to read before she turned to God. Caught alone behind the potted palms, except this time it's worse. And it's my own fault. I just had to... get away from everything. I'm so tired, Addie."

Addie put a hand on Lucy's arm. "You can ask your friends for help, you know."

"Really? Everyone says, 'Call me if you need anything.' But they never mean it." Tears welled in Lucy's eyes.

"Oh, my dear." Addie got her handkerchief out of her bag and looked up at Mr. Hunter. "Would it be all right for us to go upstairs for a few minutes so Lucy can compose herself? You can entertain Bunny when he gets back. Help yourselves to the food, but save me some fruitcake."

He nodded. He must see that Lucy was at the end of her tether. Surely he couldn't still suspect her?

They climbed the steep stairs, and Lucy turned into the tiny room on the right. A small carryall was tucked into a corner; she had brought a few things after all. The mattress was bare, its stuffing coming out in tufts.

"You've slept here?" Addie asked, aghast.

Lucy wiped her face with a sleeve, and Addie gave her the handkerchief. "Not very much. You wouldn't credit it, but it's so noisy in the country. I could hear the mice in the walls and the owls and the pigeons cooing in the rafters and the wind and the rain. Mostly I just lay there, wishing I was dead."

"Lucy!"

"Well, it's true. What do I have to look forward to? I've done stupid things. Behaved badly."

Addie swallowed hard. "Do you know a girl named Mary Frances?"

Lucy looked puzzled. "No. Why, should I?"

"Definitely not. You haven't experimented with any drugs, have you?"

Lucy snorted. "Don't be ridiculous. As if I have the money for them. I had to get Bunny to buy the train tickets and the fish paste. But I suppose I'll pay him back when I'm Mrs. Bernard Dunford." She broke out into heart-wrenching sobs.

Chapter Thirty-Nine

"The ladies went upstairs for a minute."

Dunford set the mugs down. "What f-for?"

"Oh, you know. To talk about woman things. Lady Lucy was upset."

An understatement. She was desperately unhappy. Unhappy enough to kill? Dev's list of suspects had shrunk alarmingly, and right now she was number one on his list.

"Why?"

"Dunford, if I knew answers to questions like that, I would probably be a married man." At this point he'd welcome answers to any sort of question.

"I've asked L-Lucy to marry me a th-thousand times. But she never s-says yes." The young man slapped cheese between two pieces of bread and wolfed it down.

"It's been hard for you here, has it?"

"Y-you d-don't know the half of it."

"So tell me," Dev said. He grabbed an apple slice to keep Dunford company. The truth was, those sandwiches earlier had been terrible and he probably could have eaten the whole picnic himself.

"I d-do whatever she w-wants, but I still d-don't think she

l-likes me enough." He pushed Lady Adelaide's open purse aside and hopped up on the table. There were no chairs in the room, so Dev settled himself on the wide stone window ledge. Dunford crammed some fruitcake in his mouth and drank all the water in one mug.

"What does she do for *you*?"

Dunford goggled at him. "What d-do you mean?"

"It seems like you're on a one-way street. To make a marriage work, you'll have to compromise. Both of you need to do things for each other. Make sacrifices." Dev suddenly felt very wise. It was right comical, him giving anyone relationship advice. He didn't have time for one, and the only woman who intrigued him was unavailable anyway.

"I've made s-sacrifices. You'd b-be s-surprised at wh-what I've done," he muttered.

Dev felt a prickle race up his neck. "Are you making a confession, Mr. Dunford?"

"You think I'm a chump. S-so does L-Lucy. S-so d-did—no, no. You're not g-going t-to t-trap me."

So...

Not Lucy after all.

Dev wanted to slap himself for not seeing it sooner. He'd been led astray by cherries and stuttering and the sheer improbability of it all, but in his way, Bunny Dunford was just as desperately unhappy and desperate as Lucy Archibald.

Dev suspected Dunford was no longer a nondescript, conventionally upstanding member of good society.

Not one of us.

"I'm not trying to trap anyone." But he wouldn't mind an explanation.

"You c-come here, all f-friendly, b-but you think one of us is a k-killer." Dunford picked up the other mug, his hands shaking.

"Why would you say that?"

"It's got t-to be one of us. K-Kit or Greg or Nadia or P-Prince

Andrei. M-maybe even P-Pip. We were all there, every t-time s-something happened, weren't we?"

"Do you think it was Lady Lucy?"

"N-no!"

Dev thought the poor deluded young man might defend her to the death. Not his own, he hoped.

"Who then?"

"That's what you're g-getting p-paid to find out," Dunford said.

"Apparently I need help." It had started to spit rain, and drops pattered along the wavy glass. "Are you sure you want to stay here tonight? You'd be much more comfortable at Compton Chase." If he could somehow arrange for the Cirencester force to meet them there—

"Why? So L-Lady Adelaide c-can t-talk L-Lucy out of marrying me? N-not after all I've d-done."

"What exactly have you done?" Dev asked. All his senses were alert. He didn't have visions like the young medium he'd met last year, but he was feeling something.

Something very unpleasant. Malevolent. Urgent. And the women needed to be protected. Dev hoped they stayed upstairs forever, or at least until he had Dunford subdued.

"L-leave us alone! We were f-fine b-before you came. L-Lucy is going to m-marry me—I'll make her—and that's that."

"That might be difficult if one of you is behind bars."

The effect on Dunford was electric. "You c-can't prove anything! Whoever m-murdered those people w-was very clever."

"Like you."

Dunford picked up Lady Adelaide's purse and drew out a small revolver.

Oh, hell.

Dev hadn't been shot in a while, and that had been just fine with him. He was more surprised than hurt, catapulting backwards on his arse at first, then pitching to the floor and winding up against the table leg. He supposed that was good—he could have crashed out the window just as easily.

A quick glance downward showed a smoking bullet hole in the tweed fabric of his second-best suit, but the thick leather notebook in his inside pocket had acted as armor. There was no blood that he could see, which boded well. However, he did feel as if his chest had been hit by a large shovel, maybe ten or eleven shovels, and tried to snatch a breath.

It was all rather miraculous. Dunford's aim had been impressive, yet here Dev was, relatively unscathed, only his dignity at risk.

But Dunford didn't need to know that yet.

Up above, the women screamed and clattered down the stairs. Dev took some pride when Lady Adelaide stopped shrieking first. Lady Lucy rushed toward Dunford but stopped when she spotted the gun.

"D-don't move, any of you."

Not a problem for Dev. He had to think. He tried to relax up against the turned wood of the table leg, but its carved embellishments dug into his back. Such a fancy table for the humble surroundings he thought, somewhat beside the point. Still, he'd been less comfortable in the flooded and fetid trenches, so counted himself lucky.

He'd be luckier still if Dunford would put the gun down.

"Is he dead?" Lady Adelaide choked.

"I h-hope so."

"Oh my God." Lady Lucy sank to her knees. Lady Adelaide rushed to her, defying Dunford's instructions. Dev kept his head down, but looked up through his lashes. He had never seen her looking so furious—Dunford had better watch out.

Look over at me, he said silently. Remarkably enough, she did, her eyes filled with tears. He gave her a wink and watched the joy spread over her face. Somehow she managed to conceal her relief from Dunford and hugged Lucy for all she was worth.

"I th-thought you'd l-like what I did for you, L-Lucy," Bernard

Dunford stuttered. "Just d-desserts, and all that. I'm your a-avenging angel. H-he wanted to arrest me, b-but it r-really was all your idea."

"Like it!" Horror was written all over Lady Lucy's face. "Oh, Bunny, what have you done?"

"You r-ragged on the Hardinge girl all the time, how she was no b-better than she should be. How her father was a c-crook and prospered, while yours was an honorable man and still b-bankrupted. Hardinge was a w-war profiteer! Why should his d-daughter be allowed to spend his ill-gotten gains on d-drugs and d-drink, and 'screw everything in p-pants,' as I think you said. She only got what she d-deserved. She was a *tart*," he spat.

It was clear from her expression Lucy recalled her own words, but that didn't make it any easier to accept Bunny's translation of them.

"You did all those…things? But why kill Tommy Bickley? He was just a kid."

"He s-saw me g-give Penelope the flask, y'see. He w-wasn't as stupid as he looked and w-was asking me q-questions about the night she died."

Lady Adelaide was on the floor a few yards in front of him. No theatrics or heroics, please God, just her steady, stubborn good sense. Except for bringing that gun! If they ever got out of here, she was due for a stern talking-to, possibly a spanking.

And then he might try to kiss her. He could claim his brain was scrambled from the attempt on his life. Anyone would empathize.

"Why did you poison my sister's drink at the Savoy?" Lady Adelaide asked, as if she were inquiring about the weather. Keep him talking. Keep him too distracted to remember he held the gun and all the cards.

"It w-wasn't meant for her. W-Wheeler and Trenton-D-Douglass are d-disgusting. Perverts. W-why should men like them live when your brothers d-died, Lucy? I only m-meant to m-make him sick. W-warn him someone *knew*."

When Dev had interviewed the man before, there was hardly any trace of a speech impediment. The stress was getting to him, and he could barely get out three words in a row without tripping over his tongue.

His agitation might prove his eventual downfall.

Eventual was the operative word.

Lady Lucy shut her china-blue eyes. "And you killed Roy Dean because he was to inherit the family business and I thought it was unfair to Pip because she was female."

Just as Lady Lucy could never inherit from the Earl of Marbury, not that there was anything worth having, judging from Dev's current surroundings.

"You said so, d-didn't you? It w-was so easy. When I d-dropped the cherries in his drink, I had a vial of nicotine in my hand. No one n-noticed a thing."

"And Mary Frances needed to die. She could identify you, since you bought the poisons from her. Was she blackmailing you?" Lady Adelaide asked. "Or perhaps she turned you down, too?"

Jesus, Addie! If she'd wanted to enrage the boy, she'd succeeded.

"As if I w-would touch her! If anyone d-deserved to d-die, it was she. Grasping l-little bitch. The Forty Dollies! More like the Forty Whores. Trollops and thieves. I d-did it with the greatest of p-pleasure, and I'd do it again! Watch me!"

And there was Dev's case solved. If he could get into the Yard to turn in the paperwork.

Bizarrely, Dunford began to sing a song that had come out a couple of years before. Everyone and his uncle had recorded it, but none sounded as macabre as the murderer.

> *Who's sorry now?*
> *Who's heart is aching for breaking each vow?*
> *Who's sad and blue?*
> *Who's crying too?*
> *Just like I cried over you.*

He pointed the gun at the women, his smile a fearsome thing. The man had lost touch with reality, which made him more dangerous than ever.

How quickly could Dev roll up onto his feet and attack before Dunford shot him again? Judging from the pain in his chest, not very.

"I made them all p-pay, didn't I? T-time and t-time again. I only d-did what you w-wanted and c-couldn't d-do yourself."

"I *wouldn't*, Bunny. Play God. It's one thing to criticize or gossip, but to kill—for *me*—you've ruined everything. I wish *I* were dead." There was no doubt in Dev's mind that if she were in possession of Lady Adelaide's gun, she would use it, preferably on Dunford first.

"W-we can go away. To P-Paris. Or S-South America. I have plenty of m-money." Dunford sounded less sure of himself now. Less like a man and more like a boy. How old was he? Twenty-two or twenty-three?

"Are you mad? You just killed a policeman. They'll never let us go. I hate you, Bunny Dunford!"

His face was a mask of fury. He cocked the gun at Lady Adelaide and Lady Lucy as they cowered on the floor.

Which one would he shoot first? Dev decided to clear his throat. "Fortunately for you, I'm not quite dead yet." The words came out on a wheeze.

Lady Lucy screamed again, and Lady Adelaide held her, whispering something in her ear.

"Shut up!" Dev wasn't sure whom he was addressing, but Dunford turned the pistol on him.

This was it. He couldn't miss at so close a distance. All those nights of reading—Dev wondered if his comparative religious studies would pay off wherever he was going. He shut his eyes, trying to remember a prayer that would deliver his soul to a higher plane.

No real regrets. Dev had done his best, although he wished he'd solved this case a little sooner.

Dunford fired. A click echoed around the stone walls, and he fired again. "What the…?" Dunford threw the gun down in disgust and snatched up Dev's knife from the table. He looked even crazier than before.

One bullet? Lady Adelaide must be extremely confident of her abilities. If they put this incident behind them, Dev would like to see her on a firing range.

"Nothing needs to be decided right now," Lady Adelaide said soothingly. "We're all frazzled. Why don't I fix us some tea, and you can put the knife down, Bunny."

Dev wanted to laugh. Trust Lady Adelaide to come to the conclusion that tea would cure everything, even a gunshot wound and criminal impulses.

Of course, the last time they had confronted a murderer together, a pot of hot tea had come in very handy. Maybe she hoped history would repeat itself.

"There is no t-tea, you stupid t-twat. Shut up, I said." Dunford glanced down at Dev. "Why aren't you d-dead?"

"Just lucky, I suppose. I'm probably bleeding to death internally. I can help you, you know. Get you out of here."

"How?"

"Lady Adelaide's car is outside." Every word cost him. His lungs seemed unwilling to fill with air.

"I d-don't have a license."

Dev stopped himself from laughing. What was breaking the driving laws when one had already murdered a bunch of people?

"I can drive."

"Dev! No!" Lady Adelaide cried.

"I t-told you to b-be quiet. Stay still or I'll c-cut you."

"Really, we can leave right now. I just need a little help getting up," Dev said. A crane might come in handy.

"I'm not getting tricked b-by you," Dunford sneered. "Lady Adelaide, you'll take me."

No. *No.* Dev hoped Lady Adelaide would forgive him. "Have

you driven with her, man?" he rasped. "Even with her specs on, you'll be taking your life in your hands. I thought we were going to die on the way over here, truly I did. Woman drivers—you know how they are. You'll wind up in a ditch."

Once he got the fellow out of the gatehouse, he could see about driving into a ditch himself. Lady Adelaide had plenty of other cars.

"He's trying to be chivalrous, Bunny. Don't believe him—I'm a perfectly safe driver."

Damn it. He'd thought *no heroics* hard enough, but she hadn't gotten the message.

"I'm a more valuable hostage. The police won't shoot one of their own."

"Nonsense. *I'm* a marquess' daughter. Widow of a war hero. Imagine the scandal if something were to happen to me. The press would have a field day. You'd be made *famous*, Bunny. Everyone would know the name of Bernard Dunford."

Damn her to hell and back. Dev could see the poor fool's eyes light up.

Lady Lucy stumbled up. "No. I'll go with him. This is all my fault."

"Of course it isn't, Lucy," Lady Adelaide said. "You had no idea the lengths he'd go for you."

"I l-love you, Lucy. We can be happy. I know it."

"Are you utterly insane? What if I burn the bacon? How do I know you won't put Harpic in my milk, or strangle me in my sleep if I snore and disturb you? Or shoot me, since it seems you know how to use a gun?"

"We'll all go," Dunford said, that ghastly smile back on his face.

Chapter Forty

Mr. Hunter had winked at her again when he staggered up from the kitchen floor, his hands bound, his mouth stuffed with Dunford's handkerchief. A scorch mark was visible in his suit jacket, but no blood that she could see.

There must be a bullet lodged somewhere in his body.

Addie would never forgive herself if he died. This was all her fault. She'd insisted on coming. Supplied a murderer with a gun. Had been too stupid to see that harmless Bunny Dunford wasn't harmless at all.

Where was the nearest doctor? If she knew, she'd drive there. Let Bunny stab her too.

He'd already slashed through Lucy's jumper when she told him she wouldn't tie up Inspector Hunter with an old length of clothesline. Droplets of blood had dripped down her wrist and shaking hands as she'd finally relented. Then Bunny had tied hers together, whistling as if he were on a walk in the country. He'd been so quick, Addie didn't have time to leap upon him and pummel the stuffing out of him.

She was behind the wheel now, with that idiot—that *murderous* idiot—pointing Inspector Hunter's knife much too close to her face. Addie imagined Mr. Hunter somehow plunging forward and garroting Bunny from the backseat.

She relished the image.

She was becoming nearly as unhinged as Dunford himself.

Addie glanced backward. The detective's eyes were closed. He didn't appear to be in pain, however. A tear spilled down her cheek.

"G-get hold of yourself," Bunny growled, "or I'll have to d-drive myself."

"I thought you said you couldn't."

"I c-can. Just d-don't want to. Too many things to p-pay attention to. It's n-not r-relaxing."

None of this was in any way relaxing. Addie shifted gears and crept along a narrow lane. It was raining very lightly, just enough to cause the surface of the road to be slippery. Squinting through the windscreen, she really didn't have the first idea where she was at the moment, but Bunny did not know that. None of it was familiar. She expected a signpost at any turn. Or a farm wagon. A herd of sheep. Any distraction to give someone time to do something.

Could she drive around in circles indefinitely until they ran out of petrol? Bunny did not know this part of the world, and Addie wasn't so sure now either. She'd taken one too many short cuts.

"We need to put the top up."

"A l-little rain won't hurt you. C-can't you g-go faster?"

"The road isn't very good—it's wet and I might skid. We'll lose an axle or puncture a tire. You wouldn't want that, would you? We'd be stuck here."

"I'd b-be b-better off on foot at this r-rate."

"Let me know if you want me to stop and let you out," Addie said sweetly. "There's an umbrella in the back."

"Shut up!"

They rode on in silence. Addie wondered how this dreadful situation would impact Lucy's life. Would she feel forever guilty that the man who claimed to love her had killed for her? How did one go forward after something like that?

Addie slowed the car to a crawl.

"What's the m-matter n-now?"

"I can't see—my glasses are speckled with rain. And the gauge is telling me the engine is overheating." It told her no such thing—there was no such gauge—but maybe Bunny wasn't aware of that.

"B-bullshit! P-pull over. I'll drive myself."

"Why don't you let all of us go? We're miles from anywhere. No one will stop you."

"You'd l-like that, wouldn't you? N-no. Lucy is c-coming with me. You t-two—I haven't d-decided what to do with you."

"Mr. Hunter needs medical attention."

"T-too bad. G-get out of the car."

With the knife wavering near her face, Addie complied. She stole a look into the back seat and received another wink.

Was Devenand Hunter really all right, or was he trying to reassure her by being brave? She knew he'd been wounded in the war—he and her gardener had talked a little about it last August. But no one enjoyed getting shot.

Addie now had the chance to do something. Bunny couldn't have two hands on the steering wheel and still hold the knife. He inexpertly ground the gearbox and they pitched forward, picking up speed over the rutted road.

"You're going too fast."

"Shut up! Again. If you s-say one m-more w-word—" He pulled the knife from his breast pocket—"I'm going to fix your pretty little face."

Addie had no intention of becoming his next victim. Could she grab the steering wheel without getting all of them killed? She shut her eyes, feeling sick to her stomach as the car bounced around at a speed that felt far from safe.

And then Bunny shouted and the car swerved. "Jesus Christ! What was that?"

Addie opened her eyes. There was nothing on the road in

front or behind them. She was about to offer to drive again, then remembered Bunny's threat.

She would be quiet. And she might use the time to pray.

A figure appeared suddenly in the distance. Was there any way she could signal their distress? She might toss her hat out of the car. But what would a farmer do with her green velvet hat? He'd just think she was crazy for throwing a perfectly good hat away, though the rain was ruining it drop by drop.

But there was a hatpin. Why didn't she think of that before?

Her hand rubbed her neck, then went a little further. She was about to tug the green glass tip free when Rupert smiled and blew a kiss from the middle of the road, just a few feet away.

Both she and Bunny screamed. He tried using the fly-off handbrake, but the Lagonda had been designed to function in a different manner from most motor cars. Bunny lost control, falling against her shoulder as the car slid sideways, Rupert now cross-legged on the bonnet and holding onto the windscreen for dear life.

Or death, she supposed.

Inspector Hunter dove over the driver's seat, viciously elbowing Bunny out of the way. He was now in Addie's lap, a perfect target for her hatpin.

She did not hesitate, and more screams ensued. Mr. Hunter knocked Bunny unconscious and removed the knife from his jacket with one hand, while somehow taking charge of the Lagonda with the other.

The car stopped abruptly. Rupert blew Addie another kiss from the bonnet, and disappeared.

"Are you all right?" both she and Mr. Hunter asked at the same time.

"You first."

"No! You're the one who was shot."

"I'm going to need a new notebook. The bullet's embedded in it."

"And not in you?"

"Not in me." He pulled the clothesline out of his pocket and tied Bunny's arms behind his back with efficiency. "Thank you very much for the flimsy knots, Lady Lucy."

"I was an excellent Girl Guide. Slipknots were my specialty. It's a wonder Bunny didn't notice," Lucy said in a shaky voice.

"Do you suppose you can get him off me?" Addie asked. He felt like a wet bag of cement on her, or possibly something worse. She pulled her hatpin from his shoulder. No point letting it go to waste.

"How thoughtless of me." Mr. Hunter got out of the car, walked around and opened Addie's door. He hauled Bunny out and dropped him to the mud. "Oops."

"What now?"

"I think we have to find a telephone. Do you know where we are?"

"Not really."

Mr. Hunter removed his necktie, and gagged Bunny with it as he was beginning to make a commotion on the ground. "Lady Lucy, you ride up front with Lady Adelaide, who is, I might add, an excellent driver. I'll sit in the back with the prisoner." Bunny flailed and groaned but was unintelligible. None too gently, the inspector shoved him back into the car, then proceeded to put the top up on the vehicle. As he did so, Addie inspected the angry-looking slice on Lucy's arm, wrapping the worst of it with a clean handkerchief from her handbag.

"I'm sorry about the revolver," Addie said, once the car was moving again.

"Spilt milk."

Did that mean he forgave her? He could have been killed! For that matter, they all could have rolled upside down into a ditch after Rupert's stunt. Addie was surprised at her husband's recklessness. The Lagonda had been his favorite automobile, after the Hispano-Suiza that he'd died in.

And Bunny Dunford had seen him.

Addie coughed. "Did you see what spooked Bunny on the road?"

"There wasn't anything. Not even a badger," Lucy said. "He always claimed to be a nervous driver. I guess he was telling the truth for once."

"Well, I'm grateful for whatever he imagined. But you screamed too, Lady Adelaide," Mr. Hunter said.

"I panicked." It was more or less the case. Rupert had that effect on one.

Epilogue

Bright Young Poisoner Locked Away for Life

Addie put the scissors down. The newspapers had made a tremendous fuss over the last few weeks, but somehow Mr. Hunter had kept Lucy and Addie out of all of it. He'd received a special commendation from Commissioner Horwood for not only solving the murders, but the apprehension of several of Mary Frances' confederates. Jewelers and furriers across London expelled sighs of relief and had offered the inspector a generous reward, which he declined. There were still plenty of Dollies on the loose, and he was determined to send as many of them "away" as he could.

Bunny had been judged unfit to stand trial. His babbling about kissing ghosts was the kiss of undeath, and he had been remanded to a mental institution for the rest of his life. It was only fitting—if one killed four people, and tried to kill several more, one was definitely not of sound mind. Addie had tried to feel sorry for him, but failed.

She did wonder if Rupert was expressly breaking some rule or other by haunting him, but she couldn't ask. She'd not seen him since that awful day on that soggy country road.

Did she miss him? She really didn't want to consider that. In life, he'd been an awful husband.

But he'd saved her life twice in death and kept her out of the "pokey." Was he finally where he was supposed to be?

She had quite an assortment of clippings now to go into her secret scrapbook. It hadn't been her idea. One day before they'd left for New York last fall, Beckett had presented her with a stack of newspapers. She'd saved every one that had mentioned the events at Compton Chase in August, and Devenand Hunter specifically.

Addie had sworn off murders, had given away all her mysteries, but she couldn't throw the newspapers away.

So she'd cut neat lines and glued, moved to record the most unusual period in her life so far, when she thought she was losing her mind. Maybe she had. Some people kept invitations and theater tickets—she seemed to be memorializing death itself.

But now there was something much happier to include on the blank pages of the scrapbook: today's announcement in *The Times* of the engagement of Prince Andrei Alexei Andropov and Miss Nadia Kristina Elena Sanborn. Addie wondered if she'd be invited to the wedding.

The postcard she'd received from Kit Wheeler on the Cote d'Azur had been dutifully pasted in too. On it, Kit had simply written, "See? I was right."

The little snot.

She wondered if he and his lover were happy and safe in France. Wondered too about Trix and Ollie Johnson. The Thieves' Den had booked another band, and it was still the place to throw off one's inhibitions and dance until dawn. But a newer club had opened a few weeks ago, the Southern Belle, which was stiff competition. Addie hadn't been, but Cee said it was all the rage, with paper magnolias in vases and plenty of bourbon flowing. Waitresses in hoop skirts somehow managed to deliver drinks without knocking the tables over, and young idiots took bets as to how many of them could hide inside the hoop without being seen.

Cee and her mother were back in London and staying at Addie's Mount Street flat while the builders put their finishing touches on the Dower House at Broughton Park. So Addie had Compton Chase all to herself, if one didn't factor in the servants and Fitz, who was anxious for his walk.

She checked her watch. "All right, you furry reprobate. Come on." The dog danced around her legs, nearly tripping her. She headed out into the garden, admiring Jack Robertson's handiwork. He was young and ambitious, a very hard worker who had achieved miraculous results with only a couple of village boys to help. She knew he sketched garden designs in his off hours, and one day hoped to market his skills in the wider world.

Addie couldn't hold him back, even if it meant he might take Beckett away with him. However, the course of true love was not running especially smoothly at the moment, as Beckett had somewhat cinematic expectations of her leading man, and Jack was definitely a no-nonsense hero. Addie smiled. She looked forward to planning their wedding, right here in her beautiful garden.

Spring was full of promise, and Fitz was on the trail of new scents, heading off into the woods. She whistled to him, and he came with reluctance. "Time to walk up the drive and greet our guest. He should be here any minute."

She'd been a little too nervous to wait inside, and certainly did not want to be caught with the scrapbook. Was it too forward of her to hang about the gatehouse? At least it was in much better shape than Lucy's love nest. She shivered a little, remembering.

Addie prevented Fitz from jumping in the ornamental lake to go after the ducklings, and she walked up the tree-lined avenue at a stately pace after the dog, her sensible country brogues cushioning her footfalls. She didn't wish to "glow," as her mother called it, when she saw her visitor again. No lady of consequence allowed herself to *sweat*, or even speak the word out loud.

She also didn't wish to look as if she was trying too hard, hence the ugly brown shoes, a tan pleated skirt, and an argyle sweater set in pink, white, and mint green. Beckett had been disappointed at her choices but had at least approved of her hair.

Addie heard the Morris before she saw it, and called to Fitz. The visit would not start propitiously if the dog got run over first thing. He raced back, tongue lolling, and she picked him up in her arms, where he proceeded to writhe and lick the powder off her chin.

The car stopped and idled. "May I give you a lift, madam?"

Addie grinned. "I don't ride with strange gentlemen."

"I'm really not so strange. Just slightly eccentric."

"It's lovely to see you. How was the drive?"

"I made excellent time. My mother has sent me with some *laddoo* for you, but I admit I ate a few on the way."

"What are they?"

"Here. Have one." He opened the box that was on the passenger seat, and handed her a perfectly round small sphere.

"Mmm," she said, after taking a bite. "None for you, Fitz. Raisins. And pistachios?" She popped the rest into her mouth.

"Yes. The ingredients vary, but they are often served at important occasions."

Was this an important occasion? Addie hoped so.

You've cut your hair," he said.

"It was time for a change." She tucked some curls behind her ears, still a little uncertain about the hairdo.

"It suits you."

"I thought most gentlemen liked long hair."

"I'm not like most gentlemen, as you know. Remember, I'm eccentric."

Addie walked around the car and slid in, putting the box of sweets by her feet. "Don't even think about it, Fitz," she said, clutching the wiggling dog. Then to the inspector, "Thank you so much for coming. I wanted to make it up to you somehow, after almost being the cause of your premature demise."

Mr. Hunter's dark eyes moved over her clothing. "I hope you aren't armed today."

"No, I've locked the gun up in the safe, at least while you're here."

"That's good news." He put the car in gear and headed toward the house.

"You've been well?" she asked.

"Busy. Still alive. I count myself fortunate." He'd told her on the telephone that he'd only been badly bruised by the bullet that could have killed him.

Addie would never forget thinking he was dead, and that it was *her fault*.

"Well, I hope you can relax," she said, feeling quite on edge herself. What if it had been a mistake to invite him? What if he expected—

No. Detective Inspector Devenand Hunter was too much of a gentleman to expect anything. Much too honorable.

Addie would try to change that. She had two days.

AUTHOR'S NOTE

The Forty Dollies are based on a real girl gang that confounded and fascinated Britain for several decades. Known as the Forty Elephants, presumably since many of them hailed from the Elephant and Castle district in London, they wound up resembling elephants after they packed stolen goods into their specially made petticoats. They were glamorous, ruthless, and reckless. When the police got too hot to handle in London, they'd travel further afield and rob fresh marks. Working in groups, one would distract the shopkeeper while the others brazenly carried out trays of diamonds and other valuables. I'm not sure how Maggie Hughes managed to conceal three fur coats stolen from Harrods under her dress, but she wound up with a sentence of twelve-months with hard labor. For more information on "Britain's First Female Crime Syndicate," read Alice Diamond and the Forty Elephants by Brian McDonald.

And for those of you (like me) who thought Connie Francis was the first to sing "Who's Sorry Now," the song was first published in 1923!